Morgan Marquette

Morgan and Katrina

Copyright © 2019 by **Morgan Marquette**

All rights reserved. No part of this publication may be reproduced, distributed or transmitted in any form or by any means, without prior written permission.

Author's Note: This is a work of fiction. Names, characters, places, and incidents are a product of the author's imagination. Locales and public names are sometimes used for atmospheric purposes. Any resemblance to actual people, living or dead, or to businesses, companies, events, institutions, or locales is completely coincidental.

Book Layout © 2017 BookDesignTemplates.com
Cover Illustration by Naomi Ledesma
Cover Design by Heather Anderson
Edited by Melissa Carmean
Cover Font: Irianis ADF Std

Morgan and Katrina/ Morgan Marquette -- 1st ed.
ISBN 978-1-7334704-0-7

To all of the Katrinas who ever were or ever will be

Contents

Roll Over Beethoven..1
Help!...9
A Day In The Life...15
Nowhere Man..21
Got To Get You Into My Life...29
Can't Buy Me Love...33
And Your Bird Can Sing...45
Think For Yourself...53
Act Naturally...59
Ob-La-Di Ob-La-Da..63
Eleanor Rigby..67
Nobody's Child..77
Here Comes The Sun..89
Do You Want To Know A Secret?.................................97
Hey Jude..103
Carry That Weight..109
Ask Me Why..113
Devil In Her Heart..119
I Need You...125
For No One..137
The Night Before..145
I Don't Want To Spoil The Party................................149
Because..171
Yesterday...183
The Two Of Us..189

Roll Over Beethoven
Katrina

"Sit up, Katrina. You're ruining your dress."

I immediately leaned forward, making sure to keep my back straight as a pin. *A lady isn't friends with the back of a chair*, I remembered. I ran my hands down the edges of my dress, hoping Mother would appreciate the extra attention I was giving to it. But when I glanced up to see if she had noticed, she was looking in a different direction. I frowned. Following her gaze to see what had distracted her, I spotted two strangers walking into the room. Mother greeted them one at a time. I had noticed all day that she would lean in and whisper to anyone who entered the room. This time was no different. Sometimes the people would look at me, then back at Mother, their faces falling for a second before looking back up with a smile and nodding. I knew better than to ask what they were staring at me for. I had gotten used to that.

My frown deepened. I didn't want to have to greet them. I only wanted to sit in this chair and rest my aching body. Thankfully, Mother didn't seem to notice that I hadn't risen from my seat. No sooner had she left me to make a beeline for the strangers than I allowed my back to curl and I sighed heavily.

Feeling relaxed now that Mother had gone, I looked around the room. I hadn't expected the space to magically change from what it had been before, but I was disappointed when nothing new came to my attention. Still the same small room I'd never been in, with its stale air and musty odor and filled with a mixture of strangers and relatives I didn't want to talk to. Still the same strange set up of chairs placed in the middle of the room in rows all facing the same direction. And, strangest of all, still the same long wooden box, surrounded by flowers, displayed at the farthest end of the room.

It's like a party, Mother had said. *Grandfather is just the center of attention this time.*

That was fine, and all. But why was everyone so sad about it? Everyone spoke in quiet voices as though something were wrong with him. Only Mother seemed to be joyful. Well, she and her close friends. Was this not a party for Grandfather? Were we the only ones that knew what was really going on with him?

"Katrina! Hello, little girl. How nice it is to see you."

I snapped to attention, sitting forward and making sure my chin was held high. *Only a servant greets a guest with a bowed head.*

"Hello, Auntie Martha," I said through gritted teeth.

Of all the people in the room I wanted to avoid, Auntie Martha was at the top of my list. She talked forever. I was surprised it had taken her so long to find me.

"My, how you've grown since last I saw you," Auntie said. Something she mentioned every time I saw her. "Have I ever told you that you look like a young Demi Moore?"

"No," I responded with little interest. I didn't know who Demi Moore was. Probably someone from television. Mother had never allowed me to watch television.

Auntie Martha always picked someone new to compare me with each time I saw her.

"Well, you do. Ten years old, and already, you have the look of a real woman! I'm quite jealous of your hair, you know. I could never grow mine as long nor as wavy, and that color is an absolutely *perfect* shade of brown."

Auntie Martha spoke with an overly sweet voice. It made me uncomfortable. She was already awkward enough in her outdated outfit (an open jacket while all the other women wore closed suit coats with belts). I was further disturbed by the deep red of her lipstick, which somehow made her already thin lips seem thinner. I thought lipstick was supposed to do the opposite, but I didn't know much about it. Only what Mother told me.

"Thank you, Auntie Martha." I lowered my head and looked away from her, hoping my silence would make her walk away.

"And... I'm terribly sorry that we have to meet under such circumstances. Your grandfather was a wonderful little old man." She paused and looked at the front of the room, where Grandfather was. "At least he looks clean."

I looked up to meet her eyes again, confused by her words. *Was?*

"He's just sleeping," I explained as though she were stupid. I was quite tired of everyone's sadness and Auntie Martha annoyed me even more. But as soon as the words left my lips, a shiver ran through me and I shut my mouth tight as I realized something. What if I wasn't supposed to tell? What if Grandfather's sleeping was supposed to be a secret and I had just blabbed it? I glanced across the room at Mother, worried that she may have heard what I had just said, but she was too busy talking to other people.

"Ah, right" Auntie Martha said, her face spreading into a warm smile. She took a moment to look behind her again, this time to glance in Mother's direction. "That's a good way of looking at it," Auntie Martha said. Then she reached out to pat my cheek. Normally I would have leaned away from it, but I felt frozen to my seat, still staring at Mother ahead of me. In the end, I simply gripped the fabric of my dress and waited for Auntie Martha to stop touching my face.

I didn't relax until she walked away. The stress of thinking Mother might know I had blabbed the secret to Auntie Martha wasn't going to leave until I was alone again. I remained still until she was out of sight whereupon I finally felt comfortable tearing my eyes away from Mother and releasing my fingers from my dress.

So, nobody knows Grandfather is sleeping? I thought. *But what would be the point of not telling them that?* My eyes floated up to the long wooden box against the far wall. On one end I could just see Grandfather's nose poking out from an opening on the top of it. I focused on the tip of his nose and squinted. Grandfather was clever. He must have had a reason for staying in there. I thought back to what Mother often said whenever she hosted parties at our house, and it hit me. Grandfather must want to overhear what others are saying about him! But the smart man was pretending to be asleep so that it would be easier to hear. That had to be it. How sneaky of him!

Not sure I would want to lay in a box just for that, though. Couldn't you just set up hidden microphones and listen later? Not to mention it had been a long time. Was he intending to pretend all day? He hadn't moved for the whole hour I'd been in that room, and he hadn't even responded when I tried talking to him earlier (although Mother did pull me away from him before he could respond). He was clearly dedicated to the task.

  The biggest proof of his dedication wasn't how still he was holding his original position, it was having to do so while that awful music played in the background. Only a ninny would be able to sit through that in silence! In fact, the thought of doing nothing but listening to Edward Elgar on repeat made me want to stick out my tongue. Although the more I thought about it, the more I realized that, technically, that's exactly what I had been doing. I may not have been laying in a box, but I was quite tuned in to the music that played throughout the room. Not even when people interrupted my thoughts and tried to apologize for whatever Grandfather was doing could I have been swayed from hearing the notes that spilled out and filled the space. Then again, I'd always paid attention to music. At home–when I was alone–I would hum along to my cassette tapes since I knew them by heart. Not that it was necessarily enjoyable. Sure, I loved music, and humming along to my cassettes was better than other hobbies, but I was so tired of symphony. It was all Mother would let me listen to. I was ready for something different. Surely there was more to music than just orchestra.

  Snap!

  My breath hitched at the sound and my body tensed as I realized I had been caught slouching. I glanced carefully at Mother and sat up. She had her fingers positioned to snap yet again, and her eyes were aimed at me like darts. A few seconds passed before she lowered her hand and turned away.

I dared a sigh and stood. What was the point of sitting if it hurt just the same as standing anyway? I plucked at my itchy tights a bit, then looked around. Nearly everyone stood in the same positions as before. Uncle Albert was in the corner, looking out a window. Some older cousins whose names I didn't remember were sitting in the back row of the chairs. Auntie Martha stood by a window, also in the back, while she chatted with a group of women who had the biggest teased hair I had ever seen. Lastly, there was my mother—with her back straight as a rod; her black dress free of lint and wrinkles—who was still greeting new arrivals. I reached up to shift the shoulders of my new dress to a more comfortable position as I watched her from a distance, then regretted doing so as she locked eyes with me.

"Katrina, darling, would you come over here?"

I approached Mother slowly, hoping she wouldn't expect me to introduce myself to the strangers. Having to do so yet again made my heart race and my palms sweat. Mother wouldn't like that. Sweating wasn't ladylike at all.

"Isn't it charming?" Mother asked, placing her hand on my shoulder as I approached. That was my cue to lift the edges of my dress so that everyone could see it better.

"Oh, it's *darling*," said one of the strangers.

"The black taffeta is simply perfect for her," said the other. "Really shows off her *father's* nose."

Mother shot a look at her friend before clearing her throat. She clutched my shoulder. I didn't understand how a dress could make someone's nose stand out, but I said nothing.

"It's from *Paris*," Mother pridefully announced. She seemed pleased with me as she let go of my shoulder. The women giggled at Mother's words and one reached forward to playfully slap her hand.

"Should I even ask the price?"

"Well, they say the best things in life are free, but I'd beg to differ; they can keep them. My father's money is finally going to a place of use rather than that trashy record collection of his." Mother giggled. The noise was so false I could barely stand it.

"Oh, you mean the money isn't coming from child support?" One of her friends asked.

Mother shut her lips tight. The quiet women stared and smirked at her. I turned to glance at Grandfather.

I didn't know Grandfather had a record collection. They mustn't be like the records Mother owned if she called them trashy. If his records weren't concert music–what were they? I wondered if perhaps there were a way I could get to them to find out. I had half a notion to walk over and ask Grandfather right then and there, but I already tried talking to him, and Mother had promised me a swatting for it. Plus, now that I was pretty sure what he was really up to, I wouldn't want to interrupt his pretend sleep.

"Where is your other little one, anyway?" One of the women asked Mother.

Mother's face transformed into a joyful grin. She clasped her hands together. "Oh, Charles is at home," Mother replied, going right back into a

7

pleased look. "I wasn't going to let my darling boy be subject to such an *offensive* event."

"What kind of music does Grandfather listen to?" I said, my curiosity getting the better of me. One sharp look from Mother and I knew I shouldn't have asked. I held my tongue and looked down.

"So, Helen," the woman on the left said, ignoring me. "Regarding those records you mentioned– did you really throw them all away?"

"Oh, good heavens, yes!" Mother answered. "All that atrocious *noise* that he listened to! Can you believe he requested it to be played here? He already forced us to choose this *horrid,* common place rather than the Whitworth Funeral Home back on our side of town. I'm embarrassed enough as it is to have to explain to everyone why we're here. And if you ask me, I'm considering not paying for it. The service here is terrible. The makeup doesn't even *look* like Father! For how rich the man was, you wouldn't think his lifestyle would have been so lowbrow. The man survived all the way until 1982 and still he couldn't grow up. The sooner that box is closed, the better."

I frowned, still listening to Mother but watching as a man who wore a name tag shifted uncomfortably near her. There went my chances of listening to the records. Did Grandfather know Mother had thrown his collection away? I looked back over at him and raised my chin to see if he was listening. I made a mental note to ask him sometime when Mother wasn't nearby.

Was Mother suggesting that Grandfather was in that box as a punishment over the things he enjoyed? Like being in a time-out rather than pretending to sleep? Shocked at my train of thought, I grabbed for Mother's hand.

"Is Grandfather being punished?" I asked.

"God, I hope so," Mother retorted. Her blunt words caused me to gape.

"F...for how long?" I stammered, my grip tightening on her fingers.

"I already told you. Forever."

Stunned, I let go of Mother's hand and stepped back. Was this party a secret trick against Grandfather? My mind raced to figure out a way that I could warn him in time.

"The poor dear," one of the women said. "She doesn't understand, does she?"

Feeling stupid, I looked up at Mother for an explanation, but she only stared back at me with a blank expression. I didn't know what to do. I couldn't let Grandfather be punished forever! He had to be warned.

I turned away from Mother and stared at the long wooden box against the wall. I focused on Grandfather's nose poking out the top, and in that moment, I knew there was no way I could stand by while he was being tricked.

I bolted.

Ignoring the shrieks from the women behind me, I scrambled up the steps to Grandfather with dread rising in my chest.

"Papa! Papa!" I shouted, gripping the edges of the box. "Wake up! You're going to be stuck in there forever!"

No sooner had I yelled these words than Mother snatched me, pulling me backward. I began to cry; whether it was from fear of what was coming or concern over Grandfather's fate, I wasn't sure. Why wasn't Grandfather hearing me? Tears clouded my vision as a blurred crowd of worried faces passed by while Mother dragged me toward the front room. I barely had time to process where we were headed before I found myself face to face with her alone in a separate hallway. Her eyes were wide with anger, and her upper lip was curled. I braced myself for the inevitable slap. Surprisingly, the blow actually stopped me from crying.

"Perhaps this is a good time for a lesson," she hissed.

I swallowed. A lesson was not a good thing when it came from Mother.

"What happens when someone does something bad?" she asked.

I paused, unsure if this was a trick question. "They get hit."

"That's right, Katrina. You were hit because you were bad. And when we get home, you're going to be punished more. Do you know why? Because you embarrassed me, which I've strictly told you *never* to do. *That* is not how a lady acts. *That* is not how you should behave."

I nodded, swallowing again before I spoke. I understood what she was saying, and I didn't want to argue because she was right, but I couldn't help but say, "I didn't want Grandfather to be punished."

Mother's shoulders lowered a bit. She looked down and picked at her clothing, as though she wasn't listening to what I had said. I tried to say something more, but she interrupted.

"Do you believe people should be punished if they do bad things?"

I hesitated. "Yes."

"Well, your grandfather did a very bad thing. Do you know what he did? He was an embarrassment to this family. And he kept money from us.

And because of that, he's being punished—forever. He's being locked away in that box and never coming back."

My lip trembled as I pictured Grandfather being stuck in a box forever. I imagined waking up and finding myself in a tiny space with no light, unable to escape. It was a terrible thought—a thought I knew well.

"You think the closets are dark?" Mother continued. "Closet doors open. Boxes do not. Remember this, Katrina, the next time you choose to embarrass me."

My knees were shaking, and my hands trembled as I tried not to think about being locked in a closet forever. Staring at the ground in shame, tears rolled down my cheeks. Mother took hold of my chin and raised it.

"A lady doesn't stare at the ground unless she's in front of a man. Now go wash your face and don't come out until you look presentable."

I waited for Mother to leave the hallway before I turned to find a washroom.

Help!
Katrina

Every door in that long hallway that Mother left me in was either locked or opened to reveal a supply closet. I fretted at first, since I knew I couldn't go back to Mother with a dirty face. But soon enough I spotted a winding staircase that I thought might lead to a washroom downstairs. So, despite posted signs warning me not to, I found myself tip-toeing down to the lower level to see what I could find.

After hopping off of the last step in my own bit of play, I discovered another long hallway before me. The lighting was poor and came from a single open window to the right at the end of the hall. Its thin white curtains floated eerily in the wind. The sight caused me to shiver. I shrugged off the feeling by focusing on finding a washroom. I stepped quietly, scanning the area for any signs or at the very least any doors that looked open.

Finally, I discovered a water fountain between two doors to my left. Too caught up in sudden thirst to think about anything else, I decided that the washroom could wait until after I'd had a drink. The cool water just barely touched my lips when a sudden voice shouted out from behind me.

"Help! I need somebody!"

I gasped, stepping back from the fountain, and frantically wiped the water from my chin before it could drip down onto my dress. I panicked, believing someone had caught me drinking from a fountain I wasn't allowed to touch. Turning around, however, I noticed I was still alone. I was startled when the voice continued.

"*Help! Not just anybody!*"

I stumbled, looking around for the source of the sound.

"*Help! You know I need someone. Heeelp!*"

The voice was coming from inside the room opposite the fountain. I hesitantly stepped forward, as I noticed a light coming from beneath the door, and a shadow moving back and forth in it. Someone was inside, and it sounded like they were singing.

"*When I was younger, so much younger than today...*"

What kind of song was that? I stepped forward, my curiosity getting the better of me. At first, I put my ear against the door to hear better, but after a second or two of listening, I couldn't imagine who or what was in that room, which made me very curious. Was the person singing along to something they were listening to, or were they making it up as they went? Either way, it was obvious this was music Mother would definitely not approve of. But it sounded so interesting. So different. Perhaps Grandfather knew it! I longed to hear more as well as see who was singing it. What if I just peeked a little? No one was around to stop me anyway...

I twisted the doorknob as quietly as I could and pushed the door open just enough to peer through the crack.

The room was brightly lit, with white tiled flooring. There were cupboards, a counter with a sink on the far end, and a long silver table in the middle away from anything else. No windows and no decorations at all. It was a plain room, really, except for one thing. A funny looking man swiped a mop across the floor in front of the table. I flinched when I spotted him, but his back was turned, so I kept watching. He looked completely ordinary with his plain blue shirt, sleeves rolled up to his elbows, and light brown pants; that is, until I saw his hair. It was the brightest shade of orange I'd ever seen, and it ran all the way down to his shoulders.

I could do nothing but stare. Not only was his hair weird but he was acting strangely as well. He was dancing around like a complete buffoon, all the while singing. *Perhaps he's from the circus*, I thought. His movements were certainly clownlike, and so was his hair. There was a box attached to his belt with a wire connecting to the pair of black headphones that covered his ears. He was listening to a cassette player.

The strange man continued to dance, using the mop in his hands to sweep the floor in time with his singing. He looked so silly that I almost laughed out loud. I was so interested in his odd behavior, I forgot I wasn't supposed to be in the room. When he moved away from the table, my eye caught on something I should have seen much sooner–there, on the shiny metal stand behind the dancing fool, was a different man, one who lay flat and still. He appeared to be sleeping. His skin was an unsettling color. And he looked very, very, sick. My stomach lurched and horror ran through my body.

I screamed.

I didn't know why, but the sight of the person on the table frightened me so badly I couldn't help it. Immediately, the funny-haired man swung around to face me, and for a moment, we looked at each other without moving. I clasped a hand over my mouth as I realized I had given myself away. Bright blue eyes stared at me in shock behind round glasses. I couldn't move. Then, without warning, he ran toward me with his arms outstretched, and I really began to panic. Unsure of where to run, I ducked under his arms and bolted forward; a really bad decision, considering it meant going toward the silver table. I choked back a second scream, staring up at the nightmarish elder above me before realizing that the dancing man was still on my tail. Seeing this, I took off running again, and soon we were both chasing each other around the table.

"Wait! Please!" the man with the orange hair shouted. I only stopped running when the man slipped in a puddle on the floor. I heard the squeak of his shoe as it skidded to a stop. So did I, and the rest unfolded slowly as I turned around. I watched as he slipped; his arms flailing crazily, the puddle water soaking through his clothes when he landed.

I watched him grab for the round glasses that had fallen from his face. He looked up at me, then took a sharp intake of breath before blowing it out, long and slowly. Silence. I refused to look away.

"Hello," he said after a moment, putting his glasses back on.

There was a pause.

Then I ran again.

"No! Wait!" the man called after me, but I didn't stop. My only focus was the door. Getting out of there as soon as possible was the best thing for me. I was already in enough trouble that day. However, just as I had taken two steps toward freedom, my feet slipped out from under me. The world started to slow in front of my eyes, and I knew I was doomed. I could already hear Mother's voice hissing in my ear about how careless I had been. One squishy thud later, and there I was, sitting in the puddle in my new dress.

"Oh, no!" the man cried out. "Are you okay? Are you hurt?" I didn't answer. The water seeped up my tights, cold and uncomfortable. My shoulders tensed as I pictured Mother's reaction to what had just occurred. No longer did I care that I was trapped in a room with two strange men. All I cared about now was what Mother would do when she saw me. That's when the tears came.

"My dress... *my dress...*" I repeated through sobs. I picked at the folds of the fabric, peeling them off the floor, hoping to save them, but they only slipped from my fingers and made a loud *splat* against the floor. Automatically, Mother's advice about not crying in front of others came to mind, but the tears fell in front of the dancing man anyway, who was now half-bent over and slowly walking toward me.

"Shh, shhh," he said. I didn't move as he reached for me. I squeezed my eyes tight, bracing myself for the hit. To my surprise, however, he didn't lay a hand on me. He slipped his headphones over my ears, and suddenly my head was full of music. Not Bach, not Beethoven, nor any kind of classical. There was singing, but not in the way I had often heard. I didn't have a word for what the type of music was.

"*...I know that I just need you like I've never done before... Help me if you can, I'm feeling down...*"

17

MORGAN AND KATRINA

Mother would definitely not approve of what he was listening to. Why, then, would he have me listen to it? I opened my eyes and stared up at him. Slowly, he lowered his hands to grasp the cassette player on his belt and he turned down the volume a bit.

"Hi," he said, smiling. "I'm Morgan. Are you okay?"

I didn't respond.

"You're listening to the Beatles. They're my favorite. Do you like it?"

I hesitated, searching his eyes for any sign of a threat. There wasn't a single trace of anger or irritation behind his expression and that confused me. Then again, if it meant not getting in trouble, I wasn't about to question it. So, instead of saying anything, I allowed myself to look at the floor, taking a moment to really listen to the song. Anything was better than classical, really, but this music was far better than anything I had heard, and I could see why Morgan had danced to it.

"Yes," I said finally. I did like it, however, one thing stuck out in my mind. "Is this how bugs are supposed to sound?" Morgan blinked at me before furrowing his brow.

"Bugs?" he asked. "Oh! No, no. Not beetles. Beatles. Er, wait, that sounds completely the same. I, uh... it's spelled differently. That's the band's name. The *Beatles*. Like keeping time in music, not insects."

"Oh."

Footsteps came from outside the room. Morgan and I both looked up in time to see a man with a name tag rush through the open door.

"Are you Katrina?" the man shouted, looking at me. I didn't know who he was, but I assumed Mother had sent him after me. A chill ran down my back as reality hit me, and I glanced down at my dress in alarm.

"What is she doing in here?" the man demanded, looking past me. Morgan winced as he stood up. He took back his headphones and stuttered in response.

"I-I'm sorry. She just ran in here. I was trying t—"

"This is not a place for *children*," the man interrupted, stepping forward and reaching for my arm. I stared at Morgan as the strange man pulled me up out of the water. Morgan's blue eyes seemed sad. He looked down at the floor as I was whisked from the room. *What a strange man*, I thought. Strange as he was, though, I knew that I would have spent forever in his company just to escape what was coming from Mother.

"Wait," I said, but I was already too far away to know if Morgan had heard.

A Day In The Life
Katrina

Mother's punishment was more lenient than expected. She stuck me in a closet for a while, and I received a couple slaps on the arm. It was bearable. More bearable than going all day without food, or any of Mother's harsher penalties.

Maybe it was because she had to split her anger between me and Sarah. My nanny was also in trouble with Mother for having accidentally broken one of Mother's jeweled boxes. Sarah had done this on the same day I ruined my dress and it seemed Mother thought it best to discipline us both.

Normally when a servant broke an item, they were fired, but Sarah's accident that day was different because Mother's attention was divided. Not to mention, if Sarah were fired, I would be left without a nanny. So, not only was Sarah going to pay for the box, but I had to follow her all day for a week while she ran errands. I dreaded this, knowing Sarah's errands would be boring. Sarah also seemed upset about it, as she would have me at her heels at all times, pressuring her to be on her best behavior. Also, she wouldn't be able to sneak away to her boyfriend's house when she was supposed to be getting groceries or the dry cleaning, but I wasn't supposed to know about that.

MORGAN AND KATRINA

I'd discovered Sarah's secret accidentally a few months before when overhearing a phone call she was having, and I had been using that knowledge to my advantage ever since. I blackmailed her to bring me certain things, or to do favors for me without telling Mother. At first, Sarah was annoyed with this arrangement. But after a while she seemed to enjoy going behind Mother's back as well.

Our sneaky plans did not mean we got along, however. In fact, our first errand day made that quite clear.

"If you hadn't taken so much time getting up this morning, we wouldn't have left so late in the day," Sarah said, staring at me as she turned the steering wheel. "Now there's going to be a line at the dry cleaners, and they're already slow as it is." Her face was scrunched up and her voice was barely restrained. She was probably only twenty, but she already had a crease in her brow. Two heavily indented lines above her green eyes. I made that face a lot, too. Maybe by the time I was her age I would have permanent worry lines as well.

I crossed my arms and looked away from her face in the rearview mirror, instead focusing on the scenery outside.

"I didn't *choose* to wake up so early," I muttered, watching the downtown buildings go by. I was always groggy in the mornings.

"You kinda did, Ms. I'm-going-to-douse-my-new-dress-in-mop-water," Sarah shot back, giving me a look through the mirror. I made a face at her before returning my eyes to the scenery. I had been downtown before, but never to the dry cleaners.

"I can't even listen to my eight-tracks because of your mother," Sarah spat, banging her fist against the car's dashboard. "I already have to do so much around the house as it is with her stupid pretentious nit-picking! I'm supposed to be a housekeeper, not a slave. A whole week of errands without some kind of distraction is going to be hell."

I said nothing. I did recall that Mother had said that eight-tracks were starting to be outdated.

"Ugh, I can see the line from here," Sarah muttered, pulling into a parking spot. "I'll never understand why we have to take *normal* laundry to the dry cleaners. Especially when we have a washer and dryer at home." She glanced at me and squinted a bit. "Maybe if I were rich too, I'd get it."

She shifted her eyes from me, and I followed her gaze to the inside of the building across from us and saw at least seven people standing in a row. I sighed as I leaned my head back into my seat. Then, I turned slightly to the right, and that's when things went from boring to interesting.

"Sarah..." I began, once she had opened the door and unbuckled my seat belt for me. "Is that a music store?" I pointed past the payphone to the shop next to the dry cleaners. I could see the records in the window from where I sat.

Sarah glanced at it quickly, then helped me out of the car. "Yeah, why?"

I hopped onto the sidewalk and let go of her hand, watching her retrieve a basket of dirty clothes from the trunk of the car. Mother had said something about Grandfather having a record collection, but I didn't want to tell her that I was curious about records. "No reason," I said.

"Let's go. We have to get in line before anyone else joins it," Sarah said, motioning with her head to start walking and heading for the door of the dry cleaners. I reluctantly followed her but regretted not asking to go to the music shop. I dragged my feet as we passed by it, slowing to look at the instruments and posters inside. At the very far end of the store were cassette tapes.

Tapes!

They reminded me of the man with the orange hair who had let me listen to his music. What had that music been called? Beetles? No, it was spelled differently, but spelled how?

A bell jingled as we entered the dry cleaners. There wasn't much to look at once we were inside—not even a chair to sit in. There was just a counter with a line of people standing in front of it, some with large baskets in their hands, or holding clothes on hangers. Many of them smoked cigarettes. The man in front was arguing with the shop owner.

Sarah sighed. "You'd think there would be a separate line for people who are in a hurry," she said. "This is going to take a while."

I frowned. There was no way I wanted to stand there very long. I looked around for anything that could preoccupy me when suddenly I tuned into the music that was playing: Vivaldi's *Four Seasons*.

Groaning, I dropped my head. Of all things this place had to play, did it have to be this? Shuffling my feet, I tensed as a new idea formed in my head. One I had never had before. Hesitantly, I looked up at Sarah.

"Could I... go to the music shop?" I asked carefully. Quietly. The question was difficult, like the words were hard to put together. Impossible words.

Sarah looked at me with her eyebrows bunched up. "I don't think we have time after this. We have to be back in time for you and Charles to see your tutor."

She'd already looked back ahead to the counter by the time I gathered the courage to reply. "No, I... I meant by myself."

She looked down at me with a curious expression. It was the first time I had asked to go somewhere on my own that wasn't the washroom. I wasn't exactly sure why I chose to ask her that. I felt it was important to go somewhere alone, even though the idea made me tremble. I didn't know how she would react, but it was better to ask Sarah than Mother.

"Hmm. I don't think so. God forbid something happened and your mother found out that I not only broke her box but lost her kid, too? No."

Defeated, I stared at the ground. I shouldn't have expected that to work. At least I could trust Sarah not to tell Mother that I'd asked.

She stared at me for a long time after that and rolled her eyes. "Fine. We can go together after this. *If* we have time."

I thanked her but still felt like sulking. The whole point of my going alone was so that I could try and find a specific tape that Sarah wouldn't let me look at. I tried to focus on the fact that I should be grateful to go at all.

I watched as Sarah pulled change out of her purse and shuffled through it. She then glanced out the window, toward the payphone. Then, she tapped the lady ahead of her who turned around.

"That man's never going to stop yelling. We'll be here forever. Could you do me a favor?" she asked.

The woman scoffed. "I know. Who argues about a lost dime? Get over it, already," the woman replied. "What can I do for you?"

Sarah laughed a bit, then said, "Well, I need to make a phone call. And I can't leave her alone," she said, tilting her head toward me. "Would you please hold our spot in line?"

The woman glanced down at me and smiled. "Sure. Go on. I bet I'll still be right here by the time you come back," she said.

Sarah thanked her and turned to me. "Ok, look. I need to call my b... brother. So while I do that, you can go to the record store. But you can *not* tell your mom, OK?"

My heart pounded in my chest. I was excited, terrified, and relieved all at once.

"Yes, thank you. I won't stay inside too long," I promised.

"Fine. But you better not go anywhere else. I'll pick you up when I'm done here."

"Thank you," I said again. I turned to leave and sprinted toward the door before I lost my nerve.

"Hey!" Sarah called after me, but I kept running. I could feel the butterflies tickling my stomach the second I inhaled the autumn air. What would it be like to be alone? It didn't matter that it would only be for a short amount of time. It was my first time without a chaperone, and already, it felt amazing and terrible all at once.

Nowhere Man Morgan

"You look like a crumpled leaf, standing there like that."

I jumped, nearly knocking the closed umbrella that was hanging on my arm to the ground. Recovering slowly, I looked up to see Mike, the owner of the music shop, grinning at me from the other side of the record shelf. He smiled knowingly, but his eyes were kind and non-threatening. I tried to return the gesture, but it was weak. I didn't feel up to joking around.

"What happened this time, Morg?" Mike continued with a smirk. "Did you park it on a hill with the back door open?"

I shot him a look, but he had meant it playfully so I said nothing. "No," I responded eventually. "A kid got in the room while I was working."

"Yikes," he said. "Er... is that bad?"

"Well," I said, "sort of. She'll be fine. She wasn't in there very long at all. As long as she showered well enough as a just-in-case measure, then all will be fine. Honestly, it's the mother that's the real problem."

"Yeah?"

"Apparently she made all kinds of threats about suing us over what happened. I'm fairly certain it's all for the drama and she won't end up doing it. But even if she doesn't end up suing, I'm sure she won't pay for the services we gave at the very least."

"People do that?"

"You'd be surprised."

"Dang," Mike said with widened eyes. "Gettin' chewed out about it?"

I bit the inside of my cheek and turned away. "Yeah."

"Jesus, man," he said earnestly. "What are you gonna do?"

"Well, nobody spoke to me this morning," I said, "so I'm hoping if I just lay low, I'll be fine. Doesn't stop me from worrying, of course. I really need that job. I don't want to be fired."

Mike raised an eyebrow and clicked his tongue, all the while staring at me. Feeling like I was under a microscope, I shrank a bit, but I kept my eyes on him. He raised one hand to rest it under his chin and made a small "hmm" noise. Just as I was beginning to squirm, he said, "Can I ask you a personal question?"

I froze. I didn't like personal questions, and I liked it even less when people led them the way he had, but I also didn't want to be rude. Mike was a nice guy. "Okay," I said quietly, unsure of what else to do or say.

"Do you get paid a lot?" he asked. I blinked at him. He continued. "What I mean is, are you only working there because of the money?"

Beads of sweat formed around my hairline. "No," I answered after a long hesitation.

"Well, then, why the hell do you still work there, then?" Mike asked. He leaned forward and placed his elbows on the top of the shelf as he talked. "You only say negative things about it."

I relaxed slightly and let my shoulders fall, only just noticing I'd been tensing them. "I do?" I asked.

Mike snorted. "Only every time I ask about it. You get this kinda far-away look, ya know? Sure you're doing okay?"

I looked back down at the records. I hadn't realized I was so outwardly negative about work. "But I help people," I offered, looking back up to meet Mike's eyes.

He shrugged. "Maybe."

"I enjoy helping people through the grieving process," I explained further. "It's a beautiful profession."

"Yeah, maybe," Mike repeated, now with a bit of irritation. "But you don't talk about that part of it. I mean, I'm just saying that in the eight years you've been coming to this store, it always seemed like work made you glum. It's none of my business, of course. But I'd like to think I know you pretty well by now. I consider you a good friend. So, I hope I'm not being too forward in saying that I'm surprised you never went into music." He momentarily removed his elbows from the shelving unit to spread his arms out, indicating the store and its various music-related items. "That seems more your thing, especially being a Galloway and all."

I shot him a look. "Please don't. You know how I feel about my last name." Mike apologized, and I continued. "It's true that I've always wanted to do something music related. Not symphony, of course but..." I trailed off, my head filling with memories of strumming a guitar in daisy filled fields.

"I've said it before, and I'll say it again: you should be working here," Mike emphasized. "This store suits you better, and if it's not about the money, there's no reason to deny my offer. You'd be much happier here. You're here almost every day, anyway."

MORGAN AND KATRINA

I was too lost in thought to process what he said. My mind was busy remembering good days of sunshine. The memory of laughter and rolling in the grass floated by as a vision of a lost love of mine came into view. I could still see her hair drifting in the breeze. The sound of "If I Fell" started to echo through my head. My eyes blurred, which confused me. I blinked a few times before I realized tears had formed in my eyes.

"What?" I asked, trying to push the memories out of my head. "Oh. No, uhm. No, Mike. I can't. I can't do that."

"Are you okay?" Mike lowered his head and squinted at me.

I shook my head and cleared my throat. "Yes, I'm okay. Thank you for the offer, but I just can't. It... it's the health benefits and all that, you know?" I forced myself to smile. Mike opened his mouth to speak but I cut him off with a wave of my hand, feeling too antsy to leave the conversation now that I was so close to crying.

I shuffled away as fast as I could before he had the chance to say anything more. Feeling stupid over how awkward I had sounded, I kept my sight on the floor and fiddled with the umbrella handle on my arm as I walked, trying to resist looking back at him.

Eventually, I glanced back at Mike. He was moving toward the front counter, apparently having given up trying to convince me of anything.

Sighing, I decided to walk to my favorite area of the store. The Beatles section always cheered me up when I was blue, and as a bonus, their tapes faced away from the front counter.

I stopped walking when I found their shelf and turned to stare at all the hard plastic cases before me. I looked at them with longing, which was ridiculous, given that I already owned the entire collection, but I couldn't help it. I loved The Beatles. I had memorized most of their songs on my guitar. I'd never seen a live concert, but it had long been a dream of mine to do so. The Beatles and the world they created represented my happy place and standing in front of their section in the store was always a good way for me to de-stress. Or, in this case, use as an excuse to get away from an awkward conversation with someone.

Soon, I found myself picking up random tapes and staring at the cover art without really processing what I was looking at.

"You're the man who ruined my dress."

I jumped, shaken from my thoughts, and looked down to see the very same girl that had gotten into the post-mortem room the day before. Despite her accusatory tone, her big brown eyes stared up at me with intrigue. I could feel what little color I had draining from my face, and soon I was scanning the shop for the girl's mother. I didn't see her, nor did I see any other guardian the girl might have come in with. Was her presence just a coincidence? I answered slowly.

"H-hello."

"Why is your hair orange?" she asked, clapping a hand over her mouth afterwards, as though she were upset she'd asked the question. She looked at the floor for a moment.

Not expecting such a blunt question, I said nothing. The awkward silence caused my anxiety to build further.

She examined me for a moment, then spoke again. "Why are you holding an umbrella when it's sunny?"

MORGAN AND KATRINA

The familiarity of a question I was asked often caused me to relax. I tapped the umbrella still hanging on my arm with my other hand and then pointed toward the windows at the front of the store, which were mostly plastered in black discs.

"It's to protect me. Did you know that umbrellas were first invented to block the sun and not the rain?" I asked. The girl tilted her head. I decided to take advantage of her silence and turn away. The sooner I could avoid more trouble, the better.

"Mother says gloves are only for winter or special occasions."

I glanced at my hands, then back to the girl. "You have a very strong curiosity, don't you?" She didn't respond. I got the feeling that perhaps I had offended her. I apologized. She may have been making me uncomfortable, but that didn't mean there was anything wrong with her questions. "Well, I have a condition. Solar urticaria. Really rare and it's a very severe case," I said.

She cocked her head to the side and squinted. "Solar what?"

My eyes darted to the floor. "Urticaria. Solar urticaria. It's... it's basically an allergy to ultra-viol— uh, to the sun. If I don't wear my gloves and cover myself with the umbrella, the allergy will flare up and it's not pretty."

Her eyes widened. "Oh. Does it hurt?"

I managed a half-smile. "Not if I have my gloves, umbrella, and sometimes sunscreen," I paused for her to say something, but the girl didn't ask anything else. Relieved, I switched topics. "What's your name again?"

"Katrina."

"Well, Katrina, it was nice to see you again. I'll be off, now." I stepped away from her and began to walk toward the back of the store.

"Wait!" she called, quickly shuffling forward to catch up with me. "Can you show me more of that beetle band you told me about?"

I stopped. Turning slowly to face her, I eyed her with interest. "What did you say?"

Katrina shrank back as though she had been caught doing something wrong. Her hands shriveled into each other, and she lowered her eyes to the ground.

"I..." she began. But she didn't finish.

"The Beatles?" I asked. The girl's eyes shot upward in a flash.

"Yes!"

I pointed at the shelf next to her. "You're standing right in front of them."

Her eyes lit up and she grinned, turning to face the tapes. She seemed giddy just looking at them. I recalled her reaction from the day before and wondered, as ridiculous as it seemed, if she'd never heard of the Beatles before.

My thoughts turned to questioning if I had judged her prematurely. She, or rather her mother, might have caused me some grief the previous day, but it wasn't Katrina's fault that my job was at risk. What if this truly was just a coincidence and my immediate discomfort in seeing the girl here was presumptuous and rude?

Feeling guilty for how I had originally treated the girl, I looked around the store for her mother again before stepping forward to point toward one of the tapes.

"That's the one I was listening to. The one I showed you."

MORGAN AND KATRINA

Katrina looked up at me as though she'd forgotten I was there. She paused, giving me a queer expression, then slowly grabbed for a completely different tape, seemingly on purpose.

"Sorry," I murmured, pulling my arm back and looking away. Suddenly feeling intimidated, I turned away and pretended to look at the tapes in the next section. I was uncomfortable, this time due to social anxiety, and not because of yesterday. How stupid.

"Can I listen to more?"

I looked over, expecting to see Katrina admiring the tapes I had just pointed out, but instead she was staring at the Walkman on my belt. I gazed dumbly at the device before realizing what she was asking.

"Oh! Uh..." I considered her question for a moment. Her mother seemed quite overbearing, at least from what I'd been told. But who was I to deny this girl access to music? "Yeah, sure," I said, and pulled the headphones from around my neck before handing them to her. She placed them gingerly over her ears, and I pressed the play button for her. Immediately she smiled, staring off into the distance. I was happy to see someone else enjoying my favorite music.

We stood there for a while, her listening patiently, and me allowing her to. Most of the time, she would stand with a blank expression, but occasionally she'd lose herself and close her eyes, swaying her head slightly. We probably would have stood there for the tape's entire duration had I not stopped her after three songs. She seemed disappointed when I did so.

"I really like them," Katrina said. I nodded and placed the headphones back around my neck.

"Me, too. They're really outta sight, aren't they?"

Katrina shuffled on her feet for a moment, then reached up absentmindedly to play with the tapes on the shelf.

"Can you tell me more?" she asked, not looking at me.

"About the Beatles?"

"Yes."

"What do you want to know?"

Katrina paused, tapped a cassette case a few times, then shifted her gaze to me.

"Everything."

A feeling of joy rushed through me. No one had ever asked me to explain *everything* about the Beatles before. How honored I felt! I tried not to show it, but I felt like a kid on Christmas morning. Even my shoulders lifted slightly in my excitement.

"Oh, it would be my pleasure!" I said.

The lesson began with me pointing to all the different tapes, explaining each one's title and giving a description about the album. Katrina seemed fascinated and asked several questions. I found myself getting carried away with the answers, but she didn't mind at all. In fact, she pressured me to continue with the small details, drinking up my words to the last drop. No tape was left unturned. I even made sure to mention where each song was recorded and who the lead singer was. I didn't expect her to remember it all, but Katrina just kept asking and I kept spewing. By the time fifteen minutes had passed, I was completely focused on teaching her all that I could. I was eager to share my thoughts, not having anyone aside from Mike to talk to about the subject.

Katrina claimed to only have listened to classical music until she'd heard my tape, and she much preferred it to classical. She spoke quietly, as if she were embarrassed, or nervous, I couldn't tell which. I tried to make her feel better by explaining that classical music had been used in some Beatles songs, but she didn't like that. We moved on before she got too frustrated. Instead, we talked about what she wished she could listen to. Apparently, she longed to listen to anything that wasn't symphonic.

We talked for at least twenty-five minutes. Work completely disappeared from my mind. I just kept rambling and she soaked it all in. I probably would have kept talking all day had we not been interrupted by a shout from the door.

"Katrina!"

The girl and I both flinched, sharply turning toward the source of the voice. A young woman, perhaps in her twenties, was at the door staring directly at us. In an instant, my previous worries about the day before flooded back, and the joy I had felt from teaching Katrina deflated. The woman didn't look old enough to be Katrina's mother, but that didn't mean I wasn't in potential trouble, and it certainly didn't help my nerves when Katrina backed up against my leg as though she feared what was to come.

"What are you doing?" the woman demanded. Her accusatory tone startled me, and my mouth went dry as I tried to come up with an explanation for my actions. But I realized she wasn't even looking at me. She was looking at Katrina.

"I'm learning about the Beatles." Katrina said, but there was something about her response that worried me. Her face was directed toward the floor and she spoke as though she were caught doing something wrong. I could have cast this observation aside as simply a lack of knowledge about the situation on my end, but the more concerning factor was that Katrina still stood backed against me, as though the woman–a woman she clearly knew–could be an existential threat to her. She was more comfortable with me, a man she barely knew. I didn't have much experience with children, but my chest tightened at what her behavior implied.

The woman took in the information and then looked up at me.

"Is she bothering you?" she asked.

"Oh, no, no! She was just asking me about a band, and I was telling her about them. She wasn't bothering me at all. She's a very polite girl," I said, trying to smile.

"He knows a lot about music," Katrina said. She wrung her hands as she did so and still hadn't looked at the woman.

"Well, all right," the woman said, giving a quick suspicious glance at Katrina before looking again at me. "Still. Sorry about that."

I assured her that it truly wasn't a problem and that I actually enjoyed talking to Katrina. "Honestly, I don't often meet people who are that interested in this stuff. So it was a nice change of pace."

"If you say so," the woman said, unimpressed. "Well, thank you for your kindness Mr..?"

"Call me Morgan."

"Morgan, I'm Sarah. Thanks, again. I'll be taking Katrina out of your hands, now."

Katrina's face fell, but she stepped forward. She seemed a bit more relaxed than she had when the woman confronted us. A bit less fearful. Her changed behavior put to rest any concern I had previously.

MORGAN AND KATRINA

"Let's go," Sarah said, offering her hand to Katrina, who reluctantly took it. They hadn't taken more than two steps before Katrina suddenly pulled against the woman's hand to face me again.

"Can I see you tomorrow?" she blurted as Sarah sighed behind her. I blinked at Katrina, unsure of how I felt about her question. I didn't feel right denying her request, but I felt cornered regardless.

"Uh, sure," I responded. It was an automatic answer.

"Okay, see you tomorrow!" Katrina called, waving at me.

"Uh, alright," I replied. I waved back at her as I overheard Sarah tell her they wouldn't be back here at least until their dry cleaning was finished but neither of them said anything more to me directly. I waited until both of them left the store before returning to the section of tapes I'd just spent a half-hour in. So it really was a coincidence, after all.

I found myself smiling at the thought that I'd been able to speak with her about my favorite subject. It felt nice to feel so genuinely happy over something so seemingly small.

Before I had time to consider whether I would look forward to potentially seeing Katrina again, my thoughts shifted as soon as I raised my arm to look at my watch. Panic took over when I saw the time and I immediately dashed for the exit with a quick goodbye to Mike along the way. I couldn't be late for work again!

Got To Get You Into My Life
Katrina

"She looks just darling in it."

I looked at myself in the mirror and held my chin up high. Flattening my hands, I spread my arms out like a bird taking flight and turned in a slow circle. My new dress was okay. It was less itchy than the last one and definitely prettier, but I didn't quite feel like myself in it. The only thing I liked about the outfit was the bow in my hair.

"Hm," Mother murmured, watching me with a critical eye. Her arms were crossed, and her lips were pursed.

"The white really goes well with her hair," the tailor cheerily said. "Shows it off, you know? And the red sash around the middle could be accented with red ribbons in the hair instead of the single bow if you wish." His teeth were bright, and normally, I would have been polite and returned the smile he was giving me, but I was too busy feeling glum.

"Honestly," the man continued. "Your daughter would look good in anything."

Mother reacted as though someone had pricked her with a pin, but then she waved her hand in the air and turned away with a snort. "Yes, of course she would. She got it all from *me*!"

"What do *you* think?" the man asked me. His eyes were just as shiny as his teeth, distracting me too much to answer properly.

"I like it very much," I answered timidly. I glanced over at Mother, waited for her nod, then looked at the floor.

"Well, shall we box it up, then?" the tailor asked Mother.

She clapped her hands. "Yes, of course!"

The man scurried off to find a box while I stepped down from the stool to go the dressing room. Mother quickly jabbed a knuckle into my shoulder as I passed her and hissed into my ear. "We're in public. Ladies should always be cheerful in front of a man!"

I nodded and straightened my back while faking a grin. Once I was safely behind the curtain of the dressing room, I dropped my smile. Mother had been upset all day about my attitude, and yet no matter how many times she warned me, I still couldn't pretend to be happy. I felt miserable, and the worst part was that I couldn't tell her that. I couldn't tell her why.

I was upset because Mother switched plans that morning. Mother decided to take me shopping to replace the dress I ruined at Grandfather's celebration instead of going with Sarah on her errands. Which meant I wouldn't have the chance to convince Sarah to drop me off at the music shop. I had lied to Mr. Morgan, the one person who finally allowed me to listen to the music I so desperately wanted to hear. He might be mad that I had lied and I might never hear that music again. I could only hope that tomorrow would be different so that I might still have a chance to fix things.

I sighed deeply and allowed myself to sink against the wall. I wanted nothing more than to listen to that wonderful music again. I was almost in tears when I heard Mother.

"Katrina, what's taking you so long?"

"Coming!" I called, grabbing for the white dress and opening the curtain.

Mother grabbed my chin and inspected my face. "Why are your cheeks all red?"

There was a lump in my throat. I didn't dare try to choke it down. Not with her looking at me like that. "I'm hot," I lied.

"Hm." Mother stared at me a moment before seeming to accept my answer.

We walked together to the cash register, and I handed my dress to the tailor. Distracted by my own thoughts, I didn't look up at the man, nor did I pay attention to the exchange my mother was having with him. Instead, I stared off to the left and let my face continue to droop. Before I knew it, I was walking to the car, and Mother was squeezing my hand tightly.

"What's the matter with you?" she questioned. "Quit acting sad. Your brother would have behaved better!"

I climbed into the back of the car, and Mother followed behind me. I looked away from her and focused on the trees outside. The driver started the car, and slowly the trees passed out of view.

"Well, that's finally over with. I'll never understand why they always give *you* the compliments. It's so rude to ignore someone standing right next to you," Mother muttered, pulling out her compact mirror and inspecting her makeup. "Although, I suppose I should be used to that from the way your father used to treat me." My gaze traveled to the box in the front seat.

"Mother," I started to say. "Do you actually like my new dress?"

She huffed slightly and pulled out her lipstick to reapply it before snapping the mirror shut and throwing it into her purse.

"I think you look like a slut in it."

Can't Buy Me Love
Morgan

I waited at Mike's Music the whole day until five minutes to closing time, just for that girl to show up.

Mike would not let me hear the end of it. Sure, there had been plenty of times when I'd spent a long time in the shop, but never had I spent *all day* there.

"Why do you look up every time the door opens?" he had asked. "Are you paranoid or something?" I had brushed him off quickly, not wanting to explain the reasons behind my actions. I didn't want to admit that I had been waiting for Katrina, to whom I had no relation, to show up just so that I could talk to her more about the Beatles. Mike would have teased me endlessly.

The more I thought about it on my own without Mike's input, though, the more foolish I felt anyway. Keeping a distance from people was something I usually prided myself on. It was a rule I'd set for myself long ago. Mike had been the only slight exception I'd made to that rule and I didn't even think of him as more than a friendly acquaintance despite knowing him for eight years. Katrina was no different. I couldn't just go around befriending anyone who let me talk their ear off about the Beatles. No exceptions. No friends for me.

MORGAN AND KATRINA

I stepped into the store a few days later, determined to keep to myself. However, as I walked down the aisles of records, umbrella tucked under my arm, I felt the tug of regret straining under my skin. I tried to ignore it, but I found myself chewing the inside of my cheek in discomfort. Despite my trying to talk myself out of it, it was clear that the girl was still on my mind. Something had to be done about this. I needed a reminder of why it was bad to get too close to anyone, or else this was going to bug me for weeks.

My hands went straight for *Agents of Fortune.* Drowning myself in *"Don't Fear the Reaper"* sounded like a great plan for beating a harsh reminder from the past into my head. I carried it over to the record player that Mike had set aside for customers to use and began to set it up. He wouldn't mind if I played the song twice in a row if I needed it.

During the first few notes of the song, my eyes filled with tears. I was used to feeling sad whenever this particular music played, but this was a stronger reaction than normal. I really must have pegged the heart of what was troubling me if I was already clearing my throat.

Instantly my thoughts were filled with memories of the past—rolling in the grass. The flowers dancing in the wind. A row of perfectly white teeth grinning at me. Had it really been nine years already?

Oh! My eyes widened at the coincidence: the number nine. Of course, that was her favorite number. Laurelle. My "Miss Lizzy" as I used to call her. Funny how you remember little things like that, bittersweet things. The memories were difficult in general to think about. Especially the ones of her in the sunshine. Life was so different then. Promising.

I managed to get through the song without letting a tear drop, but it took a bit of sniffing and head shaking to keep them back. Perhaps it would be best to not listen to it a second time, just in case. I didn't want anyone staring.

I wasn't done moping, though. I switched tactics and returned to my usual: The Beatles. Maybe it wasn't the best decision to indulge my depressed mood but listening to "Misery" seemed appropriate. That one wouldn't make me want to cry.

"Mr... Morgan?"

I flinched, snapping out of my thoughts. Looking down, I jumped again, very nearly dropping my umbrella. Katrina herself stood next to me! I was so startled to see her–and so relieved–I couldn't help but step back. Did she always pop up so unexpectedly? No, of course not. She was probably here with Sarah to retrieve their laundry next door.

"Katrina!" I exclaimed. A balloon of happiness swelled in my chest. She stood stiffly, hands clasped behind her back, but her tone was a bit more confident than it had been before.

I grinned, but it became a frown when I noticed the girl's expression. She was staring at the wall, awkwardly playing with her fingers, obviously upset.

"Katrina?" I said again. Instinctively, I knelt so that I was eye-level with her and set down the umbrella. All thoughts of my sad feelings from before disappeared; My focus was now on what was wrong with her. She continued, however, to look at the wall.

"I'm sorry," she said eventually.

"Sorry for what?"

MORGAN AND KATRINA

She hesitated. Tearing her eyes away from the wall, she quickly glanced at me before looking down at the ground.

"For lying," she said.

"Lying?" I asked, confused. I tried to wrap my brain around what she could have meant. "What did you lie about?"

"I told you I would see you tomorrow," she whispered, her voice getting quieter as she spoke. "But then I didn't."

"Oh... Well, that's nothing to worry about," I said. "No problem at all! And I wouldn't really classify that as a lie, anyway. Everybody says things like 'see you tomorrow' and don't always mean them literally."

Katrina shuffled her feet. My words didn't appear to help at all.

"I'm sorry," she repeated again.

"Katrina, it's really not an issue. There's no need to apologize."

She shut her mouth and squeezed her lips together tightly. I stared at her for a moment, curious. What could I say to make her feel better? Then, I realized the music was still playing on the record player. If talking about the supposed lie wasn't going to help, then I would change the subject. Maybe she'd be interested in the cover of the album? It was sitting to the left of Katrina, just above her head. I reached for it quickly, saying, "Hey, what if I showed you—"

She flinched. A big flinch. And not only did she flinch; she raised her arms up protectively with a slight gasp. I lowered my hand very slowly and watched her. Her eyes were shut, and she appeared to be shaking. There was a long silence before the girl relaxed and blinked, looking up at me with curiosity.

"Aren't you going to hit me?" she asked. I furrowed my brow.

Her question alarmed me. So, too, did her behavior. Only someone who had been hit before would react the way she did. Or was I just jumping to conclusions? "Why would I hit you?" I asked carefully.

"Because I lied," Katrina responded.

I stared at her, trying to understand her train of thought. It wasn't a satisfying answer, but ultimately the reason didn't matter anyway. "Katrina, I'm not going to hit you. I would never do that," I said. Her blank stare did not bring me comfort, but I knew what I had said was true. My thoughts fluttered back to remember the way the girl had backed up into my leg the last time I had seen her. That memory mixed with the ominous question she had just asked caused concern to creep up my throat, but I tried to push the feeling down. Surely I was just overthinking again.

Reaching again for the album cover behind her, I made sure to move my arm more slowly before bringing it close to my chest. "Would you like to see what you're listening to?" I asked, wanting to distract her and I both from the uncomfortable silence.

She hesitated, glancing up at the record player and then back to me.

"Yes, please," she said quietly.

I turned the sleeve around to show her the front. "This is the first album they ever made. The song you're listening to now is called '*Anna*'."

"I like it."

"I figured you would."

MORGAN AND KATRINA

I tilted the cover so we could both look at it, but as the seconds passed, I could still feel tension hanging in the air. She was uneasy, and the cover art wasn't helping. I looked around the shop to see if there was something else that could change her mood.

"Hey!" I said, turning back to face her. "Have you ever seen someone play the guitar?"

Katrina perked up at my words. "No!"

I had her hooked; I could see it in her eyes.

"Want to see?"

She clasped her hands together. "Yes, please!"

I grinned and stood up, returning the record I had pulled back to its sleeve, and picked up my umbrella.

"You have the umbrella again," Katrina pointed out.

"Yup, I always have it, remember? My allergy," I responded quickly. I began to walk toward the back of the store with Katrina following.

"Are you by yourself again?" I asked.

"Yeah, Sarah dropped me off."

"Sarah. Is she your guardian?"

"She's my nanny."

"Oh. How old are you?" I asked.

"Ten."

Katrina and I walked the rest of the way in silence to the back corner where instruments of all kinds were displayed. In the middle of the section were a few stools that were available for interested customers to test out instruments before they purchased them. I usually didn't take advantage of this section of the store since I had my own guitar and piano at home, but oftentimes I would catch a few talented locals playing around with them for fun. Fortunately for us, the area was empty.

I went straight for an acoustic and withdrew it from its rack, pulling the strap over my head. Gesturing for Katrina to sit on one of the stools, I sat on another across from her and pulled off my gloves, laying them on the floor alongside the umbrella. Katrina stuck her hands under her thighs and leaned forward, kicking her feet back and forth a few times before settling. I debated what I should play for her, but it only took a few seconds of thinking before I knew what I wanted to do.

"Are you ready?" I asked. She nodded. I took a deep breath before starting to sing.

"Can't buy me love, love! Can't buy me love!"

Katrina grinned as soon as I started and never broke eye contact with me. I couldn't help grinning back, and after a few lines of the song, I was bouncing my foot and getting into it. I hadn't played a song for someone in so long. About halfway through the song, a strange look crossed Katrina's face. I wondered what was on her mind but finished playing before I asked.

"What did you think?" I questioned, swiping a strand of hair back behind my ear.

She giggled. "That was a funny song."

"Funny? Why funny?"

"They said they didn't need money," she said as though it were obvious.

"Well, who needs money? All you need is love, right?" I asked with a shrug.

"Everybody needs money," she said through a small laugh.

"Are you sure?" I asked somewhat playfully. Katrina blinked and sat up straighter, tilting her head at me.

MORGAN AND KATRINA

"Sorry. I didn't mean to confuse you. I just don't think money is that important," I said. My words must have stunned her because she continued to stare at me blankly   I thought I'd try a different tactic. "That's okay to have a different opinion. But can I ask why you think money is so important?"

She shuffled a bit, pulling her hands out from under her thighs and placing neatly in her lap. "Because you can get whatever you want with it," she said matter-of-factly.

"Are you *sure*?" I asked again. She squinted at me.

"Yes?" she drew the word out slowly, seeming unsure of herself.

"Well, what is it that you want?" I asked. "How much do you think it costs?"

She opened her mouth to speak but shut it immediately, looking down at the floor. Her eyebrows furrowed and her fingers curled, gripping the fabric of her dress   I felt bad having made her uncomfortable. "Hey, do you want to try playing this?" I asked, removing the guitar strap from around my neck. Katrina looked up and nodded. Her expression changed from confused to curious. But as I helped place the instrument on her lap, joking about how it was too big for her, she grew hesitant.

"I've never done this before," she said.

"No sweat. Everyone starts somewhere," I assured, guiding the strap over her head. I showed her where to put her hands and let her play around with the strings a bit before helping her strum a chord. She was quiet at first but soon relaxed and began to enjoy herself. She started to ask questions, and I answered them as best I could. Soon she was completely caught up in the moment and kept grinning, as she played the instrument for the first time. I was happy, too. It was a nice deviation from my usual routine. I felt a sense of pride introducing a child to the world of music.

We were both so caught up in what we were doing that neither of us noticed Mike walking up behind me.

"I'm gonna have to start charging you space for lesson time," he joked. I turned around and looked up at him with a smirk.

"Hey, man," I laughed. "How's it going?"

"Not bad. Just the usual. Who's this?" Mike asked, leaning down a bit and placing his hands on his thighs so that he was eye-level with her.

"This is Katrina," I explained, gesturing to her. "She's a big music fan."

Sitting with perfect posture and lowered eyes, Katrina remained quiet.

"Yeah?" Mike asked. "Niece or something?"

"No, no. Just a new friend."

"Well, cool," he said, turning to look at Katrina. "So, this your first lesson?"

It seemed to take a moment for her to realize she was being spoken to. After a moment of silence, she looked up and quickly answered, "Y-yes."

"Well, lucky you," Mike said to Katrina as he slapped my shoulder. "This guy really knows his stuff. Maybe you should consider paying him for lessons."

I glared at him, but Mike just smiled at me. "Well, I'll let you get back to it," he said, winking. I waited for him to leave, then looked at Katrina. Neither of us spoke, and for a few seconds, we stared at each other.

Finally, I managed to break the silence. "Don't worry," I said. "He's not actually expecting you to pay for anything. He knows it's just for fun."

MORGAN AND KATRINA

"Don't tell Mother I'm playing the guitar," she blurted. I was caught off guard.

I thought, for a moment, of asking Katrina why not, but she looked absolutely horrified. So I said nothing. My immediate concern was to rid her of that fear.

"I promise I won't tell," I said as cheerfully as I could. "My father didn't like me playing guitar either. Actually, he didn't support a lot of what I did. But that's okay. I may have to use his family name but that doesn't reflect who I am as a person, you know? I'm still Morgan, last name or not. So, did you want to play some more? I could give you a bit more of a lesson."

She tilted her head as I spoke. Then, very quietly, she asked, "Can there be more lessons?"

"Oh..." I said. "Do you want more?"

Her eyes seemed to shine in the light.

"Yes."

"You want to learn how to play for real?"

"Yes."

"That's great! Well, I mean, there are plenty of places to get lessons around town. I'm sure you could sign up anytime."

Katrina's face drooped at my words. "You won't teach me?" she asked.

I stared, startled by her question. "You want *me* to teach you?"

"Yes."

I hesitated. The gears in my head froze, uncertain how to form words for a moment.

"B-but I've never really taught before."

"Everyone starts somewhere," she replied, her lips tightening to suppress a smirk. I opened my mouth to speak, then quickly shut it and snorted.

"Well, aren't you clever," I said.

The thought of spending a lot of time with a new person made me nervous, but I was worried for the girl. From what I knew of the mother, I worried *she* was someone to be worried over as well.

"Sorry..." Katrina said.

I turned back to look at the girl. Her eyes were locked on the floor, and her face was downcast.

"Sorry for what?" I asked.

"For asking," she said quietly. "It wasn't proper."

Proper, I thought. The word saddened me. "Oh, asking isn't a problem at all. I've just never considered this before. Not seriously, anyway. I don't know whether I could do it."

She looked up at me, hope returning to her eyes. Suddenly feeling pressured, I found myself looking away from her before I continued to talk. "I mean, I have a job. I don't know that I have the time to teach you." As soon as the words left my mouth, I regretted them. If I had enough time to consistently come to Mike's on a regular basis, then I definitely had time for lessons. So why did I lie to her?

"Sorry, that wasn't quite true," I admitted. "I *do* have time to teach you. I don't know why I said that. The idea of teaching someone guitar sounds great. I mean, really, really great! I love the guitar. And you're pretty good at picking it up quickly. Teaching you would be fun. I guess the truth is that I don't know whether I *should*. Does any of that make sense?"

By the time I finished my one-sided conversation, I felt my ears getting hot from blushing. I always rambled when I was nervous, which was a trait I disliked about myself. Katrina looked confused, and I couldn't blame her.

"Sorry," I sighed.

MORGAN AND KATRINA

"You're a bit different," Katrina said, furrowing her eyebrows.

"I know," I responded sadly, my shoulders sinking. I clasped my hands together and tucked them between my knees.

"Woah, hey, what's going on?"

Startled, I looked up to see a young woman standing between Katrina and me. It took me a moment to realize that it was Sarah, Katrina's nanny.

"He's teaching me guitar," Katrina quickly answered.

"I can see that," Sarah responded flatly, turning to look at me.

"Hello," I said. The woman did not respond. I stared at her blankly before understanding what was upsetting her.

"Oh, don't worry," I explained. "It wasn't a real lesson. I was just showing her some things to kill the time until you got back."

"I don't have to pay you?" Sarah asked.

"No, no. I was honestly just teaching her for fun."

"Oh. Well, all right," the nanny said, turning her attention to Katrina. "Let's go, then."

The girl snapped her head to look at me. The lessons. I never did give the kid a real answer. Sarah followed Katrina's gaze and looked at me questioningly.

"Uh... hey, before you go," I began, standing up. "I'd like to say that Katrina really has a talent for music. She's quite the natural."

"Oh. Okay," Sarah responded blandly.

"What I mean is... her parents might want to consider real lessons for her. She could go quite far, I think."

"Oh, I see. Well, it wouldn't be easy to convince the lady of the house into doing that," Sarah said. "Thanks, anyway."

"Oh. Okay," I said.

Well, I had tried. I watched as Sarah reached out to take Katrina's hand, but Katrina seemed flustered. She didn't take her nanny's hand. She looked at me with a pleading expression. It broke my heart. Why wasn't she telling Sarah what she wanted? I stumbled into talking again.

"I mean, are you sure? Just half an hour for one day a week. I'm not kidding, Katrina would do really, really well."

Sarah stared at me for a moment. I could tell she was trying to come up with a way to not offend me rather than seriously considering the suggestion.

Before Sarah could answer, however, Katrina was suddenly by my side, chipping in. "Waiting for the lesson to be over would give you more free time to go see Benja–" Sarah shot her a look, and Katrina faltered before correcting whatever it was she was going to say. "To go run errands," she murmured.

Again, Sarah was silent. This time, however, her eyes had changed. It was as though she was no longer trying to come up with an excuse, but rather seemed to be wondering if the idea would work. She bit the inside of her cheek, then looked up at me. Still, she said nothing.

"It wouldn't cost much," I offered, trying to think of other ways to convince her. It felt like something was at stake here; something would be lost for Katrina if I didn't keep trying.

Sarah snorted and tilted her head toward Katrina. "These people live in Westbrook Heights."

MORGAN AND KATRINA

Westbrook Heights? That was the wealthiest area in the state! It was home to the snobbiest and stingiest people for miles. This kid came from a richer than rich family?

I looked down at Katrina. I was intrigued. Suddenly things started making sense. Her clothes, her posture, the way she spoke about money earlier that day. Hell, she had her own nanny. Why hadn't I seen it before? I now understood why Katrina was so interested in The Beatles. The poor thing told me she listened to nothing but classical music all day, but I hadn't taken her words literally. Now, knowing where she lived, I knew it had to be true. The whole time, she'd simply been expressing her desire to escape from that lifestyle. It was better than what I'd feared for her, but I could still sympathize with that.

"Not to be rude or anything," Sarah continued, breaking my thoughts, "but you'd have to have some stunning credentials if the head of the household were to consider you as a teacher, and by the looks of things…"

She trailed off, looking me up and down. My mouth gaped open a little, taken aback by the insult. I suppose I couldn't blame her for quick-thinking. She probably knew exactly what kind of people her boss hired, and I could only imagine how particular people from Westbrook Heights were over who was seen entering their homes.

Ready to admit defeat, I looked down at Katrina and started to shrug, but my thoughts changed completely when I met her dazed expression. She seemed to be slowly deflating beside me like a snail retreating into its shell. I could practically hear her heart breaking. The poor kid.

Katrina looked up at me. My pity increased tenfold when those sad brown eyes locked with mine. I frowned, wanting to do anything to take away the disappointment on her face.

"Well, as a matter of fact," I began, raising an eyebrow. Katrina perked up and watched me carefully. I gave her a small glance and readied myself to pull out the information I didn't often share with others. "My father happened to be a famous symphony conductor. Galloway was his name."

"Galloway?" Sarah repeated, looking up at the ceiling. "I've never heard of him, but then again, I wouldn't know because I don't go to symphonies like the lady of the house does. Wish I did."

"Perhaps if you dropped his name to her, she might agree to meeting with me and discussing it. I'm not trying to pressure you by any means, but Katrina seems really interested in this and I am very supportive of children who want to learn about music."

"Very well. I'll see what she says," Sarah said. Katrina jumped toward me, gripping my arm out of excitement. I grinned at her, but as soon as she realized what she had done, she let go and stood back, lowering her arms to her sides and quietly looked at the floor.

"Let me give you my number, just in case," I said. I didn't have a business card on me, but I knew Mike had a cup of pens at the cash register. I excused myself and ran to get some, quickly writing my number on the edge of a pamphlet while Mike looked at me questioningly. I ignored him and walked back over to hand it to Sarah.

"There," I said. "Just give me a ring if she wants to talk."

"2-3-1-7-4-3-8," Sarah said, confirming what I had written, then we all exchanged goodbyes.

"What was that about?" Mike asked from beside me a minute or two later. I crossed my arms, refusing to take my eyes from the door.

"I... might have a chance at getting a guitar student." As the words left my lips, a small hopeful flutter flowed through me. The feeling caught me off-guard but it made me smile anyway.

"Heeyy!" Mike shouted jovially, hitting me on the back. "The music man's finally workin' on getting out of that old job! Well done!"

Reality slapped me right in the face with his words. My smile disappeared as quickly as it had come. Mike meant well with what he'd said, but his kind words reminded me that nice things like music lessons were things I could not allow myself to enjoy. Not anymore.

As soon as my thoughts turned cold, however, the memory of Katrina's sad eyes entered my mind. I clicked my teeth in irritation. The urge to help her rose in my chest,

The need to be careful versus the longing to cure my sadness was difficult to balance. And the fact that I couldn't figure it out made me feel weak.

"I'm a loser," I said under my breath.

And Your Bird Can Sing
Katrina

I wasn't supposed to be listening when Sarah went to talk to her about Morgan, but I just *had* to hear what Mother would say. It was far too important for me to wait until Sarah could tell me later. I was being very bad, and I was scared, but I stayed hidden behind the kitchen door, so I could hear the whole thing. But I could only clearly hear Mother whenever she spoke. I don't know how Sarah had worded her argument, but I could tell that name was what made Mother make her final decision.

"Galloway?" I heard her shout. "You spoke with a *Galloway*?"

I was so thrilled that I had jumped around in my excitement. Of course, I realized I wasn't doing a very good job of staying hidden. So, I quickly slapped my hands over my mouth and held still. By the time Sarah came to properly inform me of the news, I had already escaped to my room. I made sure to act like it was new information. Some of it really was new information, though. For example, Sarah had cleverly not mentioned to Mother that the lessons were for guitar, knowing that Mother hated that instrument. She simply told her they were lessons from someone with strong connections.

"When do I start?" I asked Sarah.

MORGAN AND KATRINA

"I'll call him sometime in the next few days," she told me.

A week after Sarah's talk with Mother, Morgan was on his way over to meet Mother at the house and discuss terms. Standing next to Sarah, gripping her dress and looking out the window, I waited for Morgan to arrive. I wasn't sure what to expect. Remaining hopeful seemed like the best idea but worries crept over me as I watched the driveway.

"What if Mother doesn't let me?" I asked.

"Let them talk it out," Sarah answered. She paused, then added, "There he is."

I stretched my neck to see out the window. A black car pulled up the drive. How funny it would be to see him here! I grinned up at Sarah, but she wasn't looking at me.

"Go on," she said. "Get out of here before he comes to the door. You know your mother said you shouldn't be in the room."

I frowned but obeyed without question. Slumping my shoulders, I tried to walk slowly. That only earned me a glare from Sarah, though, so I dropped the act and scurried up the stairs.

I was halfway up the stairs when the doorbell rang. I turned around to watch, not caring that I was disregarding what I had been told to do. Sarah opened the door and I grinned immediately as the familiar bright orange hair came into view. Morgan was wearing the same outfit I'd seen him wear in the music store— the blue shirt with rolled up sleeves and brown pants. His hands were gloved, as usual, but his umbrella was open this time rather than tucked under his arm.

Sarah appeared as taken aback as I was but greeted him normally and invited him in without question. He looked around the entryway, surprised, as if he'd never seen a house before, but that would be silly. Sarah guided him to the left, into the living room, where Mother was waiting. That's when he spotted me. He smiled at me and waved. I waved back but then shot my arm down when Sarah turned to see what Morgan was looking at. I squeezed my lips together as she gave me a look and I scuttled further up the stairs to show that I was leaving. Of course, I wasn't leaving. I took a couple of steps up the stairs before crouching and holding onto the wooden poles, pushing my face against them as if that would hide me better. Sarah had, I recalled, said that I shouldn't be in the *room*. I wasn't in the room. I was on the stairs. The stairs didn't count.

"Hello!" I heard Mother say. She was mostly out of my view, but I knew she was sitting on the couch because I could see her legs. Morgan, who I could see, was about to sit in an opposite seat, and reached forward to shake her hand. "Welcome to Westbrook Heights, Mr. Galloway."

"It's a pleasure to meet you, Mrs..?"

"Oh, call me Helen. But for the record, it's *Ms*."

"Oh, sorry! Okay. Helen," Morgan nodded. "You have a beautiful home."

Mother snorted. "Of course it is."

Sarah had disappeared from the room, no doubt getting drinks from the kitchen for our guest.

"So, Mr. Galloway–"

"Please, just Morgan."

MORGAN AND KATRINA

There was a pause. I couldn't see Mother's reaction to being interrupted but she picked up where she left off soon enough.

"Your father was a wonderful artist. We saw him in concert many times."

"Oh, that's nice. I'm sure he would have appreciated that. He sure did love the symphony." Morgan settled back into the chair, but then seemed to change his mind, and sat back up.

"I had no idea he had a son. He must have taught you well."

"Oh, he didn't talk about family much. Very focused on his work, you know. He... he certainly taught me many things," Morgan replied, looking away from Mother. Sarah returned with a tray of lemonade. She set it on the coffee table between them.

Mother glanced down at the tray and cleared her throat. "Sarah."

"Yes, ma'am?"

"What's wrong with the lemon slices?"

Sarah and Morgan looked down at the glasses at the same time.

"Too thick?" Sarah asked.

"I don't know why I have to keep you reminding you of that. Especially when we have a *guest*."

Mother waved a hand toward Morgan, who awkwardly shrank at the gesture.

"I don't mind thick slices," he said.

I bit my lip, waiting for Mother's reaction. But instead of sounding insulted by Morgan's words, she was cheerful.

"Well, I guess you're lucky this time."

Sarah nodded and straightened her back.

"Now then," Mother said. "I apologize for the maid. She tries her best, you know. Hopefully the lemonade is still okay for you, Mr. Galloway?"

"Uh, just Morgan is fine. And, uhm, to be honest, I think she made the lemonade perfectly. Lemons are one of my favorite foods so the thicker the slices, the better."

"Wonderful!" Mother said. Morgan glanced to Sarah. The maid, meanwhile, looked as though she were holding back a smile as she handed Mother a cup. Morgan reached for his own and they took a moment to sip their drinks. Sarah moved out of the way and stood in the corner of the room. From that angle, she was able to spot me right away, and her eyes went wide. She subtlety motioned that I should go upstairs, but I pretended to ignore her. Instead, I focused on Morgan.

"So. Music lessons," Mother continued. "I can't tell you how excited I was when Katrina's *au pair* told me about you. I had no idea that a man of your stature was teaching! All this time I've been putting off lessons because I couldn't find anyone with the right qualifications and now here you are."

What? Since when had Mother considered getting us lessons?

"Your flattery is too kind," Morgan said with a chuckle. "But you should know, if this is a direction you want to go, this will be my first student. I've never taught before."

"The very first?" Mother's voice raised with interest. Her hands came into view, sitting atop her thighs politely. She must have leaned forward.

"Yup."

"Goodness me," Mother said. "So you're saying I'll be the *first* person to employ a *Galloway* for private lessons?"

MORGAN AND KATRINA

Morgan flinched, then nodded. "Yes."

I dared a glance at Sarah. She was intently staring at me. I feared she would make another move to tell me to leave but instead she nodded, throwing a glance toward Mother. I nodded back and smiled. It was a warning. *Be careful.*

"So, what kind of services do you provide?" Mother asked. "Would you be teaching instrument instruction or music history or?"

"Oh, I can do both." Morgan responded. He grinned. "I play the piano. I play the guitar. Sometimes I even play the foo–"

"Guitar?" Mother interrupted with a tight voice. Morgan's grin vanished and he swallowed.

"Yes?"

Mother cleared her throat. I shot a nervous glance at Sarah but she wasn't looking at me. I gripped the wooden poles tightly.

"I did not picture guitar," Mother said. "Guitar won't earn any money. I assumed traditional instruments would be the focus. Piano or violin, perhaps. A career can be made with those."

"Oh..." Morgan began carefully. "Well, I'm afraid I don't know violin. I could teach either of the other two but I must admit I had strongly hoped guitar would be your number one choice."

"Well, I don't want guitar."

Morgan looked uncomfortable. He took a moment to think about what to say, then started again.

"Are you sure? It's my specialty. And forgive me if I'm being too forward, but in the music store the other day—"

I frantically waved my arms. *Morgan mustn't tell Mother that I had played the guitar!*

Sarah looked alarmed as I stood up, motioning ridiculously in the air, but I couldn't let her distract me. I had to get Morgan's attention as quickly as I could. Luckily, I could see that he spotted me from the corner of his eye and he did a double-take when he noticed me practically dancing on the staircase.

"—I saw, er, well, I saw..." Morgan fumbled over his words. "Sorry, uh..."

"You saw what?" Mother asked patiently. Morgan cleared his throat.

"I meant to say... there seems to be growing popularity with the guitar these days. I've seen a lot of people, girls especially, taking it on. I'd bet your daughter would do wonderfully at it. You'd be keeping up with the times."

I breathed a sigh of relief as I dropped back into a crouching position. Thank goodness he saw me in time. I don't know what would have happened had Mother learned the truth. Pulling my hands away from the railing poles, I slipped quietly down the steps another few inches so that I could see her face. Both her arms and legs were crossed and she was staring at Morgan with an expression that meant it was her way or no way at all. Frowning, I gripped the wooden poles in my new stair position, feeling like a prisoner in a jail cell.

"My daughter Katrina? Oh, right. Sarah must have given you the wrong information over the phone," Mother said, plucking at her skirt and pulling off an imaginary fuzz. "Mr. Gallo-, I mean, *Morgan*... I didn't request an appointment with you to discuss lessons for Katrina. I had hoped you would teach my son instead."

The entire room seemed to freeze. Morgan's shoulders raised and I could see Sarah reacting in a

MORGAN AND KATRINA

similar manner. I stared at Sarah in horror but she shook her head at me. Morgan seemed stunned, blinking quickly a few times in a row. It was clear that none of us had expected Mother to say such a thing.

Mother reached for her lemonade and sipped it before ordering, "Sarah, go ahead and retrieve Charles."

The maid shuffled off without a word. She walked straight for me, our eyes locked on each other. I stared hard, my thoughts racing and demanding answers. Sarah walked past the railing and took the opportunity to whisper, "I didn't know," before moving out of sight. I turned my head to look at Morgan in panic. He glanced briefly at me, still stunned, then he faced Mother again.

"I think there may be some mistake..." he said to her. But Mother ignored him as she waited for Sarah. She walked past me with Charles in tow, who was proudly puffing out his chest to show off his favorite sweater vest. I quickly moved out of the way so that when Mother turned to watch them walk in, she wouldn't see me. But I returned to where I had been before, as soon as I could. If I hadn't already guessed that Mother had planned this beforehand, I would have known by the way a bit of hair was sticking up in the very center of Charles' blonde head. Mother always did that when she wanted him to look extra cute.

Sarah returned to her place in the corner while my brother walked straight for Mother.

"Hello, darling," she said in a cheery voice, reaching her hand for Charles to join her on the couch. She adjusted his little bowtie before turning to look at Morgan with an overly bright grin. My hands shook and my throat was closing up.

Morgan, meanwhile, stared at Charles with no clear expression.

"This is Charles," Mother said, squeezing my brother's shoulder. "He's very much interested in learning from you."

Morgan swallowed, then spoke. "This is not what I came here for."

"What do you mean?" Mother questioned, wrapping an arm around Charles and laying her head against his for a moment before pulling away. "You *are* looking for a student, yes?"

"Yes, but–"

"You have an available student right here."

Charles began to pick his nose. Morgan's fingers curled in.

"This is not who I thought I would be teaching."

Mother paused, closing her eyes and breathing in for a moment before letting out a short, forced breath.

"I realize you came here thinking of Katrina but you haven't even given my boy a chance. I guarantee he has double the talent you think she has. And besides, boys are little bundles of joy."

"You don't understand," Morgan said flatly. His tone was serious. "I'm not doubting his ability. He's too young."

"Oh, but surely if you heard how much I would be paying you–"

"Money has nothing to do with..." Morgan began to say, but then drifted off with a sigh and leaned back in silence.

I was miserable; practically sinking into the steps. I stared at Mother, silently pleading her to change her mind. Charles didn't care about lessons.

MORGAN AND KATRINA

He was only being agreeable because he didn't know any better. I doubted he even knew what was going on. Tears were slowly rolling down my cheeks.

Turning my focus from Mother to Morgan, I noticed that he was staring at me. I hadn't expected this and as such responded by freezing in place. His head was lowered. His blue eyes peering over round glasses into mine. I blinked. He did not. Then, he turned away from me, and looked at Mother.

"I'm sorry," he said. "I can't teach him. But..."

Morgan paused, looking at Mother with a serious expression. She gently tilted her head, curious as to what he would offer.

"If you'll let me teach Katrina instead, I'll agree to no guitar."

I pressed my face as hard as it would go against the wooden poles. Wasn't guitar what we wanted? I furrowed my brow.

Mother squinted, and her lips were pursed. She turned her head, looking down at Charles and chewed the inside of her cheek.

"Unless..." Morgan continued. "You don't want to be the first person to hire a *Galloway* for private lessons."

Mother breathed in and let it out slowly. She did not like being cornered. She hated it. I didn't breathe at all.

Facing Morgan once more, Mother raised an eyebrow at him.

"Fine. But I expect only the best results, Mr. *Galloway*."

Wiping my eyes, I leaned back from the railing and rested my head against the wall; my eyes traveling to the hanging chandelier in the entryway. Morgan had actually done it! He had convinced Mother to give me lessons!

"Very good," Morgan said. He didn't say it with any emotion, but I hoped he was as happy inside as I was.

"Shall we talk specifics?" Mother asked in a somewhat irritated manner, patting Charles' leg and glancing at Sarah, who swooped in to pick up my brother and left the room. I grinned stupidly at her as she passed by.

"Lessons!" I dared to whisper at her.

"Benjamin!" she whispered back before disappearing. I bit my lip happily and looked down at the steps. I was so lost in my excitement that I barely heard Mother call for me.

"Katrina?"

A single finger snap broke through my thoughts, I looked up to see her staring straight at me. A chill ran down my spine. Her voice sounded innocent yet her expression seemed suspicious. I stood up, eyes locked with hers. It took me a moment to realize that she was calling me into the room, not accusing me of snooping.

Walking down the stairs slowly, I tried to focus on what I would say once I was in the living room. Mother wouldn't confront me about my spying on them until Morgan had gone, so I didn't have to come up with an excuse for that yet. Then I remembered one of Mother's instructions for when a guest was in the house: *A lady doesn't walk into a room with a slouched back.* Keeping my back straight and my chin raised, I stepped into the room and tried my best not to look at Morgan.

"Yes, Mother?" I asked in the most polite voice I could muster.

"This is Mr. Galloway," she said, waving a hand toward Morgan. "He's going to be your new music teacher.

MORGAN AND KATRINA

I could barely hold back a grin. I turned slowly, gripping the fabric of my dress, and curtsied to him.

"Looks like I passed the audition. Please, call me Morgan," he said, smiling.

"It's nice to meet you, Mr. Morgan," I responded. "I look forward to your lessons."

He grinned at me, his eyes shining. I allowed myself to smile back, having never felt as happy as I did in that moment.

Think For Yourself
Katrina

Mother had agreed to lessons every Tuesday at 4pm, starting right away. I made sure to thank her for what she'd given to me. *A lady is always gracious*, after all. She accepted my thanks but said she really would have preferred Charles to have the opportunity.

As much as I looked forward to the lessons, there *was* one thing that disappointed me–no guitar. The music studies part seemed interesting, as that suggested I would get to hear more cassette tapes but how was I supposed to enjoy piano knowing it was the same instrument that boring classical was played on? Plus, we already had a piano at home. I could play that anytime I wanted. Not that I wanted to.

I tried switching my thinking to being grateful that I could at least get out of the house. Mother could have easily insisted the lessons occur at home but thankfully she and Morgan had agreed on having them at his house where he claimed to have all kinds of useful tools for teaching. She was reluctant to this idea at first as she claimed she liked the idea of being able to watch him teach, but luckily she changed her mind after Morgan had asked, "So you don't want your daughter to learn in a *Galloway's* specialized study room?". Which only led to me wondering what kind of house he lived in. Was it white like ours? Did he have more servants or less? How many cars did he own? I had so many questions.

It was an agonizing wait for Tuesday to come, but when it finally did, I found myself bouncing in my seat, watching anxiously as Sarah tried to find the right house.

"Are we there yet?" I asked.

"For the final time, *no*," Sarah said, "but soon. This should be the right street."

I lifted my chin to better see out the window. Scanning the area outside, I spotted what appeared to be an example of what Mother called "the common neighborhoods." They were usually smaller houses with one or two cars in their driveways and they were often close together. I frowned, feeling that Sarah must have gotten lost. Soon enough, she pulled into the driveway of the smallest house on the street.

Already puzzled enough, I turned my head to look to the left of the small house, where I spotted a large light brown building in the place a neighbor's home might have been. As a matter of fact, I recognized it.

"Isn't that where Grandfather's party was?" I asked Sarah.

Sarah turned to see where I was pointing and she nodded.

"Huh. Yeah, actually. I guess your music teacher lives right next to the funeral home."

"The what?"

"Uh... Nothing," Sarah muttered.

I stayed quiet, waiting for Sarah to open the car door and unbuckle the seat belt for me. The memories of Grandfather in that box came back to me and I was nervous just thinking about the man I had seen on the table in the basement. Perhaps I could ask Morgan about him sometime? But by the time we reached the front door of the house, I had become too distracted to really think about the sleeping man.

Sarah had barely touched the doorbell when Morgan opened the door.

"Hi," he said, giving a small wave.

I grinned wide while Sarah greeted him. For a while we all stared at each other, but just as I was starting to feel a bit uncomfortable, Morgan invited us in, stumbling over his words as he did so. I practically jumped forward, eager to see what his house would look like, but frowned immediately at what I saw.

There was no foyer at all. The front door led straight into his living room. Or at least I thought that's what it was. There was a couch and a chair around a coffee table so it had to be at least a parlor of some kind. But the odd thing was that directly behind the couch was the kitchen. I could see where the carpet changed to tile and the only thing separating the two rooms was a counter that jutted out from the wall with two stools underneath it.

I was still staring in disbelief when I heard Sarah behind me. "I'll pick you up in about an hour." Unable to look at her, I simply mumbled "uh-huh" without moving. The sound of the door shutting echoed behind me, but I was too busy gawking at the small space around me to care.

I finally managed to turn my feet and look at the rest of the room. A small piano was in the corner, along with some tapes and records set up beside it. A few decorations were on the walls, mostly framed album covers. I recognized one of the Beatles ones but didn't know the others. Big black blankets were hanging where windows would be. The only light coming into the room was from the lamps or overhead lighting in the kitchen.

When I spun to face Morgan again, I couldn't help but stare dumbly at him. He was looking at me while playing with his fingers. It almost looked like he was sweating.

"Sorry," he said. "I tried to make it as comfortable as possible. I don't really have company over."

I didn't know how to respond to this.

"Is everything okay?" he asked, fidgeting and shifting his weight. "If it's messy or something just let me know. I do try to keep it clean all the time, I swear, but I admit I went a little crazy this morning trying to make it look nice and I–"

"No, it's not dirty, it's very clean," I said, feeling bad that I might have upset him. "It's just... it's so small," I managed, looking away from him and focusing on the counter with the stools. I spotted a little wooden bowl full of yellow candies.

"What?" Morgan asked, following my gaze.

"Your house," I said. "Why is it so small?"

Morgan paused, looking back and forth between me and the counter. He tilted his head while blinking. Then he breathed a sigh of relief and chuckled a bit.

"Oh! Yeah, compared to your house it's, uh...." He sighed and then cleared his throat. Then grinned at me. "So, you think my house is small?"

I nodded.

"It *is* pretty small, actually," he put his hands on his hips and looked around the room. "But it's just a house. Big or small, it isn't the building that makes you feel home, you know?"

"Why are your windows covered?" I asked.

"Keeps out the light," he said, shrugging. "I have a severe allergy, remember?" I said nothing, feeling stupid for not realizing something that now felt so obvious. I watched him as he walked over to the edge of the couch and he pointed down a hallway that I hadn't noticed before.

"Down there and to the left is the bathroom, if you need it. And over there," he switched direction and pointed toward the piano in the far corner. "Is where we'll be having our lessons."

I glanced at the piano, then stepped forward to peer down the hallway. There was one open door to the left, one closed door straight ahead, and another closed door to the right.

"Bathroom, bedroom, garage," Morgan said. I slowly lifted my head to gape at him.

"You only have one washroom and bedroom?" I asked. He bit his lip as if holding back a laugh.

"I suppose you think I have a maid, too?"

"Doesn't everybody?" I asked. This time he laughed hard.

"No," he said, moving away from the hallway and walking toward the piano bench. I frowned, feeling embarrassed and not wanting to move. Morgan must have noticed my discomfort, because no sooner had he looked back at me than he quickly dropped his smile.

"I'm sorry," he said. "I didn't mean to make fun of you. You didn't know."

I said nothing. After a long pause, Morgan said, "You can take your shoes off if you'd like."

"Mother says I should never take my shoes off in front of a man or he might get the wrong idea."

Morgan gazed at me. Another long pause. Did I say something wrong? I was beginning to think there was something wrong with *him*, when he finally replied.

"Does your mother also say to remove your shoes before standing on the carpet?"

"Of course!" I answered, frustrated that he would even ask something so silly. But instead of being ashamed of his question he only smiled at me. It was kind of a sad smile at first. Then he pointed down. Of course. I was standing on carpet. My face grew hot and I bent down to take them off. I opened my mouth to apologize but Morgan spoke before I could.

"Don't worry," Morgan said, grinning. "I don't care about shoes on carpet. And I won't get the wrong idea if you decide to take them off."

Leaving my shoes alone, I gripped the sides of my dress. I wanted to hide somewhere, but instead I turned away from Morgan and approached the piano bench. Without taking my shoes off, so he knew I respected his rules.

I didn't know what to think of Morgan's home. All I knew was my own. My own home. My own life. "Mother says only poor people have small homes. Is that true?" I asked, placing my hands flat upon my lap after I sat down.

"Well, I don't think that only poor people have small houses. Some people just don't want to clean a whole house, or need a lot of room," he said. "But yes, I'm poor," he stated simply. I was shocked by his admittance and stared up at him in alarm. He only smiled at me.

"How about I explain how I was thinking these lessons should go?" he said. I nodded, feeling guilty. "I figured since we have an hour, I'll spend the first half teaching you piano. The second half I can talk to you about music in general. I'd like to expose you to different styles and explain how the same instrument could sound different depending on how you use it. For example, I went and bought tapes for us to listen to so we can explore different styles of music."

"Like the Beatles?" I asked.

"Sure! But more than just them, too. We can look at other types of rock and also music you've probably never heard of. Pop, jazz, reggae, folk, country, et. cetera. We'll explore and talk about their differences and their similarities."

The air felt lighter when he said that. It was thrilling to learn that we would be exploring different styles! But almost as soon as I got excited, I started worrying.

"Mother says classical is the only style that matters."

Morgan shrugged. "Everyone has their favorites," he replied, "but that doesn't mean the others don't exist."

I quietly stared down at the piano, my fingers plucking the lower keys.

Morgan bent to look at me. "Your mother never said I couldn't teach you other styles. She only said no guitar. And even then, that was just teaching you how to *play* guitar. She didn't say I couldn't have you listen to other people playing it. Plus, the piano can be used for more than just classical."

I glanced at him before quickly looking back at the piano. I was torn, feeling grateful for the chance to learn about different styles but unsure about the instrument in front of me and whether Mother would know what he was teaching me.

"Hey, there's no harm in trying," he said, gesturing toward the piano.

MORGAN AND KATRINA

I again stayed quiet as he spoke, this time shifting my hands to tuck them between my thighs and lowering my head. Morgan was in the middle of explaining how I would learn how to read sheet music when he trailed off, and I could feel him staring at me.

"Katrina, you okay?"

I paused before answering.

"Mr. Morgan, Mother says classical is the *only* music that matters."

We stayed quiet a moment. I bowed my head even lower, feeling more and more glum with each passing second.

"Katrina," Morgan began. "do *you* believe classical is the only music that matters?"

"Well, no, but Mother says—"

"Do you always do what your mother says?" he interrupted.

The words caught in my throat and I froze. I looked up at Mr. Morgan with a stunned expression, unsure how to respond. But he just smiled. It was a kind smile but there was a hint of something else that I couldn't put my finger on.

"Need I remind you that I told you back in the store that The Beatles sometimes used classical in their own music?" he added after a while. "Wouldn't you want to be like a Beatle?" My eyes snapped open at this and his smile got wider. I turned my head to look at the black and white keys in front of me with newfound interest. I reached out to touch them with one hand, allowing myself to feel their cold smooth surfaces, rather than sadly plucking at them as I had done a moment before.

"But I don't have to show you any other music styles if you don't want to. Your mother never said we couldn't, but she did imply that teaching you piano was her main goal. We can always just focus on you learning to read sheet music and playing classical piano."

My head shot up to look at him. "No!" I said, accidentally pressing down on two of the keys and causing a sound to escape. Retracting my hand quickly, I put my head down, embarrassed at my reaction. It wasn't ladylike.

"I was hoping you'd say that," Morgan said.

I nodded, telling myself to never touch the keys without his say-so. Morgan turned around and crouched in front of his cassette tape stand, carefully plucking a number of them from the top.

"Oh, and Katrina?" he said, looking down at the tapes and sorting through them.

"Yes?"

He peered at me from over his glasses. "You can just call me Morgan."

I smiled back. "Okay."

Act Naturally
Morgan

People from Westbrook Heights were exactly what I imagined them to be. Or, at least, Katrina's family was. Everything about them was excessive and just screamed "I'm better than you." Even the nanny/maid held an air of entitlement about her. They flaunted their money, their noses were stuck in the air, and they thought poorly of anyone who wasn't of use to them. I didn't know whether to laugh or to be concerned.

That was my opinion after the interview with Katrina's mother, anyway. I couldn't believe that woman's behavior and I thank whatever gods above that I didn't have to be stuck hosting the lessons at their house. I surprised myself at how well I hid my anxiety though I think I cringed more times than I should have through the encounter.

I remember wondering, as I drove away from their house that day, if I would regret fighting for Katrina to take lessons from me. After all, with a mother like that, I wondered if it were possible that Katrina could prove to be quite the brat once I knew her better. It was a silly thought. Katrina hadn't been anything like her mother. She'd never thrown a tantrum, nor had she insulted me. Sure, she'd had her moments, but I was certain she was speaking from a place of curiosity rather than snobbery. I think she realized how rude she could come off as sometimes.

In truth, Katrina had been far too fascinating for me to be truly frustrated with her. Her personality and way of being in general was very interesting to observe. Sometimes she'd be stubborn as hell and stamp her foot like a spoiled child but the next moment she'd be close to tears, believing she wasn't good enough to do anything. The shifts in her nature were sometimes so quick they were hard to follow. For example, I once offered to take her coat, but she reacted as though a snake had bitten her the moment I opened the closet door. Yet as soon as I closed it, her nose raised high into the air as she threw her coat carelessly onto a nearby chair. Were these mood swings just typical rich kid behavior, or were they due to something darker? Regardless of where they came from, it didn't change the fact that whenever she made the slightest mistake while playing piano, she'd look up at me as though she were afraid of me.

Her fear couldn't have been *from* me, though. After all, she'd once before asked if I was going to hit her, which made me believe someone else had been doing so. And after that interview with her mother in their home, I was very untrusting of the mother's behavior. Not that I had any physical proof of what I thought she might be doing. I looked Katrina over for bruises or scratches–any physical sign that someone was hurting her–every time she came over. I always found nothing. But that didn't mean that someone didn't abuse her in ways that could be hidden, whether it was the mother or someone else. Regardless, I kept needing to assure myself that it wasn't me she was afraid of. It had to be someone else, someone at home. The most I could do to alleviate my anxiety was to gain her trust and, perhaps, ask her one day if things were okay at home.

Over the course of several lessons I learned not to stand too closely and to always speak in a calm voice. That seemed to have helped a bit. But she was still wary of me. It was almost suspicious, how fearful she was. I had been trying hard not to overthink it, and to remind myself that her fear was most likely just a problem rooted in her own home, but that didn't stop me from worrying that I could be doing something wrong as well.

At least the lessons themselves were going quite well, which was nice. In only a few weeks, Katrina had made excellent progress. I'd actually had to slow her down at times because she was always in a rush to learn anything and everything she could. I wasn't sure if she was worried lessons would suddenly end or what, but whatever she was feeling, it caused her to absorb everything like a sponge. I told her countless times that it was best to go at a steady pace, but I was still reminding her each lesson.

To try and satisfy her need for "more, more, more," I let her borrow my tapes to take them home. Admittedly, I was a little nervous entrusting a 10-year-old with my tapes, but so far, she'd taken good care of them. Letting her listen to music at home had helped her focus more on the piano during lesson time so, in the end, it had been worth it.

There was no question over whether Katrina benefited from her lessons. With each passing week, her smile was brighter than the week before. She'd even asked to extend the lessons, or to stay longer. Each time she did that, I didn't want her to leave, either. I liked that she felt safe with me. I had yet to ask her about her potential abuser and what life was like for her at home, other than the superficial things, that is. But it seemed that when Katrina went home, fear gripped her, and uneasiness gripped me. I needed to learn how bad things were for her, but she would have to tell me herself. She'd already revealed several things just by being somewhere that wasn't her mother's house. I didn't feel that she was in mortal danger. But something was wrong. And I needed to know how wrong it was.

Yes, the lessons were definitely worth it for her, but when I asked myself if they were worth it for me, I found that I didn't have an answer.

Which was odd. I loved teaching Katrina. I was happy whenever she came over and I looked forward to giving her all kinds of new information. I was having a good time getting new lesson books for her. I even discovered that going to work wasn't as much of a chore.

Then again, I couldn't deny that as soon as Katrina was gone, I would return to my old feelings of anxiety and depression. I hadn't realized just how overwhelming the feelings were until Tuesdays brought with them that short hour of freedom. When I was teaching Katrina, I could forget about the days of old. The fields of grass, the sunshine, and even my old flame.

Yes, Laurelle—and all those ever-present memories of her—would disappear as soon as a lesson began. It was a reprieve I never thought I would enjoy. The thought that I could forget her completely, hurt in a way that I couldn't describe. How could I forget the one person whose heart I still yearned for even all these years later? Surely if I ever had the chance to meet her again, I would never let her out of my sight. I could apologize for what I'd done and she'd take me back. Maybe now that so many years had passed, she'd have changed her mind about having children. About motherhood.

No. That could never happen. Besides, I couldn't allow myself to be distracted by my own pain. What I needed to be paying attention to was Katrina's pain; her fear and where it came from.

In the end, I told myself that everything was going to be fine. There was nothing to worry about.

I really needed to just let it be.

Ob-La-Di Ob-La-Da
Katrina

I loved The Beatles!! I had been thinking about nothing but The Beatles for weeks. Every day, all day, it was only The Beatles going through my brain. No symphony, no classical, just pure rock music.

The Beatles influenced everything I did. When I was supposed to be paying attention to my schoolwork, I was secretly singing Beatles songs in my head. When I was supposed to be holding still as Sarah dressed me, I was quoting them to her without her even knowing. Whether I was lazing around in my room or sitting up straight during dinner, there was nothing I could do but think about their music. Sometimes I even got in trouble for humming to myself, but I couldn't help it. They were wonderful! And beautiful! I'd never experienced anything so amazing!

I was so glad Morgan showed them to me. Actually, I was just glad that I met Morgan. Each week I looked forward to his lessons and I know it wasn't just because of the music. Morgan was so weird and interesting that I never knew what to expect from him. Sometimes he'd be really confusing, like when he once said that he'd never changed the furniture in his house a single time since he moved in. Other times he made me really happy, like when he told me I could be anything I wanted when I grew up. I was happy anytime I saw him—so happy that I wished the lessons were every day rather than once a week. I even asked Sarah if the lessons could be eight days a week, but she didn't understand my joke, so she told me no without hesitation, which frustrated me. I thought she would have wanted more time to herself since more lessons meant more time for her to do as she pleased, but perhaps she was afraid of asking Mother. I understood that. I would be, too.

Maybe I could be a Beatle someday. That would be nice. I didn't play the piano well enough yet, to do that, but Morgan said that, with enough practice, I could do anything. I liked the things Morgan said. They weren't like the things Mother said at all. It made me feel like there was another world out there, and it was all for me. I just had to wait to get to it. Until I was an adult, I would only have bits of it here and there. Eight years seemed like forever to me, but if being able to do what I wanted for myself was anything like my music lessons–that was a world worth waiting for.

When I told Sarah that I wanted to be a Beatle, she snorted. I think she thought it was funny because I was a girl, and the Beatles were all boys, but when I asked her about it, she just said, "Do whatever you want. I don't care." So, I've decided I want to be a Beatle just like Morgan said I could.

Morgan warned me not to get too caught up in what he called "Beatlemania." Despite being the one who introduced me to them, he said that, to truly learn music, you had to learn to appreciate all genres, even if you didn't like some of them. I wasn't sure how to feel about that at first because I wanted to listen to the same songs over and over, but Morgan said I should keep trying new things. Once I got over my initial rejection of that idea, I found that he was right. I didn't know what I would find and yet, sure enough, there were new interesting bands that I discovered along with unusual music styles I hadn't expected to enjoy. Though, of course, The Beatles remained my favorite. I requested to listen to them every lesson and, more often than not, Morgan would oblige with a smirk.

I kept the content of the lessons secret from everyone except for Sarah, mainly because Mother would have been upset if she found out I was listening to rock and roll. There were a few times that I *had* to tell Mother about what was going on during my lessons, though. Luckily for me, she really only wanted to know things about Morgan himself. Such as, what was he like? What were his living conditions? And, her most often repeated question, was he dating anyone?

To my surprise, Mother didn't seem to care about how small Morgan's house was. Or that he only had one washroom. But I still couldn't get over how small and sparsely decorated his house was. How could his kitchen and parlor be in the same exact room? At least the place was clean, but how was that possible when he didn't have a maid?

There was also the matter of Morgan's clothing. What kind of person only wore one outfit? Every time I saw him, he was wearing the same blue button-down shirt and light brown pants. Sometimes he wore gloves and carried an umbrella if he was going outside, but that was it. Did he not own other clothing? Or was it just a uniform like Sarah and the other staff wore?

MORGAN AND KATRINA

I began to assume that he was far poorer than I realized. Mother said he was just an eccentric. Sarah said he was a boring recluse.

Regardless of what he was, I hoped the lessons would last forever. I never wanted to stop learning from him. Morgan may have been different from anyone I'd ever known, but that's exactly what I loved about him. His teachings opened my world up. I never would have discovered The Beatles without his help. I felt so happy! I felt so free! Ob-la-di, ob-la-da!!

Eleanor Rigby
Katrina

"I'm still thirsty," I said.

"Tough. It's out of my hands, now," Sarah responded, turning the steering wheel to the right and guiding the car into Morgan's driveway. "I asked you before we left if you wanted anything more to eat or drink but you said no. So, now it's up to him, not me."

I crossed my arms, muttering that I hadn't wanted anything until now. Looking out the window, I glared at Morgan's house.

"Don't forget that he's taking you home after your lesson," Sarah reminded me, pulling the car to a stop.

"I *know*," I said, waiting for Sarah to open the door for me. I was impatient as she unbuckled the seat belt; it felt like she was purposefully going slowly. As soon as I was free, I slid out of the car onto the gravel as quickly as I could, managing to duck under Sarah's arm as I did so. She attempted to snatch my hand, but I ran ahead so I could be the one to press the doorbell. Sarah muttered behind me, something about "rich brats" but I didn't care.

"Hello," said a familiar voice when the door opened. I grinned up at my teacher, a feeling of comfort washing over me the moment I saw his face.

MORGAN AND KATRINA

"Hey," replied Sarah, finally catching up with me. "Sorry, we're a bit late."

"Nah," Morgan said. "You're fine." He motioned for me to come inside and I hopped into the house like a toad, being sure to make a stomping sound on the mat.

"Alright, well," Sarah said, remaining behind on the front stoop. "I'll leave her to you, then. You remember the way back to the house?"

"Yup, I'm all set," Morgan responded. I ignored the rest of the conversation and focused on jumping onto the piano bench, swinging my legs back and forth once I was settled. Looking up at the music book, I tucked my hands under my thighs and hummed a short tune to myself.

"Well, I can see you're ready to go," Morgan said to me, shutting the door and chuckling. But before I could respond, the phone rang.

"Oh, shoot. Hang on, sorry," he said, shifting his attention to where the phone sat on the kitchen counter. I watched as he scuttled over and picked it up. A song entered my mind as I watched him.

All I gotta do is call you on the phone...

"Yes, hello?" Morgan answered. "Oh, hey... Yes... Right now? Ah, I'm in the middle of teaching someone at the moment..."

Morgan glanced over at me. Suddenly feeling sheepish, the song in my head disappeared and I turned away from him to pretend I was interested in the piano keys. I ran my fingers along them absentmindedly, flinching when I accidentally pressed a few. Fearing this would get me in trouble, I shot a look at Morgan, but he wasn't facing me. I slid my hands back under my thighs.

"Oh, geez, you did what? Well... I mean, I guess I could... It's just... No, yeah, I understand I'm the only one who knows how to do it, it's just..." he paused, shooting another look at me before staring at the floor. "I can run over but it has to be quick... Super quick... Okay, be right there." Morgan hung up the phone and sighed, walking over to the closet near the front door and opening it.

"I'm so sorry," he said, removing a coat from inside and putting it on. "They need my help at work. Should be really quick. Would you be alright if I left you here for ten minutes or so?"

I didn't answer. I didn't want him to leave but I understood if he had to.

"I know, I'm sorry," Morgan continued, grabbing for his gloves and umbrella from a small table next to the front door. "This isn't protocol, and normally if I needed to leave the house for anything, I'd bring you with me, but I can't do that in this situation. Will you be okay?"

I felt the need to sit up straight and rest my hands on the tops of my legs. He waited for me to nod before speaking again.

"You could practice your playing or you could take my headphones there from the table and listen to any of the music next to the piano. You know where the bathroom is and in the kitchen there's cups if you want water from the sink. I'm going right next door, so not far at all. Okay?"

"Okay," I responded, not understanding why he seemed a bit panicky. Maybe there was a big problem at the place he was going? Regardless, I'd been left alone before. Like in my room or the closet if I'd been bad. I went to the music store by myself, and that went fine.

MORGAN AND KATRINA

"I'll lock the door so no one else can get in," Morgan added, opening his umbrella and then the door. "Okay, bye! Sorry! I'll be right back!"

And with that he was gone. I watched the door for a few seconds, expecting him to come back in any moment. But he didn't, so I moved my head to look at the piano keys instead.

I said I would be fine but the sudden quiet made me realize that I wasn't sure what to do now that I was actually alone. It felt like I needed to hold perfectly still and not touch anything, which was odd because usually I was comfortable being by myself. But being alone in your own room was different than being alone in someone else's house. After a few minutes of doing nothing but listening to the clock tick on the wall I felt rather stupid. Every time I had been here, I had been allowed to play the piano or use the washroom or even touch a wall if I wanted to.

I reached out and pressed down on a few piano keys, letting the sound fill the room. I smiled, then giggled a bit, my back crumpling as I relaxed. This was fine.

What I *should* have done was practice my piano playing. But the unusual circumstances made me want to take advantage of the situation. What could I do now that I couldn't do before? My eyes drifted up to the covered windows. Morgan's house was very strange.

I shifted my body so I could look at the rest of the room. No maid, barely any decorations, a room that was both a kitchen and a parlor. I wondered what other weird things were in the house.

I stood up and walked around the room, inspecting each item closely. It was the first time I'd really considered that Morgan didn't have a fireplace.

My eyes landed back on the piano bench. At home, our piano bench was full of music sheets and yet only now did it occur to me that Morgan had never opened his. He always had the sheets I needed out and ready for me before I arrived. I wondered what other music was hidden away in there.

I approached the bench and lifted the heavy lid. As I expected, music sheets were scattered about inside. I rifled through them with little interest—that is, until I spotted a photo. I picked it up gingerly, then glanced at the front door. But the door made no sound to suggest someone was there, so I looked back at the photo.

It was Morgan sitting on a blanket in the middle of a bright field. A girl was next to him. She was very pretty and was holding up a hand with two fingers raised. They were smiling and there was a guitar between them. It was just an ordinary photo but for some reason, I felt uncomfortable looking at it. Hadn't Morgan said he couldn't be in the sun? I let the photo drop back inside the piano bench where it landed upside down. Before I let the bench snap completely shut, I noticed the numbers "1973" on the photograph.

I grew bored after a few minutes and I decided to walk around a bit. I paused when my toes reached the place where the carpet turned into tile. Morgan said I was allowed to go into the kitchen, but I took a moment to stare at the front door again and listen. I heard nothing so, I stuck a foot forward and stepped toward the counter.

It was a plain kitchen. Not that I didn't already know that from seeing it before from the living room. There was nothing on the kitchen table. The counter with the stools held nothing but the phone and a small wooden bowl filled with coins, keys, and yellow candies. The other counter, next to the sink, had some bananas but otherwise was empty. I took note of both the microwave and the fridge as well as what I assumed to be a closet to the right of the cupboards before returning my eyes to the sink, more specifically, the faucet. Suddenly, exploring the house wasn't what I wanted to do. I just remembered that I was thirsty.

    I tried to guess which cupboard would have cups in it. It wouldn't matter, though, if I couldn't reach them. So I pulled a chair from the table over to the counter and stepped up onto it. My eyes went wide when I opened up the cupboard directly above the sink. Four bowls, four plates, and four cups! Who only owned four of any kind of dish? I instinctively opened the next cupboard just to confirm, and sure enough the only thing in that one was a box of cereal and some bread, along with a jar of peanut butter. Once my initial shock passed, I felt bad for having reacted in such a disgusted way. He was poor. I should have expected that he wouldn't have the usual number of dishes. I grabbed a cup before closing both the cupboard doors.

    Morgan said that if I wanted water I could get it from the sink? Did he mean that I should drink from the sink water? Wasn't that only for washing? Drinking water came from... from...

    The more I thought about it, the more I realized I had no idea where drinking water came from. Sarah always brought it to me if I was thirsty, so I never saw where she got it from. Did she get water from the sink? I had always assumed it came from the fridge or from a drinking fountain.

    Hesitantly, I stepped forward.

    I opened the fridge and peered inside, nervous that I would find it to be as empty as the cupboards. To my surprise, however, the fridge was rather full. There was lettuce, cheese, milk, butter, apples, lemons (actually a lot of lemons), a pitcher of what appeared to be lemonade, some kind of meat, and a few other things; all normal items placed on the bottom shelf or in the door holders. I was glad that he wasn't so poor he didn't eat.

There was one odd thing. Sitting there, flat and neat, were rows upon rows of clear plastic bags, all filled with a red liquid. I had never seen bags like that. They might have been juice.

As soon as I spotted them, the front door opened. I shrieked, spinning around as fast as I could, instinctively hiding the glass cup behind my back as Morgan stepped in.

"Hey! I'm back! Again, I'm really *really* sorry abou—"

He paused after closing the door. I watched his puzzled expression closely as he turned to find me in the kitchen. When he finally spotted me, he smiled, but that smile faded once he noticed the fridge door hanging open. Thinking I was going to get in trouble for letting the cold air out, I quickly shut it with my foot, taking care not to reveal the cup behind my back. This action seemed to be the exact wrong thing to do, however, for as soon as the fridge door closed, Morgan's eyes went wide and he managed to race toward me at a speed I didn't know was possible. I gasped and stepped back, flinching as he threw his hand hard against the fridge door and leaned over me like a looming statue.

"What are you doing?" he demanded. As he yelled, I could have sworn that his eyes briefly changed color. Yellowish. My shoulders shook and my knees wobbled. I shrank like a tiny bug before him. Never had I seen him act like this. What *had* I

MORGAN AND KATRINA

been doing? My mind went blank as I stared up at his face. I felt myself shrinking under his shadow and gripped the cup harder behind my back.

The cup!

"I... I... I was just... getting a drink," I managed to say through my chattering teeth. I felt foolish for having hidden the cup. I brought it around to show him, but my hand trembled and I could feel my breathing stutter.

Morgan looked at the cup. I could feel the tears welling up in my eyes but I tried my best to hold them back. It was a long time before Morgan turned to look at the fridge, rubbing it briefly with his hand. Blinking, he turned back to face me again. His eyes were a bit softer. He remained quiet, then moved to take off his coat and walked past me to place it on a kitchen chair. Morgan stared at the floor as he moved. A single tear rolled down my cheek. Was he going to punish me? Would I never get to have lessons from him again? I was frozen as I watched him.

Morgan walked over to the door to the right of the cupboards and placed his hand on the doorknob. Immediately, my shoulders rose and my mouth hung open. That was the closet. Would that be my punishment?

A prickling feeling swept up my shoulders and I squeezed the cup in my hand. More tears fell. I couldn't help it. My breathing became more staggered. My entire body braced for the worst.

"Katrina..." Morgan began, carefully, opening the door, "I'm sorry I never explained that my fridge is off limits. Why don't I get you a water bott–"

"*PLEASE DON'T PUT ME IN THE CLOSET!*" I screamed.

Morgan jumped, and turned to look at me. I was crying full force, unable to control the fear that had taken hold. I didn't want to be put in the closet. I didn't want to be alone in that darkness, surrounded by nothing but my own imagination. Most of all, though, I didn't want to be put in that darkness by the one person in the world I really trusted.

"*Please*," I repeated, my lips quivering. I thought I heard Morgan say my name, but I couldn't really hear him. Too absorbed in my sobbing and paralyzed from fright, I squeezed my eyes shut while coiling my arms to my chest. I dropped the cup in my hands which shattered on the floor. I had made things even worse and who knew what he'd do in response. I hid my face in my hands and wished I could sink into the floor.

"*Katrina...*" The voice was gentle, quiet, and near. I refused to lower my hands, unable to stop crying. From the sound of Morgan's voice, I could tell he was kneeling in front of me. I braced myself for being grabbed and thrown into the closet, but his soft words caused my shaking to steady.

"Katrina, I'm going to pick you up and move you, but I promise I won't put you into the closet. Actually, it's not even a closet to begin with. It's just the pantry, so there's nothing to be afraid of. I just want to get you out of the kitchen so that you're not standing on broken glass. Okay?"

I didn't respond. I couldn't respond.

"I'm putting my hands on your waist now so I can pick you up," Morgan said. I flinched as he lifted me but still kept my hands over my face.

"No closet," he reminded me as I felt movement. I recognized the feeling of the carpet as I was lowered. But I wasn't convinced. It was entirely possible that there was carpet in the closet too and if I opened my eyes, I might see that I had been tricked.

"Okay," Morgan said, removing his hands. "You're in the living room now." When I didn't move or say anything, he asked: "Katrina? Are you alright?"

I opened my eyes, so that I could see a bit through the spaces between my fingers. My sobs had softened, and I was sniffing instead of crying. My chest still shook any time I tried to take a deep breath, but tears were no longer falling. I slowly curled my fingers down so I could peek over their tips.

Morgan's face was the first thing I saw, concern etched all over it. I had never seen him look so worried, nor had I seen his eyes filled with so much sadness. He was kneeling before me, watching me carefully. When I looked around, I found that he had told the truth. I was in the living room; nowhere near the kitchen closet. My eyes returned to meet his but I didn't answer his question.

He waited. I don't know how long we stayed there, in silence, staring at each other. My eyes were now fully uncovered but I kept my fists tight against my lips. His eyes seemed very blue, more blue than I remembered.

Slowly, very slowly, I shifted a foot forward. Keeping my eyes locked on Morgan's until the last second, I stepped toward him and leaned into his shoulder. He hugged me gently, his arms barely touching me.

"Feeling better?" he asked. I nodded into the fabric of his shirt.

"Good." He paused before speaking again. "Katrina. May I ask you a question?"

I nodded.

"Who puts you in a closet?" His voice was still calm, but there was anger in his tone. Now that I knew what his anger sounded like, I could find it underneath his words. I didn't want to answer him. The way he asked–it sounded like he thought my punishments were somehow wrong. Or bad. I didn't want to tell him an answer he wouldn't like. But I didn't want to lie, either.

"Mother," I said eventually, shifting my face so he would be able to hear me better.

His mouth hung open, and his lips moved a few times before he said anything. "She *locks* you in a closet?"

"Yes."

He was quiet a moment.

"Why?" he asked.

"Because I'm bad," I answered, baffled that he'd even ask. How strange that he didn't understand why. But, then again, it was also strange that he wasn't punishing me. I clearly had to have done something to anger him or else he wouldn't have rushed toward me so quickly.

"So," he began, sounding a bit confused, "you get locked in a closet for a few minutes as a punishment?"

"Oh, no," I responded, staring at the strands of his orange hair that fell in front of my eyes. "Usually I miss dinner."

"*What?*" Morgan shouted, suddenly gripping my shoulders and pushing me away from him so he could look at my face. I was startled by the movement and flinched, staring at him in shock. My expression must not have been what he was expecting, however, as he apologized immediately.

103

"Sorry," he said, removing his hands from my shoulders. He looked away for a moment, took a deep breath, then returned his gaze to me. "Hey... uhm... is everything okay at home?"

I tilted my head at him.

"Like," he began again, "you feel safe there? Comfortable?"

My eyes drifted upwards as I thought. *Safe. Comfortable.* I knew what the words meant but I wasn't sure how to connect them.

"I have a lot of stuffed animals," I said.

"Oh," Morgan responded. His half-smile returned. His eyes didn't smile, though. "That's nice. Not quite what I meant but I'm sure they're all lovely."

An awkward silence followed.

"Katrina," Morgan said after a minute. His voice was very serious. "I want you to know that I would never ever, *ever* put you into a closet. Nor would I ever hit you."

"Okay," I said simply.

"And if you ever need to talk to someone, I'm here for you. Anything you need, from me to you, I'll be there. All you gotta do is call, okay?"

I nodded. He nodded too.

Suddenly I became aware of the fact that my eyes were most likely puffy and red. *A lady never shows her tears in front of a man.* I sniffed hard and blinked, lifting my head.

"I'm sorry I broke the cup," I said as politely as possible.

"Oh, don't worry about that," Morgan said. "Who needs four cups? I only ever use one at a time, anyway."

He glanced at his watch before taking a deep breath. "Well," he began, looking around the room. "How about we just listen to some music today and not worry about piano?"

"Can you sing some songs on your guitar?" I asked, rubbing my nose with my arm.

"Sure," he said, stretching his legs to stand up fully before retrieving his guitar from the corner of the room. "What would you like to hear?"

"Beatles," I said, my lips pinching together as though I had just told a funny joke. Morgan grinned at me.

He was smiling, but his eyes were still sad. "How about *Eleanor Rigby*?" he asked.

Nobody's Child
Katrina

"Well, that's time," Morgan announced, looking up at the clock on the wall. "Gotta drive you home now."

"*Awww...*" I whined, letting my shoulders slump. I loved listening to the guitar.

"Sorry," Morgan added, pulling his guitar strap over his shoulder and setting the instrument on the coffee table. "There's always next time."

I nodded before sliding off the couch and walked obediently to the door. Morgan got his coat from the kitchen and his keys from the little wooden bowl on the counter, all the while carefully avoiding the glass shards which were still on the floor. Finally, he scooped up his black gloves from the small table by the door and the familiar umbrella.

He hesitated when he approached the door. I looked up at him curiously, unsure as to why he was waiting. He seemed to be thinking hard, so I didn't say anything. When he turned around, he looked down at me with such an expression of worry that I felt awkward looking at him. Before he said anything, he knelt down and looked me straight in the eye.

"Katrina. Are you okay with me driving you home?"

MORGAN AND KATRINA

Mother's servants drove me home all the time. Was he concerned that he wasn't allowed to drive me since he wasn't our butler?

"Sarah said it was okay," I answered. He winced.

"That's not what I mean," he said, biting his lip. "I need to know if you're okay with going home. Do you *want* to go home?"

Again, his question confused me. I looked at his piano in the corner of the room, and at the guitar on the coffee table. Was he asking if I wanted more time for lessons? Because of course I would choose staying there over going home.

I smiled at him. "Do I get to hear more music?"

He frowned. Then sighed. "Never mind. Just..." He looked me over head to toe, as if searching for something. I wondered if I accidentally spilled something on myself. I too, looked down and scanned for any problems.

"Don't worry about it," he said eventually. Then he patted my arm, stood up, and opened the door for me.

We approached his car, which was parked in the driveway. It was always in that spot whenever Sarah dropped me off and I didn't expect it to be anywhere different. I recall thinking it was odd that he never seemed to use the garage like we always did. That was, after all, the best way to protect your car, at least according to Grandfather. Wouldn't Morgan be risking his car getting damaged by leaving it out all the time? Sure enough, as we got closer, I noticed a few small dents and scratches on it that I was positive were because Morgan wasn't storing it properly. But before I could voice my opinion on the matter, I was distracted by a new discovery. The car's windows were pitch black, like the windows of the limo at home that we used for special occasions. Was his car just a short limo I'd never seen before or did some cars actually exist with these darkened windows? No sooner had I scrunched up my face at the sight of them than I released my tension and felt guilty for judging. Yet again, I had forgotten that Morgan was not only poor, but also "eccentric", as Mother put it. I needed to stop judging anything that seemed strange to me.

"Okay, should be unlocked," Morgan said, shaking me from my thoughts. I watched him walk around the front of the car toward the driver's side. When he noticed I wasn't moving, Morgan looked between me and the car for a moment, then snapped to attention.

"Oh!" he said. "Sorry." He scuttled back over to me and opened the front passenger's door. I only looked up at him, not knowing what else to do, or what he wanted me to do. Did he want me to sit up front?

"Uh..." he said, clearly just as unsure as I was.

"Sorry," Morgan said, immediately closing the passenger door and pulling the latch of the rear door instead. I smiled and climbed up into the back seat. Happily, I scooted myself to the middle seat, then, turned my head, waiting for Morgan to reach in and buckle my seat belt. He closed the door without even bothering to look inside, however, so I grumpily buckled myself in.

"Alright, here we go," Morgan said, collapsing his umbrella and setting it on the passenger's side floor. He started the car and we backed out of the driveway onto the main road. Once we were going straight for a bit, Morgan fiddled with the stereo.

MORGAN AND KATRINA

"Here's a tape I don't think I've played for you," he said. "It's the Beatles but this time they're working with a guy named Tony Sheridan, too."

"Okay," I said. I'll admit I wasn't listening too carefully. I was too busy looking out the window and watching the trees and houses go by.

As I was slowly passing an orphan's home one day... I stopped for just a little while to watch the children play...

I wasn't used to being in a car that didn't belong to one of our servants or that we didn't own. Morgan was not a servant of the house. And we did not own this car. Although one *could* argue that Morgan was being paid to drive me home so perhaps in a way he would be considered a temporary servant of the house. Well, no, that was silly.

"Morgan?" I asked, my thoughts shifting.

"Yes?"

"Where did you go earlier?"

"You mean after the phone call?" he clarified.

"Yes."

"When I'm not teaching you, I work at the funeral home next door," he explained. "I'm a mortician."

"What's that?"

He perked up and pointed at the stereo. "Oh, hey, this song was recorded with Pete Best, by the way," Morgan blurted. "Sorry, anyway, back to your question. What's a mortician? I take care of people after they die."

"After they what?" I asked.

"After they die. You know, after we pass away at the end of our life."

I stared at the radio for a long time while I tried to decipher what he'd said on my own before giving up.

"What does that mean?"

Morgan seemed to flinch. He glanced back at me before focusing on the road again. "What? To die? You... you don't know about that? No one told you what that means?"

"No..."

"Weren't you at the funeral home I work at for a viewing?"

I paused before answering. "You mean Grandfather's celebration?"

"Sure, if that's what you guys called it. That's actually a nice way of looking at it. Did your family all get together in a room with your grandfather in a casket? One of those long boxes?"

"Yes."

"That was a viewing. Did you not understand what was happening?"

"No, I did. Grandfather was pretending to sleep so that he could overhear what others were saying about him."

Morgan didn't respond. I didn't feel like I was in trouble necessarily, but still the silence was uncomfortable, and I didn't know how to fix it. Instinctively, I found myself telling him more just to fill the quiet air.

"Mother said he was going to be locked in that box forever as a punishment for being bad."

The car jolted as Morgan hit the brakes, and the wheels let out a small screech against the road. I stared up in alarm as Morgan whipped around to look at me with a horrified expression.

"She *what*?!" He shouted, his right hand gripping the passenger seat while his left still held

111

the wheel. But before I could reply he had already started to turn back forward and was frantically trying to spin the wheel so that the car would no longer be in the middle of the road.

"Wait, wait, wait..." he repeated while looking out of different windows of the car and trying to park on the side of the street. I found myself holding my breath, unsure of how to react.

Once we were properly out of traffic's way, Morgan turned to face me once more.

"Your mother told you what?" he repeated. His face was full of the same amount of concern he had shown back at his house. I hesitated, unsure if I should say the same thing as before or if I should lie. I didn't like upsetting Morgan, even if he wasn't upset with me. And I didn't think he was because he was still being nice to me.

"Grandfather was bad so he's going to be locked away forever," I said, eventually deciding I could be honest.

"Katrina..." he trailed off. "Oh, honey." His eyes squeezed shut and his fingers raised to lightly press against both temples as though he had a headache. He released them after a moment and spoke again. "Your grandfather is *not* being punished."

I didn't respond, choosing instead to watch him carefully.

"Do you understand? Your grandfather did nothing wrong. At all. He wasn't being punished. I don't know why she told you that but she didn't tell you the right thing. That's neither what was going to happen to him nor what *did* happen to him. He's perfectly fine."

"So, I'll see him again?" I asked.

Morgan hesitated. "Well... no. No, you won't see him again."

"Why not? You said he was fine," I accused.

"Well, he *is* fine. But that doesn't mean you'll see him again. That's where the dying part comes in. You see... well, I..." Morgan started to fidget, looking away from me and glancing in different directions. He seemed frustrated, mumbling a few things under his breath before looking at me again. "I'm sorry. Death is sort of a... sensitive topic for some people. And it's generally a parent's job to explain it to their child. And I'm not your parent. But your mother should know."

My heart felt like it had cracked, yet I couldn't tell if I felt more angry or sad. Wasn't he the one who pulled the car over to talk? Now all I could think of was the reminder that Grandfather was lying awake in a dark box somewhere in constant fear, and Morgan was the one who put that thought back into my head! Why would he say Grandfather was fine but refuse to explain how? I stared up at him feeling hurt and upset. He stared back at me with a tightly closed mouth before his expression slowly changed to one that looked to me like pity. For a moment I thought he would change his mind and explain what I wanted to know, but soon enough he turned away from me, and faced forward in his seat, crossing his arms. I found myself staring at that bright orange hair, both wanting to cry into it as well as yank on it. Why was he ignoring my question?

...I'm nobody's child... I'm nobody's child... Just like the flowers... I'm growing wild...

I frowned and looked at the floor. I didn't have anything to say and apparently neither did he. For a while we just listened to the tape that was still playing. Morgan didn't move a muscle. I could feel tears forming in my eyes until Morgan finally broke the silence with a quiet voice.

MORGAN AND KATRINA

"Death is what happens to all of us eventually," he said. "It can happen anytime and anywhere. One day, all of us will be done living. We just stop existing. I suppose you could say it's like falling asleep, except this time you won't wake up. You know how your heart beats inside your chest? It's like a clock that will stop ticking after a while. And that's normal. It happens to all of us eventually. Your grandfather's heart stopped ticking. But he lived a long life, and he did what he chose to do with that life, as we all do. It was his turn to rest eternally after working so hard, and you and your family got together at the funeral home to celebrate that life he worked so hard on. To say goodbye, to honor what he did, and to wish him well. He wasn't being punished. In fact, it was the opposite. You all respectfully told him you cared for and missed him. It was a beautiful act of love and I'm sure he was happy that you were there to see him one last time."

I stared at him, making sure I paid attention to everything he said. Morgan's words were calm and gentle as he explained. I may not have understood all of what he meant but I was glad he was trying anyway. Not once during his explanation had he turned to look at me as he spoke, but after he finished, he finally shifted to glance my way.

"Does any of that make sense?" he asked.

"Sort of," I replied.

"It's kind of a weird thing to think about. Hard to understand, but that's the best way I can explain it. Going back to your original question, my job is to help people go to sleep for that last time. Sort of like tucking them into bed, I suppose. Making sure their bed looks neat and tidy and that they're as comfortable as can be, you know what I mean?"

"I think so," I replied. My nanny had done that for me plenty of times and I always liked it when she did. "You're like Sarah."

"I suppose so. I just happen to put different people to bed every day rather than the same person over and over. And I don't know them personally."

"I see."

"I'm sorry no one ever explained it to you."

"Thank you for telling me," I said. It seemed like it was a really hard thing for him to do.

Morgan nodded at me. "Do you have any more questions?" he asked. I shook my head. He faced forward and took hold of the car's steering wheel and sighed. "Alright, let's go, then."

I leaned back in my seat, trying to process what we just talked about. Grandfather wasn't pretending to sleep like I thought—he died. He wasn't being punished like Mother had said, and what happened to him was normal. Dying was normal and happened to everyone. We all die once our life is over. I bit the inside of my cheek as I tried to figure out what that meant. How do we know when it's over? What was it like to die? If it really was like sleeping the way he said, would I one day fall asleep and just not wake up? Or would I purposefully go to sleep knowing it was my turn next? I certainly didn't think I was ready to do that anytime soon.

I sighed, clicking my teeth together and letting my cheek rest against the back seat. Instead, I tried to focus on the trees passing by. They flew past quickly and I vaguely wondered how close we were to home.

My thoughts drifted again, and I frowned at my sudden remembrance of the broken cup. How kind Morgan had been, how careful. I hadn't gotten in trouble at all. No punishment, no being put into a closet. He hadn't lifted a single finger against me. My eyes floated to look at the back of his bright orange head. Why hadn't he gotten angry? Was he really not mad at all that I had broken something? I went to look at his face in the rear-view mirror, when suddenly I became startled.

I couldn't see Morgan's face in the mirror. I stared hard, positive that I wasn't seeing correctly. Shifting in my seat, I attempted to sit up straighter and even used my hands to lift myself up a bit in order to see the mirror better. Perhaps he was sitting lower and the mirror was at an odd angle? But no, even when I stretched myself to the right as far as I could go, the mirror only showed the headrest of the driver's seat and then, once I settled back to my original position, my own face behind it.

"You okay?" Morgan asked, turning his head to glance back at me before focusing on the road again.

"Yes," I responded automatically, still staring at my own dumbfounded expression in the mirror. Was it broken? Could a mirror stop working like that? I finally tore my eyes from the mirror and stared at the floor. I tried to think of a time where I would have seen someone else besides myself in a mirror. Ah! Sarah! There had been plenty of times where I had seen both Sarah and myself in the car mirror at the same time. So what other reason could there be for Morgan to not appear in this one?

I stayed quiet the rest of the drive, choosing to ponder the question rather than talk to Morgan. He didn't seem bothered by the silence.

When we arrived home, the strange occurrence still hadn't left my mind. Not having an answer for it nagged at me. I was so distracted that when the car stopped, I unbuckled myself rather than waiting for Morgan to do it.

"You alright?" Morgan asked. I got out and looked down at my toes for a moment. It felt stupid to ask about the mirror and I didn't want to be embarrassed, so I debated for an awkwardly long time if I should say something. Finally deciding to take the chance, I lifted my head, only for Morgan and me to speak at the same time on accident.

"Listen, if this is about the death thing—"

"Why couldn't I see you in the mirror?"

Morgan's eyes went wide. I could see his fingers slowly clench the umbrella handle and his face expressed nothing. It felt as though I had asked a question he didn't know the answer to. I felt bad for asking. I hadn't meant to insult him; maybe I could fix the situation by automatically assuming the obvious.

"Is it because you're poor?" I asked. Morgan didn't relax but this time he at least responded.

"Yes."

He said the word very carefully, keeping his eyes fixated on mine. I shrank slightly under his piercing gaze and eventually looked away out of embarrassment.

"I'm sorry," I said, whether out of pity for his poverty or my own shame I wasn't sure. Either way, I waited until he shut the car door and walked toward the house before I approached my home.

"Ah, Mr. Galloway," a butler announced as he opened the door. One I recognized but whose name I didn't know. Usually, I associated him with the kitchen.

"Hello," Morgan responded, wincing slightly when his name was said. I remembered a vague detail from back in the music store—Morgan telling me that he didn't like his last name. But I said nothing. "Here's Katrina for you."

"Thank you," the butler said, moving out of the way as I walked into the house. I turned to wave, still feeling embarrassed for asking about the mirror. Morgan nodded at me with the same sharp look as before.

"Hey, Katrina?" he asked, looking down at me. I was startled because his friendly tone of voice did not match the suspicious expression on his face. Guilt washed over me as I promised myself that I would never again point out something so stupid as a broken mirror.

"What?" I asked, focusing on the question. He knelt down and lowered his voice so that only I could hear.

"Do you know what I do when I'm afraid?" he said.

I stared at him.

"I sing the Beatles. If I'm ever sad, I just sing their songs and then I feel better."

I didn't understand why he was telling me this, especially when his face looked like I was sure mine did when I thought I was in trouble. It was all I could do to nod.

Morgan nodded back. And then he was gone. I was left to consider the day to myself, alone in my room.

When Sarah returned to help me get ready for bed, I was unable to contain my curiosity.

"Sarah?" I asked. I was standing in front of my full-length mirror, waiting for her to return from the dresser with my nightgown.

"What?" Sarah asked flatly. She had been irritated ever since she'd returned from her errands. I didn't need to ask to know that her boyfriend was the reason for her snappy attitude. It happened at least once a month if not more and I had grown accustomed to ignoring it.

"What's a poor person's mirror look like?"

Sarah, who had been holding my nightgown up for me to slip into, lowered it quickly and shot my reflection a look.

"Is this some kind of weird metaphorical question?"

"No," I said, not bothering to ask what that meant.

"Then I don't understand," she replied, lifting my nightgown again and waiting for me to put it on.

"Well, I couldn't see Mr. Morgan in a mirror today. I wondered if that was because he's poor and he can't afford a working mirror."

Sarah snorted and moved away from me, taking my day clothes and putting them into the laundry basket. "I wonder if I had grown up like you, if I would have come to stupid conclusions too... No, there's no such thing as a mirror not working. What is he, a vampire?" she asked. I could tell she was mocking me. Of course she didn't believe me. I rolled my eyes and stepped toward my bed before hesitating.

"A what?" I asked.

"I called him a vampire," Sarah said, turning around from the basket. Noticing my unmoving stance, she added, "I was joking."

"I know that," I said. "But what's a vampire?"

"You've never heard of a vampire?" Sarah asked. Her tone made me feel stupid.

"No."

"Oh. Well, it's a creature with sharp fangs that sucks your blood and can't be in sunlight. Apparently, they also don't have reflections."

I stood motionless staring at Sarah, the gears slowly turning in my head as I took in what she told me. After a moment or two of silence, my jaw opened to gape at her.

"Did you say sucks your blood?"

"Yeah," Sarah confirmed. "Have you seriously never heard of vampires biting your neck with their fangs and draining all the blood from your body?"

Immediately, I covered my throat with my hand. "No!" I blurted. Sarah sighed at me.

"Katrina, I was *joking*," she said irritably, motioning for me to get into bed.

"I know," I said, lowering my hand and scurrying to do as I was told. I tried to hide my concern as Sarah straightened my comforter, but the truth was that I was getting more and more frightened as the seconds passed. The only thing I could do to help ease that fear was reach for my bunny doll and wrap my arms around her.

"Ugh, the ass," Sarah muttered. "'I'll always be true', he said. 'I'll write home every day' he said."

"What?" I asked, too busy in my thoughts to have heard what she had said.

"Nothing. Just Benjamin," Sarah said, practically spitting the name at me. "When you grow up, never date a man who acts like an imbecile!" I stared at her blankly, not knowing what to say.

"Just go to bed," she snapped, walking to the door and leaving the room.

It was dark and quiet. A thousand thoughts raced through my mind. *A vampire*, I thought. Was it possible? I stared at the door of my room, curling my fingers around my bunny doll's head and pressing my chin against her ears. Was I really being taught music by a vampire? How would I find that out? Surely, I couldn't just ask him directly, right? After all, if Sarah was telling the truth, a vampire sounded dangerous. Then again, Morgan didn't feel dangerous to me. In fact, he always seemed quite nice. So, maybe I *could* just ask him.

A chill ran down my spine, however, as I thought about confronting him. No, I shouldn't do that. If there was any chance of him being dangerous then bringing it up wasn't a good idea. I'd have to be sneakier than that. Possibly even bold.

Could I be bold? I stared down at my bunny doll, feeling unsure. I turned the doll in my hands to gaze into her eyes, half-expecting a reply.

"What if he hurts me?" I asked the doll. I was only met with silence.

The memory of my feet touching carpet in Morgan's home the day I broke one of his cups came to mind. He had sat me down so gently and carefully. Could I picture the same man hurting me? One thought of Morgan's kind eyes and I nodded to myself while kissing the top of my bunny doll's head before setting her aside to rest next to me.

Bold. For the first time ever, I'd have to be bold.

Here Comes The Sun
Morgan

All week I continually convinced myself that everything was fine. There was no reason to be suspicious. No reason to fret. I had to be calm. Very calm. Admitting that I felt stressed and nervous underneath it all would be death. I had to keep it together because if I didn't, that would be accepting the possibility of two things that I desperately wanted to deny.

The first was the risk of being exposed. I was almost positive that it wouldn't happen, but after nine years of trying hard to hide, being discovered was my most common fear. After the events during the drive home with Katrina, my obsession with keeping the secret hidden increased tenfold. Strangely enough, however, despite this fear having been a constant in the back of my mind for years, it was the second concern that heavily outweighed the first. Yes, of course, I was worried that Katrina would figure out my huge secret and spill the beans to everyone around her, but that didn't terrify me nearly as much as the possibility that she was being abused at home. I would have exposed my secret to the entire world if it meant a child did not have to go through that kind of pain. I felt so guilty for not having said anything to her before. The image of her anguished face, believing I was going to lock her in a closet, haunted me more than any previous fear I ever had. If only I could grab her and run to save her from what terrible things she must face at home.

I wanted to deny it so badly. God, I felt so stupid for letting it happen right under my nose. I had had my suspicions from before, of course, but now that they were confirmed by Katrina herself, I felt worse. Then again, what could I logically do now that she'd told me? I'd been providing her with a safe place, though not often enough. I had no tangible evidence of her abuse. There was no one to call who would care about my suspicions, and I had never seen bruises on her. Plus, it was entirely possible that the girl was just super sensitive and she had over-dramatized the situation, although I doubted it. However, she was a sheltered rich girl. If she was used to being waited on hand and foot with no real common sense of the world around her, maybe she just didn't know how to handle someone's anger?

Continuing my rationalization of everything, I rehashed my reaction to having seen her in the kitchen. I wish I'd handled it better. There was no reason for me to have scared her so badly. I never told her the fridge was off limits, so that was my fault. She must have seen what was in there. It was right there in the front, where anyone could see. And I'd left it there. I was culpable for that. Never having guests, never connecting with others, I never thought about rearranging my home, especially for a child.

I shook my head and placed my forehead in my palm.

She didn't know that sink water was drinkable. I doubted she recognized what she'd seen. No, I wouldn't have to worry about her.

Nothing to worry about at all.

When I heard the knock on my door at the usual lesson start time, I had a moment of panic, like in the old days. It was a brief reminder of what it was like to picture police at your door, waiting to arrest you. Getting over that fear had taken a long time and it was strange to feel a bit of that familiar response. The feeling passed as quickly as it had come, I opened the door for Katrina and Sarah.

"Hello!" I greeted them as normally as possible. Hopefully, it was believable. I had practiced saying 'hello' out loud just moments before. Sarah greeted me back while Katrina hesitantly stared up at me. Looking down at the girl, I noticed she was wearing a long scarf wrapped tightly around her neck despite it being a warm day. I grinned as wide as I could. *Calm, remain calm.*

"Ready?" I asked, pulling my eyes from the accessory and trying to focus on the girl it belonged to instead.

"Yes," she said, her wary look disappearing as soon as I spoke to her. Her attitude turned matter-of-fact and she marched into the house like a dedicated soldier. I glanced at Sarah, who only shrugged and waved goodbye. I closed the door and looked for Katrina.

I found her scanning the room, a hand to her chin in contemplation. She wasn't moving forward, simply turning slowly in a circle and inspecting the room. Anxiety crept up my throat and clogged my airway. It was hard to breathe around. There wasn't anything in the room that she hadn't already seen and yet I felt the sudden fear that perhaps she would find something I wouldn't want her to see. I cleared my throat.

"Ready to play piano?" I asked, hands behind my back, waiting.

Katrina jumped, apparently having forgotten that I was present in my own home, and turned to face me.

"Yes," she responded automatically. Then she gave a small worried look before shaking her head quickly and saying, "No, wait, I want a snack!"

I tilted my head, puzzled by her request. When she averted her eyes, I squinted at her. Typically, she would ask, not demand it of me as though I were her servant.

"Okay..." I said, letting the word hang in the air so she knew I could tell something was wrong. As if hearing my thoughts, Katrina clasped her hands together innocently and smiled at me. My suspicions only increased.

Moving toward the kitchen, I found Katrina following me very closely, like a puppy at my heels. When I turned around to look down at her, she would freeze and pretend that she wasn't following me at all.

"What kind of snack would you like?" I asked, going to the pantry. I turned to see that Katrina had stopped following me as soon as she reached the fridge, glancing awkwardly at it before smiling at me again. *Calm*, I thought. *Remain calm.*

"Oh, I was thinking, uh, something, uhm..." she looked around the kitchen as she spoke. "Something cold."

"Cold?" I asked.

"Yeah, like from the fridge."

I raised my eyebrow at her. She looked away immediately but eventually returned the gaze. We stared at each other. I removed my hand from the pantry door and stepped closer to the fridge, closing some of the gap between us. Instead of opening the fridge, I leaned against it, crossing my arms and legs while lifting one foot to angle it against the floor with my toes. After last week's lesson, I had already taken the precaution to hide anything in my fridge that I didn't want anyone to see. A simple rearranging of the items inside. But she didn't know that. Nor did I want to establish that the fridge wasn't off-limits anymore on the off chance that she dug through it sometime in the future while I wasn't in the room.

"What do you want specifically?" I asked. Katrina shuffled her weight between her feet.

"Maybe we can open the door and I can see what you have," she said.

"You've seen my fridge. You know what's there."

She wasn't happy with this answer. In fact, she seemed frustrated. She looked away from me.

"You know, it's a good thing you're not learning violin because if you were, you'd have to remove that scarf from your neck."

Katrina stared up at me in shock. I trained my eyes on hers like a hawk cornering prey. As soon as I believed I had the upper hand, however, Katrina's expression turned from surprise to irritation. Her hands clenched into fists and she raised her chin confidently.

"I've changed my mind. I don't want a snack. I want a drink," she stated. She added a sensible nod when she said the word *drink*. I tilted my head slightly.

"Oh?" I asked.

"Yes. I want juice," she said, crossing her arms assertively.

MORGAN AND KATRINA

"Ah, the lemonade" I said, assuming she meant the pitcher I had in the fridge.

"No," Katrina said defensively. "I want the red stuff."

A sharp jolt ran through my body. I tried not to show it. My arms shifted uncomfortably and I briefly looked away from the girl.

"What red stuff?" I questioned.

Katrina lifted her head higher.

"The red stuff that's on the top shelf of your fridge."

My fingers trembled and my throat began to close up again. I tried to remain calm, but my shield was breaking. My brain shouted at me to come up with an excuse.

"Oh. That?" I asked, stumbling over my own words. "That's just..."

Just come up with an answer! She'll believe anything! I thought.

"Oh, *that* juice. Yeah... it's... just juice," I said finally. I ignored my brain as it repeated the word *idiot*.

Katrina opened her mouth to speak but fell short of words and closed her lips. Furrowing her brow, she appeared to consider something for a moment.

"So I can have some?" she asked.

"No," I said flatly.

"Why not?"

"Because..." I began, but my mind went blank. I tried to will myself into thinking faster but it wasn't working. I looked around the kitchen in vain, as though an idea would pop out from an object near me. And then it happened.

"It's medicine," I said, this time with confidence. I stood up straight and it was my turn to lift *my* chin. Katrina squinted at me.

"Medicine?" she questioned. I could feel her distrust but I refused to sway. The calm feeling trickled back into my system. Now if we could only get back to the lesson...

"Yes. Medicine that only *I* can take and no one else. You can't have any and I'd rather not talk about it."

Katrina took a step toward me. "You called it juice," she said, pointing an accusatory finger at me.

I instinctively took a step back

"Yes, well..." I began, but again I was out of excuses. I felt cornered.

"It's not juice," Katrina interjected, "and it's not medicine either."

"Er, well," I started, giving a sort of general shrug. "I mean, one could technically argue–"

"It's *blood*!" Katrina shouted. Immediately I jumped, so shocked by her tone and also, specifically, by the word *blood*. My mouth dropped open in horror at her accusation and I shriveled like a prune.

"It's blood, it's blood!" she kept screaming, now pointing at the fridge rather than me. I put my hands up flat in defense, shaking my head slightly and trying not to succumb to panic. The calm I had tried so hard to hold onto all week had quickly slipped from my grasp.

"No, no," I said, keeping my hands in front of my chest and gesturing between myself and the fridge with no real clarity. "It's not. It's not."

"It is!" Katrina insisted. I had never seen her stand so boldly. She had always been so meek, at least whenever she wasn't letting a sarcastic comment slip, anyway. I didn't have time to consider her developing confidence, though, for she continued to spit out even more horrifying accusations. "I couldn't see you in the car mirror last week! *And* you drink blood!"

The hair on my head stood up on end. How stupid I had been. I hadn't even thought about being careful in the car when I agreed to drive her home. I could lie about what was in the fridge, but I couldn't lie about what she'd seen–or not seen–with her own eyes in that mirror.

"And," Katrina added, her voice dropping to almost a whisper. I turned my head slightly at her strange expression, my eyes fluttering down to her legs as I noticed her foot spinning slowly to a running position. My shoulders rose in alarm, as if predicting what was about to happen.

"You can't be in sunlight!" Katrina screamed at the top of her lungs, bolting from the kitchen as fast as her legs could carry her. I yelped and called out for her but only half her name escaped my lips. I jutted my arms forward in an attempt to snatch her but she was already gone, and I had no choice but to chase her. Katrina high-tailed it past the couch and ran straight for the front door. I was close behind, but I was still unable to catch her. I only paused when I realized she had stopped, her hand poised on the doorknob and staring at me with an expression that made me feel she was reconsidering her actions. I hesitated, hands still outstretched and frozen in place, refusing to move until I knew what she was going to do. Then I gasped as she grabbed my umbrella and flung the door open. In an instant, she had disappeared through it, slamming the door forcefully behind her.

"KATRINA!" I screamed, rushing forward and opening the door. Desperately wanting to follow her, I was forced to halt as soon as the bright light from outside blinded me. I gasped again, backtracking immediately into the shadows of my home. Breathing sharply and squinting, I traced the front yard for the girl.

"You're a vampire!" I heard her call. My vision finally adjusted to the sudden light and I could see her standing in the middle of the yard, holding my umbrella tightly against her chest. Her posture suggested she was frightened, but her tone was strong, albeit desperate.

"Katrina, come back inside," I yelled, this time too panicked to be mad at her.

"No!" she said, stamping her foot in defiance despite shaking like a leaf. "Not until you tell me I'm right!"

"Katrina!" I hissed, lowering my voice and looking around the yard to see if anyone had heard. Luckily, none of the neighbor's houses sat close enough for Katrina's display to be an immediate red flag, but I was most certainly close enough to the funeral home that her shouting could eventually bring out a curious coworker, which would spell bad news. "Katrina, get back here!"

"Am I right?" she asked, still gripping the umbrella fearfully. "Tell me I'm right!" I groaned, running my fingers through my hair and beginning to pace. I couldn't go after her and she refused to come in without the truth. What was I supposed to do?

I looked around my living room hurriedly before my eyes landed on the coat closet. I rushed for it, flinging the door open before reaching for a second umbrella I had stashed away inside years ago in case I ever lost or broke my first one. Relief washed over me the moment I touched its handle, but when I attempted to open it the metal arms refused to give. I struggled with it for a moment, cursing at the horrible timing of discovering that my second umbrella was broken. Throwing it angrily aside, my eyes focused on the contents within the closet and I began to debate if I could cover my head with a coat. But before I could even decide whether this was a smart decision, I heard Katrina begin to sing:

"Here comes the sun! Doo doo doo doo! Here comes the sun, and I say! It's all right!"

She was crouched, hands over her ears and eyes squeezed shut. The umbrella was tucked under her arm. She wasn't singing at the top of her lungs, but she was still loud enough that neighbors would hear. Was she trying to make herself feel better? I didn't have time to figure that out. I was mortified by her singing. I sank against the door, my heart feeling like it was going to break. I was trapped. Nine years of hiding and here I was, having been found out by no more than a child.

"Katrina!" I called, this time trying to control the desperation in my voice. "Katrina, if you come back inside, I'll tell you the truth!"

She stopped singing, her head raising to look at me seriously. Her hands were still covering her ears and her eyes were careful. I had her hooked, but she wasn't ready to give up quite yet.

"I'll tell you. I will. But you have to come back inside before I say anything." She took a moment to consider my request. She lowered her hands before removing the umbrella from under her arm and looked down at it, turning it slowly in her hands. Then she looked up and gradually made her way toward the door. Her steps were cautious, her gaze fixated on me. It was clear she was still unsure of whether she should come in. My brain screamed at her to walk faster, to hurry so I could shut the door and not have to worry about others overhearing. But the sooner she was inside, the sooner I would have to tell her the truth, if I intended to tell her the truth at all.

    I found myself swallowing and clearing my throat as Katrina stepped into the house. I resisted the urge to push her inside when she passed and instead waited patiently for her to step all the way in before closing the door and immediately locking it. When I protectively placed my back against the door and looked down at her, she stared at the doorknob as if suddenly regretting that she had come back inside. She clutched the umbrella like a weapon, keeping her eyes trained on me. This was it. Now or never.

    "Katrina," I said, letting my hands fall completely to my sides. "You're correct. I'm a vampire."

    She screamed.

Do You Want To Know A Secret?
Morgan

"Katrina, will you please come out?"

"No!"

"Katrina, this really isn't necessary."

"No!"

"You already guessed I was a vampire, why are you hiding now?"

No response. I sighed.

"Please unlock the door," I tried, this time a little softer.

"You can't come in here," Katrina mocked. "A lady gets to be alone in here!"

"Well... yes, that's true," I agreed. After having heard that her suspicions were correct, Katrina had screamed and ran for the one place I couldn't follow her. I was forced to sit back on my heels and wait just outside the bathroom door. "Yes, you can stay in there but, Katrina, I have to talk to you. You have to listen to me, alright? It's very important."

"Wait until I tell Sarah!" Katrina said. I rose to my knees in alarm, placing both hands flat against the door.

"No, no! You can't tell Sarah!" I shouted, trying to resist pounding on the door.

MORGAN AND KATRINA

I didn't get a response, but I heard shuffling. Looking at the bottom of the door, I saw a shadow fill the space where the light had just been.

"What I told you is a secret," I said, lowering myself back against my feet and returning my hands to my lap. "You can't tell anyone."

I didn't hear anything at first, so I brought my ear closer to the door. Soft singing was just barely audible.

"Do you want to know a secret? Do you promise not to tell, woh, woh, woh, closer..."

"Katrina!" I snapped. The singing stopped. Taking a deep breath, I tried to calm my voice before speaking again. I shouldn't have snapped at her, even if I was feeling tense. "This isn't the time for singing. This is very serious."

After a few moments of silence, I heard a very quiet, "I'm listening..."

"This is a secret." I repeated. "No one else can know. Do you know what a secret is?"

"You mean like Sarah's boyfriend?" I heard. A small gasp followed. I moaned and buried my face in my hands. I was done for. All those years of hiding wasted and it was all my fault for not being careful. All the friendships I rejected, all the things I could have done with my life if I didn't have to work in a funeral home. All the years of not living a normal life. All of it would be over as soon as this girl walked out my door. I could hear the sirens now. The police looking for me, my hands in cuffs, never to see the light again. Well, I already couldn't see the light again.

"Katrina," I said once more. My voice was steady but it was very quiet. I leaned my forehead against the door and closed my eyes. "It is so *so* important that you don't tell anyone. This is just between you and me. And you can trust me. Vampires aren't bad people, or at least *I'm* not. I already promised I would never hurt you and that's still the truth. You're right, that red stuff in the fridge is blood, but I didn't hurt anyone to get it. I would never want to hurt anyone. I'm not like the vampires in all those stories."

More silence. I resisted crying. I never believed I would have to do what I was doing now; literally on my knees, begging for a child behind my bathroom door to keep the secret I had protected for so long. I was at the mercy of a ten-year-old and I was terrified. Too much was at stake to risk anything. I didn't want everything to fall apart now. Not after so long.

My heart squeezed in my chest. I sucked in a bit of air and let my forehead brush down against the door until the top of my head touched the wood. My shaking hands reached up to press against the door and my lip quivered. I couldn't resist any longer. The threat of being exposed overwhelmed me. Soon, my shoulders were shaking, and I saw two spots on the carpet begin to pool with my tears.

Before long, I heard a soft voice pipe up from behind the door.

"Mr. Morgan?" Katrina asked gently. Her question was full of concern, but I didn't respond. I couldn't. I was too afraid of the inevitable. Instead, I started to ramble to myself.

"You don't know what I've done just to stay alive," I said through my tears. "I did some regrettable things in the beginning, but I promised myself I would never do any of that again. I took on this horrible job just so I could keep a steady food supply. I cut off friendships and vowed I would never get too close to another person again. All I do is go to work

MORGAN AND KATRINA

and come home. That's it. With maybe a few runs to the music store here and there. Do you understand how lonely it is to live this way? It's awful. It's *horrible*. I don't wish it on *anyone*." I sniffed hard, not bothering to wipe my eyes, and took a deep breath.

"I miss the sun so much," I continued. "I miss *her* so much. All I wanted was a normal life with a normal family. And now she's gone and I'll never get her back. I'll never have the chance to try and convince her to come back into my life and even if she did, I'm not human anymore. We couldn't start a family even if we tried. I'm so alone now. I'm so alone and it's so dark. I'm always stuck alone in the dark."

I sniffed again. I curled my fingers to form two fists and pressed hard against the door. I thought I was done crying now that I had finished talking, but the tears only flowed more.

I nearly fell over when the door opened, but I caught myself from toppling over completely. I continued to cry, ignoring the girl that was now standing over me. Instead of looking at her, I stared at the floor and let myself weep.

Katrina didn't move. My eyes scanned upwards and I saw her feet, the umbrella lying on the floor next to them. She stood awkwardly.

"P-please," I begged. "Please don't tell anyone."

I felt her small hand touch my head. Slowly her fingers smoothed my hair before resting in place.

"I won't tell," Katrina said. "I promise." Then she began to hum. It was the tune of "*Yellow Submarine*."

Looking up, I raised my head in order to see the girl's face. She retracted her hand, all the while looking at me pityingly and continuing to hum.

I gazed at her for a while. I didn't mean to put pressure on her by staring but I had to be sure that her promise was truthful. After hiding for so long, I couldn't risk a lie. But after looking at those sad brown eyes for a few moments, I knew. She wouldn't tell. A pang of guilt struck me when I realized it was possible that she made the promise out of fright. Her humming was shaky enough that she could have been a little bit afraid, but I couldn't help that. My tears had already fallen and the rant had run its course.

My eyelids drooped and my shoulders relaxed. It wasn't a huge wave of relief but it was something. I wiped my eyes and sat back, looking at Katrina and watching her try to figure out what to do with her hands. She stopped humming and focused on the floor. I cleared my throat, trying to move past the breakdown I'd had in front of her.

"Thank you," I said.

"You're welcome," she replied. I stared at her, not having expected a verbal response from her. Normally she just nodded. She only watched me carefully.

"Well," I said, looking around the hallway. "Enough of that, I guess. Should we go back to–"

"Can I see your teeth?"

I turned to look at Katrina and saw that her expression had changed from pity to curiosity. "Your vampire teeth," she said. "Can I see them?"

I sighed and looked up toward the ceiling. "No," I replied, boosting myself up from the floor and wiping my eyes a final time.

"Aw, why not?" Katrina whined.

Well, I guess she's not afraid of me anymore...

"We've taken up too much time from the lesson already," I insisted, wanting to change the

MORGAN AND KATRINA

subject as quickly as possible. Walking away from her toward the living room, I suddenly felt embarrassed that I had poured my heart out to her. How much of it did she understand? She didn't know what death was until last week. I found myself blushing over my own stupidity and was glad that Katrina couldn't see how red my face was. I dared not look back to see how wet the carpet was in front of the bathroom door.

"I already promised I wouldn't tell anyone," she argued. "The least you can do is show me proof."

I sighed again, turned around and placed my hands against my knees, squatting lower to her level. I opened my mouth and let my canines extend downward. Katrina jumped back, gasping slightly, then grinned.

"Cool!" she squealed, quickly catching up with me as I continued to walk toward the piano.

"No, it's not 'cool,'" I said, sitting down on the bench. "It's not an easy life."

"Well, I think it's cool," Katrina said, climbing up next to me. She smiled.

"Katrina. I'm frustrated that you aren't taking me seriously. I was just on my knees—literally—crying my eyes out to you and telling you all about my fears, and while I appreciate that you made a promise not to tell anyone, I'm having a hard time believing you when you're just pressing me with questions that make me uncomfortable."

She frowned and looked at her feet.

"I'm sorry," she said earnestly. She reminded me of a small dog with its tail between its legs.

"You can ask one more question," I said after a moment's silence.

"What does it taste like?" she asked quickly, looking up at me with interest.

"What? The blood?"

"Yes."

She stared at me, looking more like an excited puppy with each second. My fate rested solely on this small girl. A chill ran down my back.

"It tastes like pennies," I said eventually, swallowing and looking at the lesson book resting atop the piano.

"Pennies?" she asked.

"Yes," I responded, grabbing the book and opening it. "Now let's put this behind us and focus on your lesson."

"Okay," she agreed, tucking her hands under her thighs and kicking her legs back and forth.

"Just between you and me," I reminded.

"*Nobody knows, just we two,*" she answered in a sing-song voice, and giggled.

I was doomed.

Hey Jude
Katrina

"*I've known the secret for a week or two... Nobody knows, just we two...*"

I was laying on my bed, staring at the ceiling and quietly singing to myself. It had been two days since Morgan told me his secret. I wanted so badly to tell Sarah but I knew I mustn't. I did ask her to tell me more about vampires (I learned about their inability to eat garlic and that they must be invited before entering a house!), but not once did Morgan come up in the conversation. Not only would that upset Morgan, but if I had brought him up, I didn't think he would teach me lessons anymore, and I didn't want that to happen.

Never had I seen anyone cry as hard as Morgan did. Sure, Mother cried all the time, but that was different: hers was either in anger or when she wanted something. I had never seen anyone cry from sadness.

I stopped singing and sat up, looking around my room with little interest. He was so upset, but why? Was it really that difficult to live as a vampire? I shifted to the edge of the bed and slipped off. Turning in a circle, I inspected the items at my feet before looking at my bedroom windows.

MORGAN AND KATRINA

Grabbing the comforter off my bed, I tried to lift it and hold it against the windowpane. I wasn't tall enough to cover the whole window, let alone figure out a way to make the blanket stay in place. Dropping the comforter, I stepped back to carefully assess the situation. Once the perfect idea struck me, I raced to my desk to make it a reality. I grabbed the chair, pulling it to the window, and stepped up onto it. I teetered, but once I found my balance, I crouched down and grabbed the comforter. I had to stand on my tiptoes to make it work. It took me a few tries, but eventually I managed to get the blanket over the curtain rod. I pulled on the shorter edge and yanked it down a bit so it would stay in place, then stepped down from the chair and repeated the process with my other window, this time with my bed sheets. When I was done, I stepped back to look at what I had done from a distance.

It wasn't effective. Not only were the sheets too thin on the left window to block much of the sunlight, but the comforter on the right window wasn't pressed tightly against the wall, so the light filtered in around the edges.

So much for trying to see what it was like for Morgan every day. I put my hands on my hips and sighed, looking around my room again in frustration.

My eyes drifted to my desk. I walked over to it and examined its contents. Pens, pencils, papers, tape... so many useless things. Nothing I needed for what I wanted to do. Then I spotted my piggy bank. Immediately, I dropped the idea of the curtains, I took the white and lavender pig in my hands and tipped it over, ripping the cork out of its stomach and pouring the coins all over my desk. There were only a few in there, so I didn't mind making the mess. I grinned when I saw a single copper penny roll across the wood. I slapped my hand toward it but missed, watching it roll off of the desk and onto the floor. I jumped for it and snatched it. Brushing both sides of the coin with my fingers, I then popped it into my mouth.

The metal taste spread across my tongue, and my face scrunched up reflexively. I nearly spit the penny out but forced myself to keep it in place. After a few seconds, the sharp taste dulled. I relaxed my muscles and tried to imagine what it would be like in liquid form. It wasn't so bad after a while, but I felt awful for Morgan if he had to taste this every single day.

"Kat-rin-a?"

I jumped, and almost swallowed the coin. Mother's sing-song voice came through the other side of my bedroom door. Judging by the distance of her call, she must have been climbing the stairs. My eyes shot to the windows where I had placed the bed spreads, knowing that if Mother saw them, I would be in trouble. I raced to the left window and tore the bed sheets down as quickly as I could. I gathered them and threw them onto my bed, then rushed to the other window and pulled the comforter down with all my might. The curtains were a bit messy looking but at least both blankets were on my bed. I didn't have time to make them look neat, though, before the doorknob turned. I frantically ran to the door, knowing it was too late to leave the room and meet her in the hallway, where I could have stopped her from walking in. The best I could do was greet her and try to block her from opening the door all the way.

MORGAN AND KATRINA

"Katrina, I just wanted to–" she said as she forced the door open without knocking. She was interrupted momentarily when the door made a small thud against my foot. She slowly tilted her head downward, then, without moving her head, she raised her eyes to look at me.

"Yes, Mother?" I asked as innocently as possible, trying to tuck the penny to the inside of my cheek since it was too late to spit it out. My heart was beating so hard I thought I could feel my shirt moving. I watched her cautiously, knowing the entire situation was too suspicious for her not to investigate, but also knowing there was no way out of it.

"Katrina, what are you doing?" she asked. I swallowed, my breathing starting to get a little faster. I knew that whatever she was originally going to ask was no longer a part of the conversation. "Why are you blocking me?"

Not knowing how to respond, I became frozen, unable to move either my lips or my foot.

"A lady doesn't keep secrets from her mother," she said. "You've never acted like this before. What's going on?"

"I'm not keeping secrets!" I blurted, but she ignored me. Instead, she pushed the door open farther, forcing me to remove my foot. She marched into the room and immediately looked at my bed. Breathing a small "Hmm," at the untidy blankets, she then looked up at the messy curtains. After a dissatisfied grunt, she turned to see the upturned piggy bank and the coins spilled out over my desk. I watched as she turned again, to look at me. Her lips were spread wide in dissatisfaction and her eyes were full of shock.

"Did the maid do this?" she asked.

"Yes," I sputtered quickly, taking full advantage of the excuse and not bothering to think of what that would mean for Sarah. Mother made a disgusted noise, straightened her back, and walked over to the curtains to take a closer look at them. Then she moved to the desk to look at my piggy bank.

"Was she stealing money from us?" she fumed. I didn't think I had to answer this, so instead of coming up with a response, I turned my focus to the penny in my mouth. Since Mother's back was to me, I rapidly tried to spit the penny into my hand before she could notice. I misjudged the timing, however, for I was just lowering my hand from my mouth to my side when Mother turned back to look at me. Her eyes narrowed on me like a snake ready to strike.

"What was that?" she demanded, slithering toward me. "Did you sneak candy? You know how I feel about you eating when you're not supposed to! You don't want to get any fatter."

My shoulders raised and I backed up against the wall, my shuddering chest rising and falling. By the time Mother approached me, she was towering over me and blocking out the light. I was so frightened that I flinched and dropped the penny from my hand.

We both silently watched the coin roll across the carpet, gently hitting the desk leg and toppling over with a soft plop.

Mother's head ever so slowly, swiveled toward me and I shrank before her accusing eyes.

"Was *that* in your *mouth*?"

MORGAN AND KATRINA

My lips parted, but I found myself transfixed by her eyes, which grew more wrathful as time passed. Her hands lifted into the air, fingers bent, sharp nails glinting in the light.

"You disgusting little girl!" she cried, thrusting her hands onto my shoulders and clutching them with her claw-like fingernails. I jumped when she grabbed me but found myself paralyzed. That is, until Mother pushed me toward the door and I was forced to catch my balance.

"Ladies do not put dirty coins in their mouths!" Mother shouted, whisking her hands from my shoulders before snatching my left wrist and dragging me down the hallway. I tried to pull away from her, but my legs had gone weak.

"No, Mother, please!" I yelled.

"People who put coins in their mouths get punished!" Mother continued, half-carrying me toward the door at the end of the hall. I began to cry and, while I already knew it wouldn't work, I tried to sob as loudly as I could in case anyone else could hear me.

Mother used her free hand to grasp the closet doorknob and tore the door open, throwing me into the darkness behind. My face collided with the fabric of the hanging coats. I tried to catch myself with outstretched hands but my knees hit the dress shoes on the closet floor first. I gasped at the contact of hard leather against my skin but didn't have time to process the pain because I knew if I didn't react quickly then the door behind me would close and I wouldn't see the light of day for hours. I whipped around and tried to block the door from being closed but I was too late. The door slammed shut, just missing my nose.

I screamed.

The cry filled the tight space. Terror gripped my entire body and I could feel the space getting smaller by the minute. I pounded on the door while tears rolled down my face in fat beads. The door shook but didn't budge. I could tell from the shadows under the door that Mother was still behind it, most likely holding it shut.

I was unable to form words. I could only sob or scream. I was so frightened that I couldn't close my eyes in an attempt to shut out the darkness. I continued to beat the door over and over, begging to be let out. Even through my fear, though, I knew that the door would never be opened, at least not until I was quiet. And even then, it would be a long time before I would be allowed to come out.

I stopped screaming after a few minutes. I was still crying but I was silent aside from the occasional sniff. Staring at the shadows of Mother's feet under the door, I waited for the inevitable dismissal that she would give before leaving me alone. She always stayed until I quieted. This time I didn't have to wait very long.

"What a disgusting thing you did," she said. Her voice was muffled but I could still understand her. "Are you a baby? Only babies put coins in their mouths. Coins are for spending, not eating."

I tried to listen to her but was distracted by my own chattering teeth. I wrapped myself into a tight ball, squeezing my eyes shut against the darkness around me.

MORGAN AND KATRINA

"You must have inherited that kind of stupidity from your father, that swine. Now stay in there and think about what you did," Mother spat.

I heard her footsteps grow quieter as she walked away. My hands shivered as I hugged myself. Listening to my heartbeat, I rocked myself slowly back and forth.

Stay in there and think about what you did.

I put a penny in my mouth. A penny is a dirty coin. A coin is not meant to be eaten, it's meant to be spent. I should never have put that coin in my mouth. Only babies eat coins. I am not a baby. Why did I put the coin in my mouth anyway?

Wait.

A flash of bright orange hair flickered in my mind. I stopped rocking myself.

Do you know what I do when I'm afraid?

I paused, allowing time to dry my tears a bit. Then, very quietly, I made a small humming noise, testing the volume of the sound against the closet walls. Would someone hear me? After a moment or two of waiting, no footsteps came down the hall, which meant the hum had not been loud enough for anyone to hear. Taking a small but deep breath, I quietly hummed the tune of "Hey Jude." I hummed it very slowly, letting it drag out as long as I could. It was shaky at first and my voice cracked partway through, but by the time I finished the song, my voice had steadied.

I opened my eyes, surprised to find that the hanging jackets touching my shoulders were far less scary than they had been before. I leaned my head into the clothing, letting the fabric brush against my cheeks. I swallowed, not understanding why I reached down and touched the shoes below me. As I ran my fingers against the shoelaces of each shoe, I found that I wasn't afraid of them, nor was I fearful of the walls that surrounded me so closely. In fact, I let myself touch each one individually, feeling nothing but smooth surfaces under my fingertips. Cold, perhaps, but not frightening. They were no scarier than the walls that covered the rest of the house.

I retracted my arm sharply and pulled it close to my chest. This feeling was strange and I didn't know what to do. I looked around the closet as if trying to find a reason to be scared, but even having literal proof of the darkness right in front of me, I was seemingly unafraid.

Stunned, I leaned back and settled into the floor, staring blankly in front of me. I was not afraid. Shaken, but not afraid.

For the first time in all my memories of being trapped in a closet, I felt my mouth spread into a smile.

Carry That Weight
Morgan

"I'm fine!" I said. Well, probably snapped a bit.

I tapped the register counter of Mike's Music with my fingers and tried to avoid direct eye contact.

"Are you sure?" Michael asked from behind the counter. "You look like death."

I scrambled in my effort to look back at him and clutched the counter in alarm. I caught myself before reaching pure panic, but I was still obviously nervous. I couldn't help it. He'd hit too close to home. "What do you mean?" I said. Mike raised his eyebrows at my display, reaching for a cup of pens that I had knocked over accidentally.

"Jesus, man, be cool!" he said. "You just look like you've seen a ghost or somethin'."

Recovering slowly, I helped him with the spilled pens and tried to force myself to relax. Perhaps leaving the house had been a bad idea. While I patted the pens back into their cup, I glanced around the shop as discreetly as I could to see if anyone had noticed my outburst. At least one customer was staring at me from across the room. They quickly looked away as soon as I locked eyes with them, but it was already too late. My pride had been struck.

I turned back to Mike with a sigh. "Sorry," I said, gathering myself and bowing my head. "I just... I have a lot on my mind."

"What's happening?" he asked. His voice dropped in tone and suddenly his words felt serious. This act of strong concern was usual for him, but I found myself remarkably unsettled this time. When he'd addressed me that way in the past, it was over things I thought were silly or unnecessary, but this time he had every right to feel that something was truly wrong. Despite knowing I should be appreciative that someone was taking me seriously, it only spiked my anxiety. I almost wondered if I wasn't panicking enough for the situation.

Looking up at Mike, I watched his eyebrows crease in pity as he waited patiently for me to answer. But I couldn't respond. I couldn't tell him the truth. What could I say? My mind could only process the problem at hand, not form an excuse for it. The more I tightened my lips to keep myself from spilling, the more I realized I needed to get out of there before Mike's questions continued.

"I... I gotta go," I stammered before pushing myself away from the counter.

"Hey, wait, man!" Mike called behind me, but I didn't look back. I barely even gave myself time to open my umbrella before stepping outside. It wasn't until the shop bell stopped tingling behind me that I felt safe.

Not that the safe feeling lasted very long. I walked as swiftly as I could down the sidewalk, making a beeline for my car, but had momentarily forgotten about the regular public while I was inside the shop. Now that I was outside with an increased sense of fear (no thanks to Mike), I became more nervous about what the other people around me were thinking.

I clutched my umbrella handle tighter to my body and tried to keep my eyes ahead of me. I hadn't felt this nervous since I first realized I was transforming into something other than human all those years ago. What an awful time that had been. The memories of it were still clear. The growing desire for a food source that I had never eaten and didn't wish to eat. Fighting the urge between what I knew to be moral and my instinct to survive. The oddity of my canines having the ability to extend at any time. Weird things such as my eyes turning a different color when I was angry. But worst of all, the painfully slow transition of my skin beginning to burn in the light.

It was a terrible time of my life. Made worse by Laurelle's rejection. It was stupid of me to have expected her to drink a bottle of so-called "eternal youth" with me. At the time, it felt like we had gone on so many carefree—and reckless—adventures, what was one more? But looking back, I was able to see the situation for what it really was: a desperate, last-ditch effort to cling to a relationship that was failing. I was ready to settle, she was not. I couldn't blame her for that.

I wondered what she'd think now if she were to ever learn that the drink I had taken was real—at least in the sense that it stopped one from aging—and not just some stunt to keep her from leaving.

I shook those thoughts from my head. Laurelle didn't matter right now. There were bigger problems to face. Currently, the one where I left the house this morning instead of staying in. Well, at least having gone straight to the music shop was a severe mistake.

I finally arrived at my car, fumbling with the keys to unlock it.

"Hold yourself together, man," I said to myself, unlocking the car and getting in. "She's a child. Nobody would believe her."

Tossing the umbrella into the passenger seat, I made a mental note that I still hadn't gone to buy a new one to replace the broken one in my closet. Shutting the driver's door and starting the car, I took a minute to stay parked and stare out of the window, clutching the wheel tightly with both hands.

I wasn't sure where to go. I didn't want to go home but I didn't want to be outside either.

Maybe I should just stay in the car? I could do that.

I briefly debated whether a carwash would be a good distraction before I looked down and remembered I still had a tape in the slot. I lowered a hand from the wheel to turn it on. Maybe some music would help.

The Beatles greeted my ears.

"*...Boy, you gotta carry that weight, carry that weight a long time...*"

I stared at the radio in astonished silence before narrowing my eyes and yelling, "Really?". I shut the music off and grumpily leaned back in my seat, crossing my arms. Even The Beatles were taunting me.

I absentmindedly chewed the inside of my lip, staring out the car window at nothing in particular.

"I should never have told her," I whispered. I stopped chewing my lip and sighed. Then, I curled my body forward, letting my forehead rest against the steering wheel. "I'm going to regret that decision for eternity," I said. "Or at least until she's dead."

I blinked, my eyes suddenly opening. There was a strange and eerie silence hanging in the air. I didn't know what I was feeling, but I didn't know how to handle it, so I quickly snapped my hand over to turn the tape back on.

"*...Boy, you gonna carry that weight a long time, carry that weight a long time...*"

A chill ran down my spine. I let the music continue to play, too stunned to move, unsure of how to process the odd experience.

Once I was finally able to break the spell I was under, I shivered and tried to shake away the creepy feeling I had.

"Back home it is," I said, looking around as if someone might be listening before shifting the car into gear.

Ask Me Why
Morgan

I heard Sarah and Katrina pull into the driveway.

This was the moment. Either I'd open the door to find both of them acting normal or else I'd be forced to smile politely as Sarah explained that this would be Katrina's final lesson. There was also technically a third option in the back of my mind that involved the police storming my house and staking me to death but that was, of course, just the nerves.

I allowed the doorbell to ring twice before I answered it. Really, I had been standing in front of the door the entire time, chewing my nails, too frightened to greet them right away. But once I finally did open the door, I put on the best smile that I could, and told myself to fake it.

Sarah was completely ordinary, with the usual look of boredom spread across her face. Katrina, on the other hand, looked smug and wore a big puffy coat despite the warm weather. The strange sight reminded me of when she had shown up wearing a scarf to protect her neck. Was she afraid of me again? No, the coat wouldn't be related to me, but it was still unusual, and thus, I kept alert for any other suspicious activity.

"Hey," Sarah greeted me.

"Hello!" I replied. "Nice to see you again."

"Yup," she said, lifting her arm to hand over an envelope. "I have this for you. It's from the lady of the house."

"O-oh, thank you." I stuttered as I took it before moving aside for Katrina to come in. Sarah nodded and waved goodbye.

When I shut the door, I was so distracted, wondering what was in my hand, that I didn't notice that Katrina had said something to me.

"What?" I asked, looking at the envelope and starting to open it.

"I said, I didn't tell anyone," she repeated. I immediately stopped what I was doing, accidentally squeezing the paper tightly in my hand as I gaped at her.

"What?" I asked again.

"I *said*, I didn't *tell* anyone." she said again. "And also I have a gift for you."

Her words were too simple. I knelt down quickly and took hold of her shoulders to force her to look at me. She appeared afraid of what I was doing and froze when I touched her, but I had been panicking all week and had barely slept. "You didn't tell anyone? Really, truly? Not even Sarah?" I stared at her without blinking. "You promise?"

"No one! I... I promise!" she said, leaning back slightly and stepping one foot backwards. I sighed and released her, now feeling bad that I had grabbed her.

"I'm sorry," I said. "I just... I was scared."

Katrina calmed once I let go and she unzipped her coat as she spoke. "It's okay," she said, slipping her arms out of the coat and shaking it onto the nearby armchair. "So, I have a gift!" She piped up, digging into the pockets of the coat that she had shimmed out of.

"Uhm, hold on," I said, remembering the letter in my hand. I looked down at it and muttered a small "whoops" as I noticed that I had crumpled it. I smoothed it against my leg then pulled out the letter inside.

To my surprise, it was an invitation.

"Oh," I said, reading it. "Katrina, your mother invited me to a dinner party at your house next week."

"Okay..." she said. She was now rocking between her toes and her heels while holding something behind her back. After reading the card twice, I set it aside on the coffee table and focused on Katrina.

"Sorry," I said. "What was it? You said something about a gift?"

"I have a gift for you," Katrina said excitedly, leaning over and looking up at me with a grin.

"A gift? What for? It's not my birthday," I said, trying to play along. Katrina tightened her lips and returned to an upright position. She looked at the floor, suddenly shy.

"For the lessons," she said. "To say thank you."

I tilted my head and waited for her to hand me what she was hiding. She revealed what was behind her back and held it out for me to take.

"A flashlight," I said, picking it up tenderly and inspecting it. I hadn't meant to sound insulting, but I was confused. It was an odd gift, to say the least.

"It's for the darkness." she said quietly, clasping her hands together and looking to the side.

I paused, my hands curling around the flashlight and my shoulders raising slowly. My chest swelled in adoration. I stared at Katrina with awe. By

161

the time she finally looked back at me I was already sniffing, and tears were forming in my eyes. She must have found my reaction strange for as soon as she realized I was starting to cry she gave an expression of alarm. She appeared unsure of what to do as I leaned forward and wrapped my arms around her. But I couldn't help it. I was too caught up in my emotion.

"Thank you," I said quietly into her ear, trying to keep myself from letting the tears fall.

"You're... welcome," she said, somewhat uncomfortably. I let her go after that and looked down at the flashlight as though it were my own child.

"I stole it from the pantry," she said proudly. Immediately the wonder of what had just happened shattered and I stared at Katrina in shock.

"You *what*?" I said.

"I stole it while no one was looking. And then I wore that big coat so I could put it in the big pocket so no one would see it."

"Katrina, you can't just *steal* something," I said.

"Why? We have, like, seven of them," Katrina said innocently. I sighed and set the flashlight on the coffee table.

"Let's just get started on today's lesson," I said, standing up straight and walking over to the piano.

"Wait, I have more vampire questions," Katrina said, skipping behind me and hopping up onto the piano bench.

"You get three," I said, sitting next to her.

"Can your eyes change color?" she asked.

"Yes. Apparently when I get very angry, my eyes change to a bright yellow. Almost like a gold but not really. Most often it's just a quick flash but if I'm really pushed to the edge then my eyes will stay that yellow color."

"I saw your eyes flash yellow," Katrina said. I sucked in a bit of my cheek and looked at her with pity.

"Sorry," I said. She just shrugged.

"Were you always a vampire?" she asked.

"No, I became one about nine years ago," I said, looking up at the ceiling. I started to reminisce a bit and got lost in the memories before being interrupted by Katrina's next question.

"How?"

"How what?"

"*How* did you become a vampire?"

I swallowed. I hadn't expected this. It made perfect sense for her to ask but for some reason it caught me off guard. "Well," I began, but I looked away from her.

"It was a rash decision," I answered eventually. When I glanced at her she was giving me a curious eye. She wanted more of an explanation.

"I was stupid and immature," I continued. "I did it for a girl."

"You *wanted* to become a vampire? For a girl?" Katrina questioned, tilting her head.

"Yeah. Wanted to prove how loyal I was to her."

"Wait, the girl in the photo?" I shot a look at Katrina. As soon as she said it, she slapped a hand over her mouth. I waited for her to explain. She bit her lip, looking down, then said, "I looked in your piano bench..."

"Oh," I said simply. "Yeah, that girl."

"Who was she? Was she the one you cried about?"

163

MORGAN AND KATRINA

Katrina didn't mean to open an old wound, but I cringed when she asked. "Oh, umm... Yes... She was an old friend. A girlfriend... Er, an *ex*-girlfriend."

"Oh," Katrina said. "Was she a vampire too?"

"No," I answered quietly. "No, she was an ordinary human. Well, not *ordinary*. She was more interesting than that. So yeah, not ordinary. But interesting. And... and wonderful. Fun and exciting, you know? I, uh... you know, that wasn't really what you were asking. Sorry. No. She wasn't a vampire."

Katrina stared at me. "Sorry." I repeated.

"You became a vampire *for* her?"

I shifted. "Y-yeah. Well, kind of... I mean, I did it as an act, really. Just wanted to prove that I wanted to be with her forever. I didn't know the blood I drank was real and so I turned into a vampire on accident. It was just supposed to be... I don't know... an act."

"The blood.?" Katrina drew out her words in disgust. She stuck out her tongue a bit as she spoke.

"Yeah. You haven't heard of that in movies and stuff? To turn into a vampire, you have to drink another vampire's blood."

Katrina seemed alarmed by this and she sat up straight. "There are *more* vampires?" she spat. I understood why she was afraid, but I raised a hand to calm her.

"Not that I know of. The blood I drank was in an old bottle and supposedly came from a guy who died yeeeears ago. There's no way to know for sure but I've never met another so far."

I could tell Katrina wasn't satisfied with this answer, but she at least relaxed for the time being and looked at the piano keys in silence. I sat quietly with her, waiting for some kind of indication that she was done processing my answers. Just as I opened my mouth to ask if she was ready to start the day's lesson, she blurted:

"Can I touch your vampire teeth?"

My face fell at her request. Seeing my off-put expression, Katrina quickly added, "Please?"

I sighed. "Fine. But then it's lesson time."

I leaned down a bit and opened my mouth. I let my canines extend downward to their full length and watched with amusement as Katrina's eyes widened. It was clear that she was suddenly hesitant, but I didn't move, instead letting her take her time. After a few seconds, she slowly raised her hand and reached out with a single finger to touch one tooth. She retracted her arm and giggled almost as soon as she touched it.

"Satisfied?" I asked. She nodded, grinning. I let my teeth return to their normal state and turned to the piano.

"Morgan?" She asked quickly, causing me to pause from reaching out my arms to the keys.

"Yes?"

"Do you miss her?"

I froze. A song lyric came to the front of my mind.

Mister postman look and see…. Is there a letter in your bag for me...

I swallowed to try and get rid of the hurt feeling in my throat. I turned to look at Katrina. There wasn't really any reason to lie to her.

"Very much so."

Katrina looked up at me blankly. I waited a minute or so to see if she would ask anything more. This time, much to my relief, she seemed satisfied.

"Alright, then. Let's get back to music."

Devil In Her Heart
Katrina

"Are we there yet?"

I tried not to sigh as Charles asked Mother the same question for a third time. Clearly, we weren't there yet or else the car would not still be moving. He was irritating enough as it were at home but sitting next to him in the back seat during a long car ride really tested my patience. I suppose I was just as frustrated as he was about how long we'd been driving, but at least *I* was mature enough to keep quiet about it.

"Hush, sweetheart, yes. Almost," Mother answered in a giddy whisper. Her voice was strange. It was full of glee, which I'd only ever heard her use whenever she was going to buy something she shouldn't. She even giggled a bit at the end of the sentence. But we weren't in a store, nor did she even have her purse on her, so why was she acting so strange? Maybe I wouldn't have paid any attention to her behavior if it weren't already for the mysterious reason that we were in the car in the first place.

"It's a surprise," Mother had said to both of us in the kitchen before rushing us out the front door despite our protests. Charles said he'd rather swim but Mother wasn't having any of it. We both would have rather been doing something else. Over an hour later, and I was staring out the car window, wishing I

had at least been given enough warning to grab my Walkman from my room. Not that it would have been a good idea, of course, since then Mother might find out that I had gotten Beatles' tapes behind her back, but, really, over an hour in the car? Where were we going and why was it so important to get there in such a rush?

Charles moaned. He was getting more fidgety than usual, and I could tell from his red cheeks that he was getting hot. Soon, he'd throw a temper from being bored. I couldn't blame him—this time.

"It won't be long now," Mother said suddenly, clasping her hands together and looking out her own window at the passing buildings. "A new opportunity to start over!"

I lolled my head to the side and let my temple rest against the door's window ledge. A lady didn't rest like that, but I didn't care. I was starting to think "lady" rules were dumb anyway.

"Look out your window!" Mother said as the car turned suddenly. "To the right!"

I lifted my head to see what the fuss was all about. All I could see was a large house, much larger than the one we lived in. It was so big that I couldn't fully see the entire thing through the car window. The color of this one was the same as ours: bright white with a dark colored roof, but around this house was the greenest grass I had ever seen and there was even a fountain in the middle of it. The size of this building plus the big lawn made this house look very fancy. Did the Beatles live in a house like this? Now that I knew that only rich people owned big houses, surely this meant the Fab Four had a house like this.

"Isn't it beautiful?" Mother asked. "Absolutely gorgeous?"

I shifted my eyes between the house and Mother. The driver got out of the car and started to circle over to the passenger's side. Charles and I both stayed silent.

"It's our new home!" Mother exclaimed, too absorbed in the beauty of the building to look back at us.

I tried not to sigh. A new house? Was that all we were brought out here for? I didn't wish to offend her but as far as surprises went, this one had to be the worst.

"We're going to move! Isn't it exciting?" Mother asked. "I'm going to announce it at the party on Friday. Come, look!"

The driver opened the door for Mother and then for Charles. I waited for my brother to hop out of the car before I slid toward the open door myself. I discovered once I was out that Mother had already taken Charles' hand and was walking him toward the front door. I had to awkwardly shuffle forward to catch up.

"A new house means a fresh slate!" Mother said, waving her hand dramatically. "New neighbors, new social circles, new interior decorations, *and*," she paused, turning around to pinch one of Charles' cheeks, "new schools!"

"Schools?" Charles and I asked at nearly the same time.

"No more tutors?" I questioned further, wanting to clarify.

"Hm, not for you," Mother replied, turning to face the house and walking forward. "Charles will be getting a new tutor. You will be going to boarding school."

I tilted my head curiously while following her.

"You mean, with other children? Away from the house?" I asked,

"Yes," she answered shortly.

I grinned excitedly. I had always wanted to attend a school with other children! Being stuck in the house all day with awful tutors was boring.

Glancing toward the fountain as we passed it, I happily skipped as we approached the house. I practically jumped up the steps to the front door.

"You both should be very happy with this new life we'll have," Mother said as she reached for the door handle. "It's thanks to you both that we're getting this new house, anyway."

Charles and I shared uncertain looks. Mother stared at us.

"Child support!" she explained as though it were obvious. Neither of us said anything, but I waved away my confusion and smiled up at Mother, finally beginning to understand why she was so thrilled. Regardless of how we attained the house it really was exciting.

"It sounds lovely, Mother!" I said, trying to appease but also being honest. "But will I have to be driven all that long way for music lessons each week?"

Mother had just put her hand on the door handle when she paused. Her whole body seemed to tense up and she retracted her hand calmly for a moment before putting it back to where it was. "Oh, you'll be quitting the music lessons," she said.

I froze. My foot hung in the air for a second too long and I nearly tripped on the brick stairs. I could feel my throat squeeze tightly and I wondered if I had heard her correctly. "What?" I asked, staring up at the back of her head.

"Mr. Galloway has provided an excellent hobby for you, and I'm sure he was a wonderful teacher, but it was just a way to pass the time, nothing more." Mother said, pressing down on the door handle and pushing it open. "You have more important things to do at boarding school."

My mouth hung open at her words. Stunned, I could do nothing but watch as she picked up Charles and carried him into the house as if she hadn't just dealt the biggest blow I'd ever been hit with.

I blinked. Tears were forming in my eyes but I was too busy trying to regain control of my limbs to worry about them. Finally, I managed to blurt out, "No, please!"

Mother snorted but ignored my plea, instead pointing out something to Charles and whispering to him.

Mobility now returning to my legs, I scrambled into the house and latched onto the fabric of Mother's dress. She turned to look down at me as I pleaded yet again.

"Katrina, stop that!" she said, swatting my hands away from her dress and smoothing it down. "You're acting like a child!"

"Please!" I begged again, the tears threatening to fall at any second. "You mustn't! I'll do anything! Please don't take away music lessons!"

"You don't need them," Mother argued, turning away from me and walking away again. I refused to be silenced and caught up with her quickly.

"I *do*!" I declared with a stamp of my foot. It echoed around the empty room and caused Mother's head to whip back and she looked at me in surprise. For a moment we just stared at one another, but one glance into Mother's piercing eyes and my hands rushed up to grasp together, without giving any thought to the action. I tightened my lips as though that would take back what I had. I lowered my head and felt the familiar racing of my heart.

"You disrespectful child!" Mother suddenly scowled. She lowered Charles to the floor before returning to her full height. She was tall and imposing. "How dare you!" She added, taking a step forward. "Who allowed you to have music lessons in the first place?" Mother continued stomping forward. My jaw clenched as I backed away. Her shadow crept over me and I felt as small as a mouse as I started to shake.

I didn't have time to raise my arms completely before she slapped me across the cheek. Stumbling, I held my stinging cheek with both hands and squinted up at her with blurred vision.

"You should be grateful for everything I provide for you!" Mother screamed. "I give you food, shelter, clothing, a private tutor, even a maid; all for you! I buy you new clothes *all* the time! Do you know how expensive that gets? Some people don't even get food, let alone new clothes! You think your life is hard? You can't even imagine what I've been through! You think it's been easy to raise a family by myself? What do you think it feels like to explain to others that you're *divorced*? And yet here you stand, complaining that you can't have your silly little music lessons! How selfish!"

I wept openly, trying to listen to what she was saying, but I was too heartbroken to truly understand. Despite what she told me, all I could think about was Morgan and whether I would ever get to hear The Beatles again. Was it selfish to think that way? Was I wrong to want the one person I felt closest to, to stay in my life?

I fell to my knees, sobbing into my hands. Mother was still yelling into my ear, her actions upsetting Charles. He whined, quietly at first, but then to a louder degree. She stopped yelling at me to try and settle him, cooing at him to be still. Once he was settled, however, Mother turned her head and continued her speech.

"Here I am, trying to provide you with a new home," she said icily. "A new place for you to be happy in. And instead of thanking me you decide to throw a fit. Absolutely disrespectful."

My shoulders shook and my chest hurt. I knew I needed to apologize to her but I was too scared to say anything.

"Unbelievable. If you're just going to be a selfish brat, then go to the car!" Mother spat, scooping Charles up with one arm. "In fact, why don't you do that anyway! If you're going to just sit there and cry then you don't get to see the rest of the house! You don't deserve to see it!"

She turned away from me and carried Charles into the next room, her heels leaving an echo behind to travel throughout the entryway. I couldn't stand, let alone walk to the car, so I stayed where I was and continued to cry.

I don't want a new place to feel happy in, I thought. *I already have one.*

What was I going to do?

I Need You Morgan

I had barely set the selection of cassette tapes I had chosen onto the counter before I was met with a suspicious look from Mike. His expression was expected, yet one look into his eyes and I had forgotten everything I had originally planned on saying to him. "Look, Mike, I'm sorry about the other day. I wasn't thinking."

Mike raised his hands to pat the air a bit and shook his head. "Hey, man. We all have those days. It's fine. Just wanted to make sure you weren't, you know, losing it. You seem better today."

I smiled weakly at him. I should have known he would take it well. Mike was always good with providing automatic support.

"Tapes for the kid?" he asked, shuffling through them with his fingers.

"Yeah," I replied. "Trying to get her to branch out from the Beatles."

Mike shot me a devilish grin as he pressed some buttons on the register. "Never thought I'd see the day where I'd hear you say that."

I snorted and tried to return the grin. "Guess we all gotta grow up some time," I joked.

"How are lessons going? You like 'em?" he asked, pointing out the total for me.

MORGAN AND KATRINA

"Uhm, yes, actually," I said, pulling out my wallet and handing him some cash.

Mike glanced at me in a way that made me shrink before he took the bills. "So... gonna quit that job?"

I frowned but didn't have time to reply before he spoke again.

"I'm just kidding you. I know, health benefits, and what not. I get it. Just want what's best for you."

"You know, actually, I feel pretty good about my job," I said. My words seemed to surprise Mike just as much as they surprised me.

"Really?" Mike asked.

I looked down at the counter, smiling softly in my bewilderment, then looked up to meet his eyes. "Yeah."

"Well, good," Mike replied, grinning. I nodded at him as he handed me my change before retrieving a bag for my tapes. We exchanged a short goodbye and then I turned to leave.

I was overwhelmed with emotion as I exited the store. Mike's teasing had caused me to think and I wasn't sure how to feel about my new thoughts. The last time Mike had brought up my job, I remembered feeling terrible. Now, it just felt dull. It was still an old wound, but somehow, I didn't feel saddened by it. Instead, it felt like an everyday truth. Simply the reality of a past decision I had made. It was peculiar to not feel the pain I had whenever I thought about it before.

Too caught up in my thinking and not watching where I was walking, I immediately bumped into someone.

"Oh, my gosh, I'm sorry!" I blurted, worrying that I had hurt this poor random woman.

Except, she wasn't random. Not random at all. As I met the eyes of the brown-haired woman in front of me, I froze.

"Morgan?" she uttered, just as shocked as I was. Her hazel eyes were wide.

"Laurelle?" I choked, confused and unsure if I was dreaming. For a moment, neither of us spoke. We just stared, dumbfounded. She broke first.

"I... I didn't think I'd see you again. At least not back here of all places!"

"Yeah, uh... I moved back years ago." I relaxed slightly but my eyes didn't leave hers. Instinctively, I reached out to brace myself against the building we were standing next to. "Wait, do you live here now?" I asked.

"Oh, no," she responded, tucking a strand of hair behind her ear. "My parents retired here. We were just visiting them for a few days."

"We?" I watched as her hand reached out to touch an item behind her; a stroller. The sight made me flinch and a wave of discomfort flowed through me. I swallowed and did my best to smile.

"This is George."

I stared at the child for an uncomfortably long time. He looked up at me briefly but was too engrossed in a colorful toy he was chewing to really care about anything else.

"George?" I finally questioned with a hint of jest. Laurelle rolled her eyes.

"It's not what you think, you dumb Apple scruff. His dad named him."

I smiled weakly at her insult before looking down at George again. The more I stared, the more crestfallen I became. When I eventually raised my head back up to Laurelle she too, seemed lost in thought, looking down at her son with a sad but pride-filled face. I didn't know what to say.

"So... you're here," she said eventually, turning to face me.

"Yeah," I nodded, looking away from her now.

"Hey, do you... want to go get some coffee or something?" she offered. I couldn't tell if it was out of pity.

"Uhm..." I said, trying to decide whether it would be a good idea. "Yeah. Yeah, actually. I'd really like that."

———

She swirled her spoon clockwise a few times before tapping it against the edge of her mug and setting it down on her saucer. I held my hands still, curling them around the warm mug in front of me in an attempt to keep from fidgeting. I watched uneasily as the creamer spun in my coffee.

We were at a small cafe, just a few stores down from Mike's. It wasn't the greatest coffee shop in town, but it was convenient. We had arrived, mostly silent. Light chit-chat passed between us at first but it drifted awkwardly into nothing after a few sentences. It wasn't until I had to help her ease the stroller through the café door that we spoke again, and even then, I wondered if she regretted making the offer to talk.

We remained quiet. I tried to keep myself from staring at her but anytime I looked away my eyes would settle on the child beside her. The child only made me feel worse, however, so my gaze would quickly shoot back to Laurelle.

She was still as pretty as I remembered her. Older, of course, but still pretty. I wasn't sure what to say at all, which was stupid because how many times had I wished for this exact moment to occur? This was my chance to fix things and dumb cold feet were going to ruin it.

"Should have brought a joint," Laurelle said. I snorted and we shared a chuckle.

"How have you been?" I asked, finally feeling my nerves settle.

"Fine, I guess," she responded, shrugging. "You?"

"Fine."

I looked down at my coffee and then glanced at George again. Laurelle caught my eye and wilted a bit, playing with her thumbs.

"Probably looks insulting."

"No. It's okay," I assured her. "Really."

"Wasn't my choice," she said.

"You never did like the idea."

She sighed. "I still don't. But that's life. Now his dad's gone and I'm stuck with supporting him. I'm in town for some help from my parents. Pretty lame, right?"

"I'm sorry," I said.

"It's not like it's your fault," she snapped suddenly, playing with her mug's handle. "It's that asshole's fault for getting me pregnant. My traveling days are over now."

I nodded solemnly, taking a sip of my drink.

"He's probably out there still, having the time of his life, the swine," she muttered, glancing out the window. I said nothing, unsure of how to respond. I had forgotten how much she used to complain.

"So, what are you doing these days?" she asked. I felt a breath of relief at the subject change.

"Well, I'm a mortician."

She gave me a disgusted look. "A what? Uh, no offense, but... why? That's not exactly music-related."

"Oh, I know," I said. "But... gotta survive somehow, you know? Plus, it's actually a very nice profession. And it's getting better all the time."

The corners of her mouth pulled downwards as she looked at the ceiling and rocked her head back and forth.

"Pretty depressing if you ask me."

I pursed my lips. My instinct was to defend myself but for some reason I didn't think it was going to work. Was she always this insulting?

"I guess neither of our lives have turned out how we expected," I said eventually, admittedly with bite.

"Yeah." We sipped our coffee at the same time. I looked out the window and watched a few cars go by. This wasn't how I expected the conversation to go. My emotions were mixed, and I wasn't sure how to sort them.

Laurelle muttered something under her breath but I didn't hear it. Judging by the tone I guessed it was another complaint. Annoyed, I turned to look at her.

"There is one thing, though," I began.

"What?"

"I'm teaching someone music lessons."

"Oh, well, hey, that's something!" Laurelle said. "You liking it?"

"Yes, very much so," I replied, smiling.

"Great!" she said.

"Yeah..." I trailed off, staring at the table and thinking of Katrina. "She's—"

"Raking that extra cash in, sweet!"

"Huh?" I said, snapping out of my trance and looking up at Laurelle.

"I said raking in that extra cash. You *are* charging for the lessons, right?"

"Oh. Uh, yeah, I guess."

"That's great! Maybe you can get more lessons with other people and quit the awful mortuary job."

"I... never said it was awful," I said, my shoulders raising a bit.

"It doesn't suit you, though."

"Well, being a mother doesn't suit you." The words barely left my lips before I realized what I was saying. My eyes went wide after I said it and I looked at Laurelle in fright. She gaped at me, stunned.

"I-I'm sorry!" I said quickly. "I didn't mean to—"

She laughed; a loud, strong, laugh. I looked around to see if anyone was looking at us. No one was but I nervously chuckled along with her anyway. Why was she laughing?

"Morgan, I didn't know you had it in you!" She said eventually. "Where was that humor when we were still dating?"

I looked at her with what I assumed to be a hurt expression on my face. But she didn't seem to catch it, despite looking right at me. She smiled, resting her elbow on the table and her chin in her palm.

"You know..." she started to say, staring at me with a whimsical eye. "You honestly haven't aged a bit."

MORGAN AND KATRINA

A chill ran down my spine, but I ignored it the best I could. I frowned as I looked back at her. I hadn't realized until just now that there were the beginnings of wrinkles on her face. Did nine years change a person that much?

She frowned, too. Looking between my eyes, she then glanced down at my gloves laying on the table, then at the umbrella against my chair. She looked away to stare at the sunlight outside, then pursed her lips as she brought her attention back to me. Assuming she had just realized only one of us had a reflection in the window, I found myself unable to meet her eyes. Staring hard at the coffee in my hands, I shakily brought it to my lips and drank as politely as I could. Perhaps if we just pretended nothing happe—

"You weren't lying, were you? Back then? That... that was real?" she said, breaking the silence. I looked up, expecting an expression of anger but instead was met with genuine concern. Surprised, I hesitated before simply nodding my head very slowly.

She was silent, leaning back and wide-eyed as before when we were outside. Then, she bent forward, eyes looking at the table and darting back and forth in an attempt to register what I had just confirmed. Her hands went flat against the table. She blinked hard, then looked up at me, still crouched forward.

"Morgan," she whispered, almost in a hiss. "If this is another joke, it's *not* funny."

"It's not a joke," I said calmly, sitting as still as possible and looking her straight in the eye.

She blinked more, sitting up normally for a moment before leaning over yet again and folding her arms up to rest her head in her hands. "*Morg*, you were telling the truth?" she asked.

"Yes."

"I... I don't know what to say."

"I know. It's okay."

"No, it's not okay!"

"No, I mean, it's *okay*," I assured. "You had every right to not believe me. I was immature, foolish, and it wasn't right for me to have pushed that onto you."

Laurelle stayed quiet, looking out the window. Tears pooled in her eyes. A few moments passed before she took a breath. "Everything you said was true, then. That phial from the old woman in the traveling fair? That was the real deal?"

"Yes. But I didn't know it was at the time."

"Wait, what do you mean?" she said, her voice now returning to an icy tone. "You said it was real."

I grimaced and looked down in shame. "I only said it was real so that you'd feel pressure." I immediately braced for the inevitable.

Laurelle pressed her lips together and nodded passive-aggressively. "Oh. Great."

"Yeah," I agreed dismally. "And then, through the biggest example of irony I've ever known, it ended up being real anyway."

Laurelle fell into her hands while I wished now more than ever that I was back in my car, never having gone to the music shop in the first place.

"It was stupid," I said.

"You think?" she spat, opening her hands to reveal her face and then smoothing her hair back with one sweep of her fingers.

"It was *really* stupid," I corrected. "And now I've got to face it for the rest of my life. It was a lesson to be learned and I'd like to think that I've matured at least a little bit from it."

Laurelle sighed, crossing her arms uncomfortably and then looking at George with a melancholy expression. "How did I end up dating two of the stupidest men in the world?"

I wilted.

"You're not... you're not hurting anyone, are you?" she asked eventually, refusing to look at me.

"No," I said, putting my hands in my lap. "Not anymore."

"Anymore?"

"Well, I... It wasn't easy learning how to live like this. I've done a lot of things I'm ashamed of. But now I'm working at the funeral home and it's gotten easier thanks to that."

Laurelle paused, slowly turning her head to look at me again. I didn't have to explain for her to understand what I meant. Her expression was without a doubt mixed with horror and I felt the need to ease it.

"I hurt no one. We get rid of it anyway. I just have to be careful to make sure I don't take in any diseases or else I will get incredibly sick."

Stunned, she looked at me in increased disgust and seemed to be about to gag. Instead, she shut her mouth tight, closed her eyes, and reached out for the stroller to steady herself. She took a deep breath and let it out slowly, finally opening her eyes again and looking at me.

"I'm sorry you had to hear that," I said. "But I want you to know that I've accepted it. I've moved on and I'm okay. I have regrets but I'm not completely unhappy."

"Morgan, forgive me, but," she paused, letting go of the stroller. "How can you possibly be happy like this?"

I hesitated. This was a question I knew well, a question I had asked myself every single day for years with no answer. Responding to it was always difficult, namely because my lack of a reason often led to my wondering if life was truly worthwhile. But sitting there, faced with that dreaded question once more, I realized that I hadn't actually asked myself in a long time—whether or not life was worth it for at least five months.

"Well," I said slowly, taking a moment to gather my thoughts, "music lessons."

"Music lessons? You mean the lessons you mentioned before?"

"Yeah..." I trailed off, crossing an arm over my chest.

Laurelle's eyes softened as silence fell between us once more. Suddenly, George began to cry. Laurelle tried to comfort him with a pacifier from a bag in the stroller but he swatted it away. She cooed at him and said his name a few times but that didn't work either. Ultimately, she had to pick him up out of the stroller to rock him before he calmed.

"Well, I'm glad you're happy," Laurelle said eventually, letting George gum one of her fingers. We sat quietly for a bit, both of us watching the child move his lips.

"It can't be easy," she said.

"Neither is your situation."

"You know what I mean." She threw me an annoyed glance before removing her finger from George's mouth and wiping it on a napkin. "Have you told anyone?"

MORGAN AND KATRINA

"No. Er, well, one person. I haven't decided yet whether I regret it."

Laurelle nodded and drank from her cup again before asking a question I didn't expect. "So, how long will you stay here before you have to move?"

"Huh? Why would I move?"

"Well, surely you can't stay in the same place for too long. People will begin to suspect."

"Suspect what?"

"Morgan, you don't age. You can't hide that forever."

My lips parted and my jaw slacked a bit.

Laurelle smiled weakly. "Still the same expressions, too," she said. Glancing down at her watch, her smile disappeared. "Shit, I gotta go."

"Oh. Okay."

Laurelle stood up, placing George into the stroller and strapping him in. I stood up too, watching her awkwardly and finding it strange that I didn't feel the need to keep the conversation going. In all my daydreams of seeing Laurelle again, I had imagined that I would talk her ear off just to get her to stay longer. Interestingly enough, now that she was about to leave, I found myself looking forward to being alone again. "Are you staying in town long?" I asked.

"Hopefully not. Just need to get a financial leg up and then I'm outta here."

Laurelle spun the stroller toward the door before turning to look at me.

"Well. Good luck and all that, Mr. Moonlight," she said. I smiled at the old nickname but the feeling wasn't nostalgic. It just felt old. I wasn't about to be rude, though.

"Same to you, Miss Lizzy."

I waved as she pushed George through the door, then kept my eyes on the back of her head until she was completely out of view. Watching her leave felt strange to me. It was like I was looking *through* her rather than at her; she wasn't the same. I must have stood still for a full minute just staring at the door and processing how I felt. The entire experience was almost funny. I remembered telling myself that if I ever saw her again, I'd never let her out of my sight, yet there I was, fully comfortable with letting her go.

Returning to my seat, I stared out the window. I tapped the edge of my coffee mug with one finger, trying to process everything that had just happened. She really was the same as before. The exact same. I could remember being with her so plainly. I had been so happy—so free. The memory of that feeling still echoed within my mind. I could feel it in my chest. So why did I want nothing to do with her?

I finished the last sip of my coffee. It was cold now but that didn't matter to me. I slid the mug away from me, wondering if today would be the last day I'd ever see Laurelle. I couldn't tell if that would be a bad thing. Would I even tell anyone I saw her? The only person that knew about her was Katrina, come to think of it, and she probably wouldn't care.

I looked at the reflection of the chair that Laurelle had been sitting in just minutes before, then my eyes floated to the reflection of my own chair. Frowning, I remembered what Laurelle had asked about in regard to moving. She was right to ask it. How long would I have gone on living without thinking of that problem myself? Had other people already noticed that I wasn't aging? Were people talking about it behind my back? Sure, men could go ten years or so without drawing suspicion but any more than that and the comments would start rolling in. In a situation like mine, I needed to think of the future constantly. If I was to continue surviving into that future, I would absolutely have to move from city to city. But then the real headaches would start. For one thing, there was my government paperwork to figure out. Then, there was the fact that I couldn't just keep moving from place to place using the same birth year information. It would be suspicious to be born in the year 1946 yet still look 27 by the year 1990. Crap.

Collapsing my head into my hands, I sighed. This was all so complicated. At least the actual idea of moving wasn't too bad. I had the funds to do it if I really needed to. Or at least, *now* I did; Katrina's mother paid enough in lessons for that. The real trouble would be finding another mortuary job because I had no other ideas for how to survive given my circumstances. The actual town didn't matter but I absolutely had to be working in a funeral home. If I really wanted to, moving would be easy as long as there was a job available.

As I was busy considering about where I would go, a crack formed in my thought process. Katrina. Where did she fit in all of these plans? Guilt washed over me as I realized I hadn't considered her. Leaving her behind would feel terrible, especially when I had suspicions of her being abused. Maybe if I helped her out of that situation, then I could leave as soon as she was safe?

Yes, that final thought caused my mind to settle completely. If I had to risk exposing myself by staying here as long as it took just to make sure Katrina could get to a safer environment, then so be it. Even if it turned out that my suspicions weren't true, and she had exaggerated everything to me, I had to at least find out the real answer.

Of course, it would be easier said than done.

Perhaps I could sleuth out what was really happening in that house during the party on Friday. If I could find proof of the abuse, then I could do something about it. And if I didn't find any proof, then there was no reason to fret and I could move without worry that Katrina was in trouble.

My excitement died slowly as I realized that would mean leaving Katrina. Not that I wished for her to be in an abusive situation, of course, but if she wasn't... Well, I had to move either way, didn't I?

I lowered my hands from my face and shoved one into my pocket to grab a pen. With the other, I reached out for a napkin and once I dragged it closer to me, I began to make notes on it. If I could just do the math right, then all would be fine. Once I was finished, I settled back into my chair and looked at the result with satisfaction. Katrina would be 18 by the time 1990 rolled around. I would be 44 by then but still look 27. In terms of stretching believability, 1990 was the longest I could go without being suspicious. If I found proof of Katrina's abuse, I had until then to get her to safety. No matter what happened, though, I had eight years to be in this town at the most. That was it.

Sighing long and heavily, I leaned back in my chair and tilted my head back into a deep stretch. I had concentrated so hard on making a plan that it took me a moment to remember I had spoken to Laurelle moments before. I snorted at that, smiling to myself at how funny life could be.

I kicked back my chair and stood up. Grabbing the napkin I had written my notes on, I shoved it into my pocket before slipping on my gloves next.

MORGAN AND KATRINA

The smile didn't leave my face as I picked up my umbrella next and headed toward the door. I felt... fine. Completely fine. Happy, even. My emotions were no longer mixed. I felt settled. I couldn't tell if I was smiling because of the absurdity of how I felt, or if I was genuinely pleased. Either way, I opened my umbrella and stepped into the light of the afternoon sun with a single song playing in my head. A song whose true meaning I had never realized until now. A song with lyrics that I would continue to repeat for the rest of the evening.

There were bells on a hill... but I never heard them ringing... No I never heard them at all...
'Till there was you...

For No One
Morgan

I had never woken up with such a sense of peaceful security. Usually I would have the pressing urge to get the day started. But not anymore. I swore there was a smile on my face before I opened my eyes. I was warm, wrapped in my cocoon of blankets, and I felt a sense of calm wash over me. No fear, no anxiety, no depression. I was cheerfully groggy and very nearly would have slept until noon had I not wanted to clean the house before Katrina's music lesson. It was a beautiful feeling.

When I finally got out of bed, I felt as though I were breathing fresh air from an open window. I wasn't, of course, since the windows had been covered the entire time I'd lived there, but the feeling was still the same. I could breathe easier and even the mere task of brushing my teeth felt merrier. I felt so elated to simply exist.

I cleaned the house in my usual manner: headphones on both ears, a Beatles tape in the Walkman strapped to my hip, and my voice carrying out to the heavens. I was lucky not to have neighbors nearby for surely, they would have been annoyed by my singing. Even if they had existed, though, they still wouldn't have been able to stop me from singing from the top of my lungs. There was joy all over my house that morning and nothing could have brought me down.

When I was finished cleaning, I still had roughly an hour before Katrina would arrive. Normally in such cases I would walk over to work and see if they needed any help (they usually did). But just as today had brought me a new attitude toward life, so had my attitude changed toward work. I didn't leave the house. I may have needed that funeral home to survive, but it didn't own me, and I didn't have to show up if they didn't call me first. Instead I got out my guitar and started to play. I had played it alongside Katrina during her piano lessons, sure, but other than that, I hadn't played for myself. Not for a long time.

When the doorbell rang, I had been engrossed in belting out "A Hard Day's Night" while laying on my back on the couch with my feet up on the arm. But instead of being embarrassed by the interruption, I was too excited by Katrina's arrival to worry about whether they had heard me. I practically skipped to the door after setting my guitar down, and grinned wide when I saw Sarah's face. Her expression was the same as always—indifferent—but I nevertheless greeted her with a cheery disposition. It wasn't until I looked down at Katrina that my attitude faltered. Her big brown eyes stared up at me as though she was ready to cry at any moment, and her lips were creased in either fear or sorrow; I couldn't tell which. She had never shown up making a face like that and my immediate thought was that she had had a run-in with her abuser just prior to coming here. That was, of course, wild speculation. Still, I was worried.

"Feeling okay?" I asked, looking her up and down for any sign of bruises or marks.

Katrina said nothing, only bowed her head and stared at the floor, swallowing in what was most likely an attempt to hold herself back from crying. I looked to Sarah for help and was surprised at her explanation.

"She's been a bit of a brat today."

"Oh," I said. Katrina walked past me into the house. I was further confused by this act since she usually didn't ignore me like a zoned-out zombie.

"Well, thanks for bringing her again," I said. Sarah nodded, then replied,

"I'll be back a half-hour earlier than usual today. She has a special appointment at the house."

"Oh, okay," I said. "That's fine." I made a move to close the door when suddenly Sarah was pointing a finger past me and glaring.

"Katrina," the nanny snapped. "You behave for Mr. Galloway."

I looked back in time to see Katrina scowling. "His name is *Morgan*," she spat, her face a mixed expression of anger and hurt.

"Behave," Sarah warned before turning away. My attention switched to Katrina as I shut the door. She stood in the middle of the room, faced away from me and staring at the wall. I walked over and knelt next to her.

"What's wrong?" I asked. Katrina refused to move for a few seconds. Her eyes clouded over with tears and finally she turned to look at me as a drop rolled down her cheek.

"Mother says we have to move," she said.

I swallowed.

"And I can't have lessons with you anymore."

"*What?*" I exclaimed. Katrina contorted with pain. She collapsed into me as she sobbed. I embraced her automatically and let her cry into my shoulder.

"I don't want to go!" Katrina shouted. I tried to lay my hand upon the back of her head to comfort her but no sooner had I done so than she pushed off of my shoulder to look me in the eye. "I can't go! I can't go to boarding school!" She looked at me with utter sadness but proclaimed confidently. "I want to stay here with you!"

"Boarding school?" I questioned, moving my hands to her elbows and furrowing my brow.

More tears erupted from her face and she folded yet again into my shoulder. This time I remained silent and simply wrapped my arms around her, letting her weep. The gears in my head turned frantically, but I had to wait until she was finished before I could ask any questions. It was more important, in that moment, that she felt better.

After a few minutes of crying, Katrina started to relax, or, at least, she stopped wailing. Her breathing was still shaky, and the tears were still coming, but she was, more or less, calm. I pulled her up away from my shoulder and had her walk over to the couch where she could sit next to me. I reached for a box of tissues and sat them on the cushion between us before saying, "Okay. Explain to me what happened."

Katrina wiped her eyes, sniffed, and then began. "Mother showed us our new house. She said we would be moving there and that I would be sent to boarding school."

"When?"

"I don't know. She said she would be announcing it at the party this week."

My whole body crumbled at her words. She began to cry again and I put my hand against her back. I wanted to say something that would help console her, but I was at a loss for words. The news was equally devastating to me and I wasn't sure how to process it either.

"Can you move with me?" Katrina asked.

I could practically hear my heart shatter.

"Oh, honey..." I said. "I wish I could."

My answer caused her to cry again. I watched her mournfully for a moment before her face changed from sadness to anger.

"Why not?" She demanded.

"Well, for one thing, it would... appear odd to people. There are certain real-life factors here. I'm an adult and you're ten years old. It would be... unwise. You'll also most likely move to an area that I wouldn't be able to afford. Not to mention, I can only live where there's an actively hiring funeral home. You may be moving to an area where I wouldn't be able to get a job quickly, and I can't survive without that, at least not safely. And, finally, you're going to boarding school."

"So?"

"Katrina, do you know what boarding school is?" She hesitated and I continued. "You won't be able to leave it. You might go home for the holidays but otherwise you stay on campus all year."

Katrina stared off into the distance for a moment, taking in my words. She looked as though she couldn't move. I couldn't blame her for that. She probably felt defeated, being unable to exert any control over her life. Understandable, given the circumstances.

I frowned, wishing I could think of something to ease her pain.

"At least you'll be away from home," I offered with a half-shrug. A lightbulb went off in my mind and I barely heard what Katrina was saying before I interrupted her with my sudden realization.

"But this is my—"

"Wait a second, that's it!" Startled, Katrina shut her mouth and looked up at me with wide eyes.

"Don't you see?" I asked. "Boarding school is perfect for you!"

"What?" Katrina said, her eyebrows curling inward, causing her to resemble a hurt puppy.

"You'll be away from home." I explained, grinning like a fool. "You'll be exposed to new things and be around other children and you'll be *safe*! It's perfect."

"But—"

"Katrina, you'll be fine. There's nothing to worry about. This is exactly what should be happening for you right now. Moving is a good thing."

Katrina's jaw hung open ever so slightly as she gawked at me. She looked puzzled and hurt. I smiled at her, waiting for her to understand what I was saying, but instead of acknowledging my genius revelation, she looked down at the couch. For a long moment she gathered herself, then raised her head and looked me straight in the eye as she said,

"Don't you like teaching me?"

My smile cracked but still I waited. Katrina waited too. After a minute or two of silence, her body slumped, and she turned away from me. Suddenly I regretted my previous words. I'd made her sound wholly unimportant to me, and my brain was screaming at me to say something, anything, but I was unable to speak as she slipped down from the couch. I watched, frozen in my seat, as she slunk toward the bathroom with her head bowed. It wasn't until I heard the click of the bathroom door that I shifted slightly and swallowed. I heard soft crying from behind the door.

I tried to remind myself that what I'd said was the responsible adult thing to do. She was hurting now, but in the end it would all be worth it, and she would see that I was correct. Still, though, I felt badly for causing her to cry, especially when I was probably the only person she trusted. Standing up, I had every intention to walk over to the bathroom door to try talking to her, but my legs refused to move. I proceeded to engage in a bizarre cycle of standing, sitting and walking toward the door, hoping to eventually make my way to the bathroom. In the end, I found myself on the piano bench, zoning out while looking at the music sheets. I must have been sitting there longer than I thought because I only snapped out of it when the doorbell rang.

Shit. I thought. I had forgotten that Sarah would be back earlier than usual. Katrina was stuck in the bathroom crying.

I stood up quickly, rushing to the door and shaking my head on the way to clear my emotions.

"Hi!" I said to Sarah as I opened the door. "Katrina's just in the bathroom." The nanny nodded as I heard a *click!* from behind me. *Thank goodness*. Katrina would come out on her own. I turned around and what I saw caused my heart to jump into my throat.

There stood Katrina, her back as straight as a pin and her chin raised high, just as she had been in the beginning. Her feet were posed just so and her wrists were bent upwards like a ballerina's. There was not a single hint that she had been crying aside from a slight redness to her eyes.

"I'm coming, Sarah," Katrina said in a higher-pitched voice than she typically spoke. She stepped forward with every movement as graceful as when I first met her, and she made every effort to ignore me as she walked by. Meanwhile, I was absolutely in shock. Until now, I hadn't realized how much she had changed since her first lesson. I had completely forgotten just how much of a rich woman's daughter she was and not just an ordinary girl. This was no longer the girl I had talked with for consecutive hours about The Beatles. This was no longer the girl who got excited over listening to new music or complained about learning the piano. This was a girl who was completely and utterly controlled by nothing more than the same society I had wanted to break her free from. She had changed so much during our time spent together that I hardly recognized the girl before me.

"Come along," Sarah said before turning away and walking briskly toward the car. Katrina followed, slow but sure, taking great care in how she stepped. I was horrified, watching her from within the shadow of the opened front door. I wanted to look away, but I couldn't.

Katrina walked about halfway down the driveway before stopping. While Sarah was busy opening the car door for her, Katrina hesitated. I watched as she turned around, looking straight at me and waiting. Her expression was blank, but her eyes were locked on mine.

Say something! I thought. *This is your chance!* But I couldn't. As much as I wanted to tell myself that I regretted everything, I truly didn't. It killed me to know that she was returning to her old ways, but I hadn't been wrong to tell her the harsh realities of the world. There would be a brief period of pain before she would realize I was right. I had to stay strong so that she could grow.

"Katrina," Sarah snapped. The girl jumped, seemingly having forgotten about the maid. Quickening her step, Katrina hopped into the car but not before shooting me one final glance, an expression of sorrow etched onto her face.

The car windows were too dark to see her once the door was shut. I stayed still as the car backed out of the driveway and didn't even wave goodbye when Sarah gave a nonchalant lift of her fingers from the steering wheel.

When I was finally alone, I could feel the tears building up. I tried to ignore them as I shut the door and returned to the couch. *Be the adult,* I thought. She had to move. She had to leave and there was nothing I could do about it. Why be upset about her leaving if it meant she could be free of abuse? Wasn't that the best thing for her? Hadn't I been planning just yesterday for this kind of situation to happen? Who cared if I was going to lose a music student over it? I could get another one.

A lump formed in my throat as I told myself this. If there had just been a little bit more time, I might have been able to talk Katrina out of being upset and gotten her to see why boarding school was the best place for her. The more I tried to talk myself into it, though, the more I knew that that wouldn't have worked. For one thing, Katrina was too stubborn to believe that, and secondly, she wasn't old enough to really understand it. In fact, why did I want to bother trying to explain it to her at all? She wouldn't get it, and she'd be hurt no matter what. The best thing I could do until she left would be to keep my distance. It might hurt her a bit, but she'd grow out of that hurt. She'd be forced to stand on her own and she'd learn that she can. She'd be far more willing to accept boarding school if she had strength in herself.

The next time I would see her would be the party, and there I would make sure to keep my distance. She'd be confused at first, but in the end it would be good. Technically, it didn't seem logical that I go to the party now that I didn't have to find out if any abuse was happening. Boarding school would take care of the problem, if there was a problem at all. But I wasn't sure I could live with myself if I didn't know the truth just for myself. I had to know. Even just for me.

I turned my attention to the piano. My brow softened as I reflected on the wonderful times I had spent with Katrina. But then my eyes began to mist over as I realized that not only had today's lesson been cut short, but that it was also probably the last lesson we would ever have. How had I not thought of that before? I was too blind in my haste to try and fix her situation that I hadn't slowed down to think of what was happening, and there was no taking back what had happened.

I felt sick to my stomach. I leaned over and placed my elbows on my knees while pressing my nose into my hands. *For her*, I tried to tell myself. *You're doing this for her.* But I couldn't convince myself.

The Night Before Katrina

What did I do wrong?

That was all I could think since I'd left Morgan's house. The question repeated in my brain, sometimes in different wording. What changed? What did I miss? I tried to think of all the things I might have said or done to make Morgan not want to have lessons with me anymore but still, after three days, I had no answer.

It was like he had changed overnight. Less than that, even. The more I thought about it, the more it seemed like he had changed right in the middle of our lesson. What happened? He let me cry on his shoulder. He talked to me and even tried to come up with an idea of how to fix my moving problem. Things were fine up until that point. Why did he change in the middle of the talk? What had I said to make him think that moving was a good idea by the end of it? Did he just decide to not like me anymore? Surely Morgan didn't change his mind as quickly as Mother did. It had to be something I did.

Did I cry too much? That couldn't be it. Morgan said it was okay to cry. And he even cried a couple of times in front of me. It must have been because I did something bad.

MORGAN AND KATRINA

I didn't mean to be bad. I didn't mean to upset him. I liked being friends with him. I *thought* we were friends. At least, before Tuesday's lesson. We laughed together, sang together. He taught me piano. We shared secrets. Weren't those all things that friends did? I was missing something. The Morgan I knew wouldn't want lessons to end. So what happened? Maybe I didn't know him as well as I thought.

No, that couldn't be it. It didn't feel right. We were friends, we had to be. He said so. Unless he was lying.

But Morgan didn't lie to me. He was always honest, even when he was the one who made mistakes. That was one of the things I liked best about him. I could trust him.

At least, I thought I could. I wasn't sure anymore and I didn't know how to feel about that. If he walked in the door right then, would I still trust him? I couldn't answer that. Deep down I felt like the answer was "Yes!" but when I tried to explain to myself why, I started to get confused.

Completely unsure of myself, I walked as though through a fog all week. "I'm so tired. I'm so tired," I would say. "I haven't slept a wink." I was so out of it that even Sarah tried to ask me how I was feeling, which would have shocked me had I not felt so unlike myself. Apparently, my response of "Will I fall asleep forever soon?" was the wrong thing to say because as soon as I asked, Sarah had shushed me and said I was being "morbid," whatever that was. I didn't care that she was disturbed, though. I didn't care about anything. All I wanted was for Morgan to like me again.

Unfortunately, my strange emotions could not have come at a worse time. Mother was very busy making plans for the party all week, and while she was excited any time there were party preparations, she was also easily agitated during the whole process. I had to step lightly. Yet despite knowing the consequences, I still couldn't bring myself to do even the simplest of tasks. I knew that whenever Mother arranged for the living room furniture to be completely exchanged out, I was supposed to model for the workmen when they came. When they arrived this time, however, I couldn't even smile, let alone walk past them with straight posture. That did end up being in my favor, though, since that meant if the workmen didn't like my behavior, Mother wouldn't be mad that I was stealing all the compliments from her. I was still taking too large of a risk, though. If Mother noticed I wasn't acting right, then she would have punished me. The idea of being thrown into a closet didn't scare me as much as it used to, but I was still afraid of her hand. Not to mention there was always the possibility she could threaten to lock me in my room for all of Friday. What would I do if I couldn't see Morgan one more time before I was sent away?

I was a mess. Crying, waiting, hoping. I felt stupid, guilty, and sad all at once. I didn't want to get out of bed, and I didn't want to do anything around the house. I didn't even want to *leave* the house. The most I did without being told was listen to some of my cassette tapes, but they didn't help me either. I kept imagining running away on a yellow submarine or being in an octopus' garden and knowing that I couldn't do that only brought more tears. Would I even have these tapes after Friday? They weren't mine. What would I do if I couldn't bring them with me to school?

I drowned in these thoughts all week. The walls felt like they were closing in on me and sometimes I would catch myself staring at nothing for a long time. I had never felt like this before. I wasn't even sure what to call it. It was almost as though I couldn't feel anything at all. Sometimes I would cry when I didn't even feel sad. The tears just came up at the most random of times. It was very inconvenient.

Crying at strange times, though, I could handle. What I couldn't handle was not knowing if I would see Morgan again after Friday. I didn't know when Mother was sending me off to boarding school, and if Friday was the last chance for me to see Morgan, then I simply *had* to talk to him. He may not like me anymore, but I at least needed to know why. What had I done to make him feel that way and what, if anything, could I do to fix it? I longed to know the truth.

All he had to do was tell me why.

I Don't Want To Spoil The Party
Katrina

I waited for him. I knew I was supposed to be downstairs talking to the party guests but I couldn't help myself. I wanted to stay at my bedroom window as long as I could, watching for any sign of bright orange hair.

I shouldn't have expected him to make an appearance right away. Mother said only bootlickers showed up at the beginning of a party, and picturing Morgan licking a boot did not make sense to me. So after fifteen minutes had passed with no sighting, I just assumed he was being polite. When a full hour had gone, however, not even the excuse that he was waiting for the sun to set would have worked. It had been dark for at least the last twenty minutes. I remained hopeful that he would show but was beginning to worry.

"Katrina."

I jumped, pulling my eyes from the valet in the driveway to discover Sarah at my bedroom door.

"You're supposed to be downstairs," she said.

I frowned at her, then turned my attention back to looking out the window again.

"Katrina."

MORGAN AND KATRINA

Ignoring her the best I could, I watched as strangers filtered into the house from the street.

"*Katrina.*"

My eyes were watering, but I dared not let a tear fall onto the makeup Mother insisted I wear.

Sarah sighed, a sign that if I resisted further, I would be in more trouble than it was worth. Finally, I tore myself from the window. I bowed my head as I walked past her.

"Your mother's in the living room," Sarah explained. I didn't respond, which was rude, but I didn't care. She must have been in too much of a rush to mind, however, for as soon as I stepped out of my room she scurried away—probably to help the kitchen.

I sniffed and clutched my dress; the very same dress Mother had bought to replace the one I had ruined when I first met Morgan. I hadn't liked it then, and I still didn't like it. It was prettier than I remembered; the bow in my hair looked nice, at least, but the dress was itchy, and so I wished I didn't have to wear it at all. Maybe someday I could stop wearing dresses altogether. Of course, Mother would be against that.

Morgan would let me wear pants, I thought.

Frowning, I shook my head to clear my thoughts and instead tuned into the sounds that echoed from downstairs. Live music played in the parlor and it was loud enough to be heard all the way upstairs; definitely Bach's Inventions. I tried to appreciate it—I really did. How many times had Morgan told me even classical had its purpose in the world? But tonight, it only made me feel worse.

I stood outside my room for a minute or two, just listening, but eventually managed to move my feet toward the stairs. The music grew louder the closer I got and, so too, did the sound of people talking. When I reached the top of the staircase, a sea of heads came into view, men and women all standing and chatting with each other, most with champagne glasses in their hands. I scanned the room, I guess to see if I had missed any sign of orange hair, but there wasn't one.

Stepping forward, I started downstairs. When I reached about halfway, I noticed the front door open, and a spark of hope lit up in my chest. But it wasn't Morgan and the feeling left as quickly as it appeared. I lowered my head and continued down the stairs, slipping into the crowd as silently as I could. A few people greeted me, but I didn't respond. I focused on finding Mother.

"Oh, ha ha, you *jest!*"

Her voice carried above the sounds of the party. I spotted her standing in the center of the living room, surrounded by a circle of several women. Mother's appearance shocked me at first. Any other time I'd seen her at parties, she flaunted the brightest of colors imaginable, but tonight she was wearing nothing but stark white from head to toe. Not only was the choice unusual by itself but compared to the outfits of the rest of the women, whose colors were practically dull against the reflecting snow-like fabric, Mother stood out like a shining light, making her presence impossible to ignore. She seemed pleased with herself as she stroked the fur wrap around her shoulders, her attitude the opposite of the women around her, who were clearly unimpressed. As I approached her, I noticed Charles standing at Mother's feet, dressed in one of his fanciest blue vests and looking uninterested as he clutched the hem of Mother's new dress. I ignored him and tried to pay

MORGAN AND KATRINA

attention to the conversation the women were having.

"Really, Helen. What's the surprise?" a woman in green to Mother's left asked. I stood just outside their circle, telling myself it wasn't polite to interrupt them, but I knew full well that I was taking advantage of not having to talk to them.

"You'll just have to find oo-ut!" Mother replied in a sing-song voice. "But I will give you a hint... It's the best thing that could happen to me right now!"

"Oh, so, your ex-husband took you back?" A woman in blue to her right asked. Mother's smile nearly faltered but she cleared her throat and recovered. Before she could reply, others chimed in.

"Did the bank finally raise your spending limit?"

"Did you contact that doctor I was telling you about? Oh, thank god. He can do miracles with *anyone*."

Mother's smile grew smaller and smaller with each guess.

"Helen, are you sure there even *is* a surprise?" one woman in orange asked. "After all, I don't see that special guest that you keep mentioning. I mean, if I promised a special guest to my friends, and then that guest was late, *I* would be just mortified."

"Katrina!" Mother suddenly exclaimed, eyes locking onto me and causing all of the women to look in my direction. "Come here and tell these lovely women about Mr. Galloway."

I shivered at the name but remained obedient, walking toward Mother and looking up at her friends uncomfortably.

"Oh, there she is," I heard one woman say.
"What a pretty face," said another.

"His name is Morgan," I said. Mother swatted at my hands, which I hadn't realized were tightly gripping the ribbons on my dress. I jolted upright and raised my chin as high as I could. "He's a very nice teacher."

"So he does exist," the woman in orange said.

"Speak of the devil!" Mother said, raising one arm and motioning toward the front hall. "Mr. Galloway!"

I frantically craned my neck. One glimpse of that orange hair and I gasped. I nearly broke away to run straight for him, but Mother's hand shot out and clutched my shoulder. I leaned forward in an attempt to narrow the gap between myself and Morgan but, of course, it barely made a difference. My heart raced as I watched him walk toward the group.

As he neared, I could tell he was nervous. He seemed almost confused, glancing around the room as if he'd never been to a party before. Then, I noticed his outfit. While he still wore the same brown pants and blue shirt as always, this time he had added a red tie and a tweed jacket with brown patches on the elbows. This surprised me, as I hadn't expected him to dress up. My shock was short-lived, however, when I spotted the collar of his jacket, which was flipped up in the back. Immediately, I became embarrassed for him. He had explained to me before that sometimes not being able to see your reflection in a mirror made things difficult, but I couldn't help but feel sorry for him. *Never get caught in public without perfect attire*, Mother had said.

When Morgan joined the circle, it took all my effort not to open my mouth, not only because of his collar, but because I wanted so badly to talk to him. I could feel myself shaking as I refused to take my eyes from him. I mentally begged him to look my way, but not once did he look down. Did he not see me?

"Mr. Galloway!" everyone echoed, greeting him enthusiastically. Morgan did his best to smile while asking everyone to call him by his first name. Mother let go of my shoulder to clap her hands happily, but I dared not take the chance to run yet.

"Hello, everyone," Morgan said, glancing back and forth between the women.

"There, you see? Here he is," Mother purred. "What took you so long, dear?"

"Oh, yeah, sorry, I was avoiding the valet. I don't have any cash on me."

"Cash? The valet is complimentary," Mother explained in a confused tone. The group hid their giggles as best they could.

"Oh," Morgan said. "I... I guess I'm just not used to parties this big. Sorry."

"Is that so? I would have expected differently from a *Galloway*," the woman in blue muttered. "At least one that could dress himself."

Silence. Morgan, his expression full of hurt, looked down at himself. He absentmindedly put a hand up to his neck to pull at his shirt which was when his fingers brushed against the flipped-up collar. Blushing, he quickly folded it down and looked sheepishly at the women around him.

"In any case, you're here now!" Mother said, clapping her hands together again. "We were just talking about you! All good things, I assure you."

"Yes," the woman in green added. "Your father was a wonderful conductor. I attended every one of his performances. Every single one."

"Wow, uh, that's a lot." Morgan replied. "If everyone did that, he'd be more popular than Jesus."

He grinned stupidly after he spoke and looked around the circle as though he'd told a joke.

An awkward pause could be felt as the women all exchanged glances in response. The green one even grasped her necklace.

"Do you see him often?" A woman in yellow piped up eventually, after she had recovered. "Your father, I mean." Morgan's smile faded but his tone remained cheerful.

"No, we're just good friends," he explained, this time causing the women to tilt their heads. Their reaction must not have been what he had wanted because he frowned to himself before looking at the floor.

"You must know a lot about music, having been raised by that man!" the woman in orange interjected.

"Well, he was definitely always trying to teach me about symphony," Morgan shrugged. "But I was never really into it."

Silence fell upon the group for the second time. My shoulders tensed. Morgan stared blankly.

"You don't like symphony?" the woman in orange asked suspiciously, her eyes narrowing. Morgan raised his head to glance at her with a confused look before a wave of realization washed over him.

"No, no!" he quickly spluttered. "I didn't mean it like that. I think all music is wonderful in its own way. It just was never my... well, it was just not... What I mean is... I'm just not a conductor is all."

"You're a *teacher*," Mother added. She placed both of her hands onto my shoulders. "And *I* was the first person to employ your services!"

MORGAN AND KATRINA

"How many students do you have?" The woman in green asked. Mother frowned at being ignored.

"Just Katrina at the moment," Morgan explained. My eyes lit up when he said my name but still, he did not look at me. I became frustrated, wanting nothing more than for his conversation to be over so that I could talk to him.

"How lucky we are!" Mother chirped. "The only people to have a *Galloway* personally employed!"

"Well, I did employ Galloway Sr. to conduct a few songs at my estate six years ago," the woman in blue pointed out.

"Yes," Mother said, nearly clenching her teeth, "I do remember that. But I meant as a *private tutor*."

"What else do you do?" the woman in yellow asked Morgan. He opened his mouth to reply but Mother interrupted with a snort.

"What a silly question, Pamela," she laughed. "He doesn't do anything else. He works like a dog as it is. We're lucky he's here and not sleeping like a log at home!"

"Well, actually, I'm a mortician," Morgan interjected. "I don't think we ever got the chance to talk about it. Teaching Katrina is something I do on the side."

If I had dropped a pin onto the floor you would have heard it. All the women's mouths were stuck in silent O-shapes, and everyone appeared to be waiting for someone else to speak. Morgan did not look surprised to see everyone's shocked faces, though. In fact, he looked around as though he'd lost something. Spotting a passing waiter with a tray,

Morgan reached out to grab one of the champagne glasses before drinking from it, visibly bored.

I didn't understand why this news was shocking to those women. Was there something the matter with what he did? I thought it was strange at first, too, when Morgan explained it to me, but now that I knew how normal it was, it didn't bother me at all. Perhaps they didn't know that there was nothing wrong with it?

All the ladies shifted their attention to Mother. I tilted my head back to look at her as well. She acted cornered, her gaze darting between all the eyes that were locked onto her. For once, she appeared to not know what to say.

"What?" I asked, forgetting I had been so upset moments before. "What's wrong?"

"*Hush,*" Mother scolded, seizing my shoulder and shoving me around so that I would be forced to look straight. But instead of staying still and obedient, I stepped forward and turned around to face her.

"But I don't understand," I tried again.

"*Katrina,*" Mother hissed, sharply focusing her attention on me. "Adults are talking." I shut my mouth and turned to face the group once more, feeling frustrated. Lowering my chin, I ignored Mother and the other women, instead choosing to glance up at Morgan from under my brow. It was then that I noticed he was looking at me. My head shot up from its lowered position with newfound hope. When I met his eyes, however, he immediately looked away. I let my shoulders droop.

"What a surprise, Mr. Galloway," Mother said. "You're always surprising me," she added teasingly. "Now, I know you said you weren't a huge fan of symphony, but what about Beethoven? Certainly you can appreciate his genius?"

MORGAN AND KATRINA

"He was a good poet," Morgan answered, swirling his champagne and watching it spin.

This time even I was confused.

"Er... Mr. Galloway," someone said.

"It was a joke," Morgan explained in a polite voice, still looking at his drink.

There was a pause before Mother erupted into laughter. A few of the other women chuckled as well, but not as loudly as she did.

"You're so funny, Mr. Galloway! Didn't I tell you he was funny?"

"He writes piano!" Charles suddenly shouted. Startled by the interruption, everyone stared down at my brother. Mother, however, continued to laugh and patted his shoulder.

"Very good, Charles! Yes, Beethoven composed for the piano. Aren't you so smart? Isn't he smart?" she added, looking around the room and beaming before placing a hand on Charles' back. "You're lucky you're so intelligent. Katrina only got the good looks of the family!"

I ignored Mother when she said my name. As a matter of fact, my attention had moved the moment she started to speak. My focus had switched to the orange hair across from me and nothing else. Thank goodness, too, because as soon as Mother finished speaking, I caught Morgan glancing in my direction for the second time. My heart skipped a beat as he opened his mouth to say something, but he must have changed his mind because, yet again, his eyes fluttered away from me and he drank from the glass in his hand. Rejected once more, I wished I could melt into the floor.

My attention snapped back to Mother as she suddenly stepped out from behind me and walked toward Morgan, talking all the while.

"We're awfully lucky to have Mr. Galloway here, aren't we ladies?" she said, standing next to him and placing a hand on his upper arm. The hair on the back of my neck prickled when she did so. "Why don't we move into the parlor and pick his brain about music? Surely he has much to say about the matter."

Stop touching him, I thought. *He's my friend, not yours...*

"I would be most interested in hearing what he has to say about my opinion that his father held many similarities to Arturo Toscanini," said the woman in blue.

Take your hand off of his arm, I thought.

"What do you say, Mr. Galloway?" Mother said, her red lips spreading into a teasing grin as she squeezed his arm.

"Well," Morgan started, smiling weakly at everyone and leaning away from Mother's hand "I think you're all going to know more than I do but I will try my best."

Mother chortled and patted his arm, then called Charles to follow her. He bounced toward her while Mother waved for a servant to come and get him.

"Say goodnight to everyone," Mother instructed.

"No!" Charles shouted, crossing his arms. Mother laughed, causing the other ladies around her to laugh as well.

"Yes, dear, it's time for bed," Mother cooed at him. "You're too young to stay up this late."

"I don't wanna!" Charles yelled, stamping his foot.

MORGAN AND KATRINA

"Isn't he adorable?" Mother asked the crowd before leaning down to give my brother a light push toward the butler. "Goodnight, now!"

"I wanna stay!" Charles shrieked as he was dragged away. Mother continued to chirp about how cute he was before turning to lead Morgan and the ladies toward the parlor.

Meanwhile, I was stuck to the floor, still unable to process how much time had passed with Morgan not saying a word to me. I was shouting at myself to do something, anything. He was right there in front of me! Yet I stood, still as a stone, staring at the back of his bright orange head.

I broke free of my still prison and bolted, nearly tripping as I did so.

"Wait!" I shouted, not caring that I yelled loudly enough to cause most of the party guests and Mother to turn and stare. Rushing forward, I pushed my way through the women following Mother, ignoring their confused faces as I passed. It didn't matter that I was being unladylike. It didn't even matter that Mother was hissing at me to behave. All that mattered was getting Morgan's attention, and I knew exactly how I was going to do it.

Mother was sure to drag Morgan away as soon as I got to him, so whatever I said needed to be immediately clear before I lost my chance. Not only that, but my words also needed to be ones that only Morgan would understand

Pouncing for his sleeve, I gripped onto the fabric and forced Morgan to look at me. As soon as his line of sight connected with mine, I shouted:

"Life is very short and there's no time!"

I felt like my eyes were drilling straight into his. I could hear Mother mutter something but I refused to look away from Morgan. His blue eyes stared back into mine. I wondered what he was thinking as he stood there, silent and unmoving. I felt like the world was in slow motion as I waited for his response.

"Not now, Katrina," came his eventual reply.

He pulled his arm from my fingers and I gasped. Continuing to gape, I watched as he turned away and the entire group led him into the other room. I didn't need to see Mother's face to know she was glaring at me. I barely heard her say, "Leave him alone, Katrina! Who put those things in your head?"

I was stunned, feeling as though Morgan had slapped me across the cheek. I stood still, my feet fixed to the carpet. I braced myself for the wave of tears to inevitably wash over me the second the fabric of his coat left my fingertips, yet, for some reason, they didn't come at all. In fact, I didn't feel sad in the slightest. I felt... angry. *Very* angry. It started in my toes and rose slowly up my legs into my stomach. My hands balled into tight fists, and as the emotion climbed higher and higher through my body, I felt my lips curling into a snarl. I spent three days crying over him and he was going to turn me away after I was obviously trying to show him that I was hurt? No, I couldn't accept that.

I folded my arms across my chest and raised my chin high into the air. Defiant and fuming, I stomped out of the living room to see where the group had gone.

I marched into the parlor, and there they were, huddled in a circle near the piano, which was now unoccupied as the band was taking a break. Morgan looked uncomfortable and leaned away from Mother as he tried to answer all the questions the women pestered him with.

MORGAN AND KATRINA

I refused to step any closer. I wanted to watch from a distance. Never had I hated anyone as much as I did him in that moment, and the more I stared at that stupid orange hair, the worse the feeling became. I was so angry I even began to mentally beg for him to look my way, just so that he could see how much fury was in my eyes. Yet the idea of him looking at me somehow also disgusted me. I both wanted to yell at him and also never speak to him again.

My anger only grew as I glared at Morgan from across the room. There was nothing I could do to tear my eyes from him. The rage kept building, even when strangers attempted to interrupt my thoughts.

"I'm busy," I would say when a party guest approached. "I don't feel like talking right now," I'd say if they asked a question.

The group didn't move for twenty minutes, which meant that I didn't, either. Even when Mother announced that dinner was finally ready and people started to file into the dining room, I didn't move. Not a foot. Not an inch. I remained as still as possible, my eyebrows locked into a tight squeeze.

I didn't move, that is, until Mother finally called out to me.

"Katrina, come now. It's dinner time."

Grumbling under my breath, I forced myself to move. No matter how angry I was, I was also hungry. Mother had insisted earlier that lunch be light to be sure I'd eat everything on my plate during the party. A miserable thought, given that I didn't usually like the food during parties.

I watched as every guest in the house moved to the dining room. They chattered happily, unaware of the anger I held inside. I followed them with a pretend smile, purposefully looking straight ahead and nowhere else, just in case Morgan suddenly decided he was up for talking.

The dining room was set up as it always was for a party; one long table in the middle with the best china and silver prepared. A few servants stood at the walls of the room, waiting to push in the chairs of all the guests as they sat.

"Now, isn't this charmingly displayed," I heard one woman say.

"Yes. You certainly know how to work with what you have, Helen," another woman said.

"It's a good thing I work with the *best,* then," Mother replied, turning around after walking to the middle of one side of the table. She waited for a butler to approach and pull out the chair for her before she sat.

I knew Mother would have me seated near her so I started to move toward her automatically. Before I could reach her, though, I spotted a flash of orange out of the corner of my eye. I turned just in time to see Morgan trying to reach out for a chair at the end of the table. Was he stupid? There were name tags next to the plates for a reason.

"Mr. Galloway, I have you over here next to me," Mother called, patting the seat to her right. "Katrina, you'll sit next to Mr. Galloway."

I resisted making a disgusted face when she gave her instruction.

Morgan appeared next to me and I jumped. He continued to walk past but glanced back with a very awkward smile.

"Teacher next to student, I guess," he said quietly.

MORGAN AND KATRINA

The sound of fingers snapping broke my concentration and I skipped forward quickly to find my seat.

Each guest took their place with ease, except for Morgan, who fumbled when the servant tried to push his chair in for him. I couldn't help but cross my arms once he had finally sat. How bothersome this all was. I didn't even want to look in his direction, let alone sit next to him.

"Oh, I completely forgot to tell all of you about what happened at my home last week," the woman in blue from before said as she looked around the table.

"What happened?" the woman in orange asked.

"Yes, tell us the news," Mother prodded.

"Well, you've all heard of the troubles I've had with my housekeeper, Mrs. Robinson, yes?" the woman began. "And you know about what my husband, William, does, of course?" She paused to lightly touch the arm of the man next to her. "Well, he had some very important businessmen expected for the evening last Sunday. We'd been planning it for weeks. The entire household knew they were coming and how important it was. And you know what Mrs. Robinson did? She had the nerve to get sick!"

"No!" the woman in green to my right exclaimed.

"What did you do?" someone else asked.

"Well, obviously I could only do so much with no one to run the staff. It was a complete disaster!"

"Oh, you poor thing," the woman in orange said in sympathy.

"Yes, what a shame," Mother agreed.

"Excuse me, but is Mrs. Robinson okay?" Morgan suddenly questioned.

I frowned. The conversation had been distracting me quite well from his annoying existence. My disappointment was short-lived, however, for as soon as the question left his mouth, the entire room turned slowly to stare at him. He shrank under the acute attention and I couldn't help but smile at how uncomfortable he was.

For a moment, Morgan said nothing. He merely looked around desperately as his shoulders raised higher and higher. Eventually, he turned in my direction, pure confusion spread across his face. I smiled wide, as innocently as possible, meanwhile shifting my crossed arms to be even tighter against my chest. So he needed my help. I wouldn't give him an inch. He hadn't helped me. There was no reason for me to save him from these women.

"*Yes,*" the woman in blue answered irritably. "She's fine."

"Oh," Morgan said quietly. "Well... that's... good..." he trailed off, bowing his head and staring at his plate.

"I'm sorry, Rose. I think Mr. Galloway might not be understanding the situation." Mother jumped in, putting a hand on Morgan's shoulder. "She's upset because Mrs. Robinson shouldn't act like that. It reflects badly on the household. Her behavior implies that her master doesn't have proper control over the servants."

Morgan immediately shot up from his lowered position and whipped his head to focus on Mother's face. "*Master*? Are you suggesting Rose *owns* Mrs. Robinson?" He accused. Mother retracted her hand in surprise and looked at him with a confused expression.

MORGAN AND KATRINA

"Well, not literally, of course! I'm sorry this is all so confusing for you. Think of it like Katrina and me. There's ownership there in a similar way."

"*What?*" Morgan wailed, shaking his head slightly.

Suddenly, the appetizer course appeared from the kitchen.

"Oh, good, I'm quite looking forward to food," one of the men across from Mother said.

Morgan was clearly lost but remained quiet. A line of servants carrying plates all came toward the dining table with perfect precision. They glided across the room like skilled birds, each holding one plate for each guest present in the room. Standing behind everyone's chairs, the servants set the plates down all at the same time while informing everyone of what they were being served. I usually never paid attention to what the food was and tonight was no exception. I did hear the word "scallop", though.

I watched as Morgan stared at his food. He lowered his head and inspected the dish closely, then looked around at everyone else's plates.

"It's seafood, dear," Mother explained, noticing Morgan's odd reaction.

"Oh, yes. Thank you," he replied. "I was just looking at what was in it. Looks wonderful."

"I told the chef to use lemon as the inspiration for tonight's dinner!" she purred with a wink. "Isn't that clever of me? I remembered it was one of your favorites."

"Yes, how nice," Morgan said automatically, not looking at her and continuing to inspect the food. He then went to reach for a utensil but quickly looked confused. His hand hovered over the multiple forks, motionless. He clearly didn't know the proper one to use.

I kicked him hard in the leg. Jumping nearly out of his seat, Morgan lowered his hand and bit his lip, it seemed, to keep from shouting. He glanced around to see if anyone had picked up on his strange behavior, then turned his head fast to look at me. His mouth twisted into a grin, but it was forced, I could tell. He first looked at my face but then saw what I was doing with my hands. I was pointing to one of the forks beside my own plate.

He caught on quickly, his pained expression fading into seriousness. Nodding, he reached out for the corresponding fork by his own plate.

"Hmph!" I snorted just loud enough for him to hear before reaching for what was actually the correct fork and piercing the scallop on my plate.

"Oh, what—" Morgan started to say in irritation, putting his wrong fork down.

"Everything all right?" Mother asked, causing most of the surrounding guests to stare.

"What? I— Yes, everything is fine. Tastes great," Morgan answered quickly. I watched in amusement as others must have seen that he hadn't touched his food yet.

The next two courses of the meal progressed in the same manner as the first: light conversation amongst the guests, Mother laughing, myself staying as quiet as possible. And then, of course, Morgan, who acted so completely out of place that I was lucky to not be directly in Mother's sight or else I'd for sure have been sent to my room for snickering. Never had I been to a party so enjoyable before. Never had I needed to hold back laughter like this before! I was having such a good time that I almost forgot how gross most of the food was. Morgan kept inspecting it each time a new plate would come out. That was the strangest behavior I'd witnessed so far. By the third course he'd at least learned to smell the food on his fork rather than putting his nose so closely to the dish, but I still didn't understand what he was doing. Did he think you were supposed to smell food in the same way people put wine glasses to their nose? Regardless of what he was doing, Morgan stuck out like a sore thumb and after the third or fourth embarrassment I wondered if Mother was really all that happy having invited him after all.

Now that we were all waiting for the entree to be served, things were starting to calm. Morgan wasn't being nearly as funny anymore, and the conversation all the adults were having around me was about politics, which I didn't understand. I was finally starting to get a little bored.

The sound of glass being tapped interrupted my thought process and I looked up to see Mother just putting her knife back down onto the table. Every guest quieted down in response and all eyes were on her.

"Ladies and gentlemen, it's time to announce my big news," Mother said.

Mother stood up from her chair and lifted her glass. I could see Morgan start to tense.

"Friends, I hope you all have been enjoying the party," Mother began, nodding and sweeping her glass around the room to acknowledge everyone, "because it's the last one I'll be hosting here."

Awkward glances filled the room.

"Wait, what do you mean?" one woman questioned.

"The last?" asked another.

"I'm confused," the woman in orange said.

"The truth of the matter is... I'm moving!" Mother gleefully shouted, raising her glass higher into the air.

How swiftly the mood had changed from light to serious. Immediately, mumblings began around the room. "Moving?" a man said in a surprised voice. "But where?"

A multitude of baffled voices came from all directions; it seemed that only Morgan and I responded without speaking a word. I sank into my chair, feeling guilty for having forgotten what the party was about in the first place. Morgan was busy staring at his own lap, fiddling with his fingers. Neither of us looked at each other. I quickly regretted being angry with him and felt tears well up in my eyes. I had spent the entire evening mocking him and wanting to hit him when here he was sitting right next to me, something I had wished for the last three days straight.

"Where are you going?" the woman in green asked once everyone's immediate reactions began to settle.

"To Saltline Shores!" Mother exclaimed. "No need to be jealous. You can, of course, visit me if you ever get time out of your busy schedules."

"But what about your life here?" a man further down the table asked.

"In what manner do you speak?" Mother replied.

"Well, she doesn't have to quit a job," another man said, "so it's really not much of a life to leave behind."

Mother frowned.

"Yes, that's true," one woman responded, "but what about your estate here? And your children's schooling?"

"Ah!" Mother responded, lowering her glass down to the table and clapping her hands together. Remaining standing, she placed one of her hands on-

MORGAN AND KATRINA

to Morgan's shoulder. "That brings me to the next bit of news. Mr. Galloway will sadly be ending his tutoring with us."

A soft "*awww*" echoed around the dining room.

"Yes, it's a shame," Mother continued, "Katrina will be going to boarding school and it's too far for Mr. Galloway to realistically travel each week. I didn't even want to try and ask him to do so. His life is understandably so busy, you know. And that's another reason why he's here tonight! A sort of farewell party, if you will."

Morgan muttered something under his breath, but I didn't hear it. No one else seemed to either, and he shook his head when Mother asked him to repeat his words.

I swallowed. The tears were so close to falling, closer now than earlier this evening when I had been waiting at my bedroom window. I couldn't raise my head to look up from the table.

"Katrina."

I blinked and looked up to see Mother smiling at me. Judging by the way she was looking at me, she must have repeated my name more than once before I finally heard her calling.

"Thank Mr. Galloway for being such a wonderful teacher."

For some reason it was this sentence that caused my heart to feel like it was breaking. I sucked in a small bit of air, squeezing my fingers against my palms in a desperate effort to control my emotions. How much further could I hold back my feelings? How much longer would the tears teeter on the edge of falling before I lost it all? Would I be punished for it? *Did I care?*

Mother stared at me with a strained expression, waiting for me to do as instructed. The room was silent. I knew all eyes were on me and yet I couldn't pull mine from Mother's face. I felt trapped in a way that wasn't the same as being stuck in a closet. This, somehow, felt worse and I didn't know why.

After a few seconds of pause, I finally blinked and lowered my eyes to meet Morgan's. Never had I seen him in so much pain. Not even when he was crying on the floor in his own home weeks before. His eyes were so incredibly blue. Would this be the last time I'd ever see them?

Two fat tears rolled down my cheeks. Two thick, warm, and troublesome tears seeped into the makeup on my face. Not once did I lift a finger to wipe them. Instead, I stood up, gripped the edges of my dress and curtsied.

"Thank you, Mr. Morgan," I managed to say through a shaky voice. "For everything."

Morgan's lips parted and he breathed in deeply. Were his eyes watering too? He said nothing, but he didn't have to. His expression was enough. The smile starting to spread across his face looked painfully forced and I knew what that felt like. We stared at each other.

Mother shifted uncomfortably behind him. I knew the moment the tears fell I would be sent away to change but I felt my feet lock into place, ready to defy the order that would be coming. I refused to look away from Morgan.

"Oh, the poor dear," I heard a woman say.

Servants began to appear from the kitchen. The main course was coming.

"Katrina, I think it's time you used the washroom," Mother scolded.

MORGAN AND KATRINA

"I... I don't want to go," I managed to say, keeping my eyes on Morgan's.

"Excuse me?" Mother demanded. She rose behind Morgan like a tower. I felt her eyes boring into me. This time, I looked up at her.

"I don't want to go," I repeated, this time with strength to my voice. My hands shook but I did not waver. I chose my next words carefully and knew I couldn't take them back once I said them. "I don't want to go to boarding school. I don't want to move. I... I would rather die."

Morgan looked alarmed, raising his hands slightly as though readying himself for something to happen. Meanwhile, the servants with the entree dishes lined themselves behind each guest's chair. I could sense that even they were watching me.

Mother gaped at me, confounded as to why I was resisting. Then she snapped her head to the side.

"Sarah," she said suddenly, searching the room for my nanny.

"Here, miss," Sarah replied, appearing from behind me.

"I think this young lady is ready for bed."

My heart jumped into my throat.

"No!" I shouted as Sarah reached for my wrist and began to pull me away from my chair. I thrust out my hands to grab at Morgan, but he was just out of reach. He looked concerned, half out of his chair already. Just as he was going to stand up all the way, however, the servants carrying dishes swooped in, preventing him from doing so.

"Stop! Please!" I cried, throwing my weight toward the floor and tearing my arm from the maid. Sarah was finding it difficult to keep her grasp on me, but she was still stronger than I was. Everyone else in the room was ignoring me. Even Mother had settled back down in her chair.

"...seared... ... cherry tomato... garlic..." was all I overheard the servants say as I fought against Sarah.

Wait! What did they say?

I stopped my struggling, momentarily allowing Sarah to drag me toward the door. I tried to raise my whole body to see what Morgan was doing. He seemed to be recoiling from the servant...

He couldn't eat that! Vampires can't eat garlic! And I was the only one who knew he was a vampire! No wonder Morgan had been smelling the food so carefully!

In one last act of desperation, I pulled with all my might, trying to rip away from Sarah. My wrist released from her grip like a sword from its sheath. I raced toward that bright orange hair in the middle of the room as fast as my legs could carry me.

"NOOO!!" I screamed at top of my lungs, stretching my arms out as far as they could go and aiming for the dish that Morgan was about to be served.

"*Katrina!*" Mother bellowed as my hands came into contact with the plate.

A crash echoed throughout the room as the dish shattered against the floor. In the next moment, Mother's pure white dress was splashed with red tomato sauce.

There was a collective gasp, then the entire room went silent. I could only hear the sound of my heart thumping in my chest. I had closed my eyes after seeing what I'd done to Mother's dress. I forced them open to see the damage I'd caused. Broken shards of ceramic were all over the carpet, mixed with spilled food. Slowly, ever so slowly, I lifted my

MORGAN AND KATRINA

head to meet Mother's eyes. She appeared stunned, head raised, her wide eyes looking down at me. Her mouth was open, the corners of her lips pulled downward like a fish, and her arms were held stiffly away from her dress, hands drooping limply. She looked so defenseless I hardly recognized her.

From the corner of my eye, I saw movement from Morgan but I didn't look. My focus was stuck on Mother.

Her limbs began to work slowly, like a robot that had just been turned on. First, her fingers curled inward, then her shoulders raised. After that, her eyebrows angled into a tight furious position, and finally her mouth twisted up into a snarling square; her teeth clenched. Instinctively I took a step back. I could feel her shadow rising over me. Her eyes seethed with hatred and I felt a drop in the pit of my stomach. The familiar sense of fear formed within me.

Mother reached out with one hand and snatched my left wrist. I could feel her long nails digging into my skin.

"I-I'm sorry! I'm sorry!" I stammered, but Mother didn't respond. She dragged me away from the table, away from Morgan, toward the servant's door at the end of the room. My heels dug into the carpet, dreading what would happen once we were in private, but I was too weak and scared to resist much.

I was so focused on Mother that I didn't have time to look behind me. Did the guests watch me go? Did Morgan watch me? Would he follow me?

Please don't leave me alone with her, I thought.

Mother stomped onto the tiled kitchen floor with me in tow. I pawed at her fingers to release their grip on my wrist.

"Please! It hurts!" I cried.

"OUT!" Mother ordered with a wave of her other hand. I shuddered at the sound, watching all the servants that had been obediently cooking scurry out of the kitchen. When we were alone, Mother released my hand and I pulled it back quickly, grasping my sore wrist with my other hand, rubbing where her fingers had left a mark. I watched the back of Mother's head carefully.

"You..." she began in a voice dripping with threat. "You utterly stupid, *stupid child!*"

I stepped back, then screamed as she lashed out suddenly, swiping her arms angrily across one of the kitchen counters. Every item she connected with was knocked from the counter onto the floor. Silverware clattered against the tiles and food squished with awful thuds. I jumped when a large wooden pepper grinder hit the ground with a terrifying *crack*. Trembling, I shrank back further. I was sobbing and unable to say anything, tears bubbling out of my eyes like a fountain. My body was frozen, and I cowered near the end of the counter. My hands shook, and I hugged myself in fear.

"You selfish child!" she hissed. "You terrible, disgusting, wretched girl! Look what you did in front of all those people! You made a complete fool of me! You would rather *die*? You don't have any concept of that word!"

She rushed toward me with hands outstretched and nails glinting in the light. Tears caught in my throat as I attempted to scream. Raising my arms to protect myself, I had barely lifted them before the full weight of her hand collided into my cheek, causing my head to snap to the side. Vision blurry and ears ringing, I collapsed to the tiles at my feet and pressed my hands against my burning skin.

"O-Oh, my God. Mr. Galloway?" I heard Mother say. Feeling dizzy, I had just enough energy to twist my body and look behind me. Was I dazed from the hit or was it true what I was seeing?

Morgan stood in the doorway as tall as a mountain. He was dark and imposing, his shoulders lifted like that of a vulture. His hands were tightly pressed into fists by his sides and his scowling mouth was stretched open to reveal a terrifying set of pointed teeth. Was his hair starting to move on its own or was that my imagination? His entire being was menacing. That was nothing, though, compared to the wrath in his eyes. Those eyes, which had previously been so gentle and blue, were now a sinister bright yellow.

Morgan bolted for Mother.

Mother shrieked, scrambling backward. Her foot landed directly onto the pepper grinder, which swiveled instantly, causing her to lose her balance. Her head snapped back like a towel and connected with the corner of the kitchen counter.

In an instant, she was lying on the floor, red liquid pooling out of her hair.

At first neither of us moved, then Morgan spun on his foot to look at me. He seemed to have returned to normal, but I couldn't look at him. All my attention was on Mother. Her eyes were open, facing the ceiling, but she wasn't blinking. Her face was twisted in a manner that I couldn't explain and the inability to describe it scared me. My breath turned to short quick intakes and I started to shake. Just as I was about to scream, Morgan appeared next to me, crouching. Immediately he clamped his hands around my head, one hand blocking my mouth and the other my eyes. The sudden darkness and the pain of his fingers pressing against my still-burning cheek only made me want to scream more, however. I felt trapped and I was too frightened to tell him that what he was doing was scaring me further.

Blinded and already having trouble breathing, I made incoherent noises as I tried in vain to push myself away from him. I fought as hard as I could to escape his hands, but my head was firmly locked into place. Unable to properly move and both of our limbs fighting each other, terror filled every fiber of my being. I didn't want to be in that room anymore. I wanted out and I couldn't move! Frantically I tried to scratch at his hands to let me go but still he would not.

"Shh, shh, Katrina!" I heard him plead, but I didn't want to listen. The more he tried to hold me down the more I feared him. I wanted him away from me. Far away!

Finally, I opened my mouth and bit down as hard as I could onto his finger.

Morgan yelped, freeing me immediately and looking down at his hand. I didn't waste any time. I kicked away from him and ran as fast I could. I ran past the spilled contents of the counter. I ran past the pepper grinder. I even ran past Mother's unmoving body. I ran because it was all I could do. I didn't know what to do but run. I passed servants. I passed the parlor. I ran even when Morgan shouted from somewhere behind me.

"Miss?" a different voice called. "Miss, what are you tracking on the floor?"

"Katrina! Katrina, oh my God, is that blood?" another voice called. I ignored all of them. I raced to the entryway and then up the stairs. I ran past my room and ran straight for the door at the end of the hall. I shakily opened the closet door and shut myself inside. It was dark, so dark that I couldn't see my hands, but that's exactly what I wanted.

I crouched down in the center of the shoes and let my hands cover my face. Crying freely, I tried to think of something, anything, that would help me feel better. Nothing was working, though. Not even thinking of The Beatles was helping. In fact, that was starting to make me feel worse.

Would Morgan know where I was? For once, I hoped he wouldn't. I didn't want anyone to find me. For a few minutes, I waited in silence, listening for any sounds from outside the door. Eventually, I could hear what sounded like a few distant screams, which caused me to press my fingers harder into my face. I knew what they had found.

"Wake up, wake up," I whispered to myself in the darkness. I repeated it over and over, trying to convince myself that everything had been a horrible dream.

But I knew it wasn't a dream. It was real, and sooner or later I knew I would have to leave the closet. Eventually I would have to face what had happened.

Not right then, though. Right then, I was safe. Right then, I was alone. Right then, I could stay in the darkness and wait until someone retrieved me.

Until then, I'd cry instead.

Because Katrina

"Honey, I know you're tired, but I just need you to answer my questions and then we'll be done."

Haze. Everything was strange. Weird, fuzzy shapes were going in and out of focus around me. Colors shifted like slow blooming flowers in the light. They rearranged themselves slowly, ever-changing in their patterns, as I continued to stare. What was I looking at? I thought I was in the living room, but nothing made sense. Was I crying? Were the tears causing my vision to be so blurry that even the furniture was beginning to spin? I felt my breath release steadily from my chest. It was calm and even, smoothly exiting my body in soft exhales. The room was most certainly turning and only I was sitting still.

Picture yourself in a boat on a river...

"Katrina? Honey? Can you hear me?"

I blinked. My eyes shifted upwards to see an indistinct face in front of me. After a few seconds, her features became clearer. It was a woman I had never seen before.

"Hi, Katrina. My name is Rita. I'm here with the police and I just want to ask you a few questions, okay? Can you tell me what happened?"

I said nothing. Instead, my eyebrows tightened. *What?* I thought.

MORGAN AND KATRINA

"Do you need some water?" the woman asked. Her voice was kind. She was sitting in front of me in a chair of her own. Her posture was polite but firm. Before I could say anything, she turned sharply to throw her hand in the air and suddenly her voice changed to irritation. "Did nobody get her water?"

Feeling began to come back into my shoulders. I hadn't realized I wasn't able to move before. The woman faced me again, a smile on her face like she hadn't just had an outburst.

"I'm sending someone to bring you some water," she explained. I moved my head a bit, finally able to look around properly. It was the living room, alright. I hardly remembered getting here. Vaguely I recalled Sarah finding me in the closet and someone leading me down the hallway, but beyond that I hadn't any clue as to how I had gotten here. How long had I been sitting in this chair?

The woman smiled at me again. I found it strangely upsetting.

"Did your mother throw a party tonight?"

Yes. The party. A lump formed in my throat as I remembered what had happened.

"Katrina, can you talk at all?"

"Yes," I said. I looked around to see more strangers in the house. There were people in uniform, some standing, some walking through doorways. A few party guests were near the front door, talking to the uniformed strangers. Not a single person was someone I knew. Feeling uneasy, I pulled at the fabric of my dress and clung to it.

"Were you at the party tonight?" the woman in front of me asked.

"Yes," I answered, turning my attention to her. Why was this lady here and why was she talking to me?

"Can you tell me what happened to your mom?" the lady asked.

A flash of an image crossed my mind—bright red blood and then the feeling of being trapped. My head seemed to lean backward automatically as I thought of the hands that had been covering my face.

"Katrina?"

I shook, snapped from my trance and forced back into reality, but still I could not respond. My mouth hung open as I stared up at the lady's face.

"It's not easy, I know," she said, reaching forward to pat my hand. I wanted to pull away from her but for some reason I remained still. "A child your age shouldn't have to see such things. I'm so sorry. But we're here now. We're going to help you. We just need to know what happened before we let you go. That's all. Can you think of anything to tell us? Even one word might help. Just one word and you'll be free."

"Love?" I offered.

The lady blinked at me. Maybe I didn't understand what she was asking. "I don't know," I said after a pause.

"You don't know what happened?"

"I..." I began to say but stopped, unsure of how to answer.

"Was there a man with you?" the lady suddenly asked.

"What?" I said, now confused.

"Was there a man with you in the kitchen?"

I blinked hard, trying to concentrate. "Yes," I said eventually.

"Can you tell me who it was?"

I gripped my dress harder. "Morgan."

A man in uniform came up behind her and handed her a cup. The lady took it, then offered it to me, but I didn't want it. She nodded at me, then set the cup down on the table near her.

"Can you tell me what he was doing in the kitchen?"

I pictured him, tall, shadowed, and terrifying. Snarling like a wild beast. And those eyes, those bright yellow eyes...

"Katrina."

I gasped, shaken from my thoughts once again.

"You all right?"

Nodding, I noticed that my fingers hurt from squeezing too hard. I pried my fingers from my dress without looking at them, wincing as pain shot through my left wrist. I quickly covered it with my right hand to ease the pain. The lady watched me carefully. Her eyes fluttered down to my hands briefly before returning to my face.

"I know it's hard," she repeated. "I'm sorry. I'm going to ask one more time. What happened to your mom?"

My throat began to tighten as I thought of what to say. I didn't want to tell her the truth but I didn't want to lie either. "She fell," I said, eventually.

"*Just* fell?" the lady clarified.

"Yes," I answered truthfully.

"What caused her to fall?" The lady asked with a strange tone, one eyebrow rising. Her stare was uncomfortable, but I couldn't look away.

"She tripped," I said.

"On what?"

On what indeed? I thought back to the kitchen and tried to picture what I had seen. Mother had tripped on a long wooden object. What was it?

"Pepper," I said after a moment.

"Pepper?" the lady mused. "The spice?"

"I don't know," I shrugged.

"There was a pepper grinder on the floor," a man interrupted from the left. The lady in front of me glared at him but then turned back to me.

"A pepper grinder?" she asked me sweetly.

I looked at the man who interrupted and then back to the lady. Neither of them said anything. Neither did I. The lady sighed.

"Katrina, are you positive that your mother tripped on her own accord?"

I hesitated, but I nodded.

"Okay." The lady settled for my answer, obviously unhappy with it but unable to do anything about it. She leaned back a little in her chair, then brought her elbows to her knees and let her hands rest against her chin. "May I ask what happened to your wrist?"

My head tilted down to see what she was talking about. Lifting my right hand, I could see that my left wrist was largely bruised. For a moment, I was genuinely confused as to why it was so purple. Slowly I let my gaze float back to the lady, but I pursed my lips, not wanting to say what had happened. In truth, I wasn't sure.

"Did he do that to you?" she asked. Immediately, my face burst into shock.

"No!" I quickly scoffed. I was suddenly angry. Why would she say such a thing? How in the world could Morgan of all people have done this to me? But then I shut my mouth tight as I remembered that he *had* held me against my will. He had gone completely against his own nature during those moments in the kitchen.

Was it possible that I was wrong about him? I bit my lip. No. That did not feel right to me. I knew him better than anyone, I was sure of it. He may have surprised me in the moment, but now I felt positive that there had to have been a good reason behind his actions. After all, he always explained exactly why he did the things he did, and surely if he were here now, he would do the same. I was just scared back then because it surprised me. Maybe if he were here now, then I could tell him I was sorry for acting the way I did, too, and I could tell him my reasons.

It made sense, but I couldn't explain that to the person in front of me. She wouldn't understand. She couldn't understand. Nor did I trust her. As a matter of fact, staring at her, I felt caught in a lie despite telling the truth. I knew that no matter what I said, she wouldn't believe me.

She must have picked up on my uneasiness, however, because she tilted her head with the smallest of smirks upon her lips.

"Who did, then?" she asked. "Did the same person hurt your cheek?"

I opened my mouth to speak but no words would come out. I swallowed, fresh tears sliding down my face, this time from frustration rather than sadness. Why couldn't I say anything?

The lady nodded. "Okay. Thank you, Katrina." I inhaled quickly as though to change my mind and speak but it was too late. She stood up, instructed me to sit still for "a little bit longer" and then moved to the far side of the room to talk with a few uniformed people in the corner.

I looked down at the floor, feeling defeated. Tears dripped down onto my dress as I mentally scolded myself for not knowing what to say. What was going to happen now? Was I just supposed to sit until they were done talking? I wanted this to be over so that I could go to my room and be alone.

"She didn't really say much, but I think I have enough to go on," I overheard the lady say. She was trying to be quiet but I could still hear her.

"Yeah?" a man replied.

"Yeah. Some kind of altercation occurred in the kitchen where Galloway grabbed the kid and the mother tried to stop him. I don't know if it was a mistake or malicious, but regardless, I don't think she tripped on accident."

"Jesus. Just a mother trying to defend her child. Poor kid."

"I don't blame her. At her age, I wouldn't have wanted to talk about what happened either."

I scrunched up my face. That's not what happened at all! Morgan didn't grab me by the wrist! And he may have frightened Mother, but she fell on her own. Not once did he touch her. I was there, I saw!

"Can you call that one housekeeper in again?" the lady in the corner asked someone, interrupting my thoughts. I watched as she waved a hand toward a different person in uniform who walked off to do as he had been told. A minute or two later, Sarah appeared. I felt a bit of relief to see someone I knew. She didn't look in my direction so I wasn't sure if she knew I was there.

"Hi there, I'm Rita, in case you forgot," the lady greeted Sarah. My nanny explained that she remembered, and then Rita spoke again. "You're the live-in servant, right?"

"Yes," Sarah nodded.

"Perfect. I think someone else spoke with you, so I apologize if I'm making you repeat anything. You've lived here a long time?"

"Yeah, I've been working here for a few years now."

MORGAN AND KATRINA

"Oh, so you knew the mother well... I'm so sorry... Are you doing okay?"

"Yes, I'm fine. A little shaken, but who wouldn't be?"

Rita nodded. "Of course. Such a shame what happened," she said. I watched as she glanced my way before motioning for Sarah to look as well. I suddenly felt put on the spot and I clutched at my dress again. Both women turned in the opposite direction to face away from me. Now they were talking more quietly, and I couldn't hear what they were saying. It was obvious that they were talking about me, though. What an impolite thing to do when I was sitting right here in front of them. Just as I was starting to pout, however, it occurred to me how many other people were still in the room, some of them staring right at me. My shoulders stiffened and I looked toward the floor again.

"I understand," I heard Sarah say. "Yes, I can do that. Katrina?"

I perked up.

"Time for bed."

Hesitantly, I looked around. As much as I wanted to leave the room, I wasn't sure if I could walk to her with so many people watching.

"Katrina, come here," Sarah commanded, snapping her fingers.

I jumped. Sarah had never snapped her fingers at me before. Forcing myself to slip off the chair, I scurried over to her with my nose lowered. I purposefully kept my eyes to the floor so that I wouldn't have to see all the heads turning in my direction. Arriving at last to Sarah's side, I did my best to hide behind her skirt.

"Okay, Katrina," Rita said to me with a smile. "You're in Sarah's care for now. We're going to contact your dad and see if he can come get you and your brother as soon as possible, all right?"

I didn't respond. Father was coming to get me? I hadn't seen him in a very long time. Was this a good thing? I didn't know anything about him aside from what Mother said, and she always said bad things. What if he was mean?

"Thank you," Sarah said to Rita. "I'll go ahead now and take her upstairs, then I'll come back down to see you all out."

"Perfect. We're just about finished up here, I think."

Sarah nodded to her, then stuck her arm down to take my bruised hand which made me wince. Ignoring my pain, I moved automatically to follow Sarah but kept my face turned back to stare at Rita. The lady was talking with one of the men from before, whispering something that included the name "Galloway".

"Sarah," I spoke up quietly as she led me toward the stairs. "Is Morgan going to be in trouble?"

"Why do you care about what happens to that guy?" she asked, stepping up onto the stairs. I wasn't sure how to reply.

"Because..." I started to say but the words wouldn't come. Instead, I looked up at my hand, staring at the purple color of my wrist. As I did, something caught my eye and my gaze floated up to Sarah's arm.

"Is that Mother's bracelet?" I asked.

She stopped moving and her head shot down to see what I was looking at. Using her free hand, she fingered at the bracelet before eventually continuing to climb the steps.

"It was a gift," she answered eventually.

MORGAN AND KATRINA

I didn't respond, instead taking one last moment to look at the people in uniform back in the living room. I wasn't sure why, but I was nervous about them. Not because they were in the house, and not because of what they might do to me, but because of what they might do to Morgan.

"Sarah," I said again once we were fully on the second level and headed toward my room. My vision was starting to blur again.

"Hush," she said. "Let's get you to bed." I tightened my lips but they were beginning to tremble.

Changing took longer than usual and was a generally uncomfortable experience. Sarah refused to touch my shoes after noticing that the bottoms were stained red. Neither of us knew what to do since they obviously needed to come off, and if one of us wasn't going to take them off, then, who would? After a few minutes of awkward silence I finally took them off myself, shaking all the while. Sarah accused me of being a baby when I started to yelp over needing my hands to be wiped off. They weren't red, but she did agree in the end that my hands definitely needed to be cleaned whether I could see anything on them or not.

I was grateful that she left to retrieve a wet cloth for my hands, but it turned out that her leaving was the opposite of what I ended up needing. Once I was by myself, hands raised in the air so as not to touch anything, I was aware of every sound in my room. The clock ticking, the creaking of the walls, even the breeze at the window; they were all sounds that I had heard before but tonight I didn't like them. They scared me so badly that I began to scream for Sarah to come back. When she ran back to the room, she scolded me very angrily, saying I could have caused a lot of trouble with the people downstairs. I apologized but did not regret calling for her given that I immediately felt better as soon as she was in the doorway.

After I was changed into my nightgown, Sarah sighed long and loud, realizing she would need a second cloth for my face. She warned me not to scream for her, and I promised I wouldn't, but it was very hard to obey. I ended up curled onto my bed under the covers, trembling with my face deeply pressed into my pillow. When Sarah returned, she screeched at me for getting makeup onto the nice covers.

All in all, the entire experience was awful. I tried to tell myself that I was just being a baby like Sarah had said, but it didn't change how I felt inside. I kept wanting to cry at every little thing, although I never did. And as time wore on, I became increasingly aware of the fact that not once had Sarah asked if I was okay.

Morgan would have asked if I was okay, I kept thinking. That simple gesture would have made things a little easier. Just that one question.

But he wasn't here to ask it. In fact, I didn't know where he was at all. I didn't even know where Mother was. Could I even be sure that Charles was still in the house? I hadn't seen him downstairs amongst all the people in uniform. Surely if I had been dragged from the closet to the living room, then he would have been taken from his bed. Yet I hadn't seen any of them. Sarah was the only person I knew, that I could confirm was still in the house.

"Sarah, where's Mother?" I asked.

"You saw," she replied, beginning to tuck the sheets around me.

"But where is she *now*?"

MORGAN AND KATRINA

"Probably on the way to the morgue."

The what? Gripping the blankets near my thighs for comfort, I swallowed in confusion. I wasn't sure if I should ask what that was.

"When is she coming back?" I questioned further.

Sarah paused in her work.

"Katrina, she's dead."

I stared at her, just as lost as I had been before. *Dead?* But Morgan said that was when you fall asleep forever. She hadn't been asleep on the kitchen floor. Her eyes had been open. I didn't have to say anything to explain my confusion because Sarah, seeing my expression, sighed in a frustrated manner.

"She's never coming back."

"I don't understand," I said.

"Look," Sarah said flatly, pressing her hands against the bed and giving me an irritated stare. "I'm not good with this kind of stuff. So, I can't really help you."

I shut my mouth. I hadn't meant to make her feel bad. Pressing my fingers into themselves, I raised my hands to my chest. My body was still shaking from before. Not even the warmth of the blankets was stopping the chill going through my body.

Sarah silently continued her work. She folded the comforter neatly across my feet and patted it to make sure it was flat. Soon she would be finished, and she would leave my room, but I didn't want that to happen, nor did I want her to leave without talking to her more. Even though she said she couldn't help me, I still felt the need to say something, anything, to get her to understand what I was feeling. She was the only person I knew in the house, and I was desperate to communicate. Words were still longing to come out of my mouth, and I had to tell someone what was going through my mind. I wished there was a song I could use to describe how I was feeling.

I want to tell you... My head is filled with things to say...

"Sarah," I said. My voice was weak. "Sarah, I don't feel well. I don't feel well at all. I don't know what happened to Mother. She didn't look right. And I don't know where Morgan is, and I don't want him to be in trouble. I think I got him in trouble and I can't fix it. And I'm scared. I don't want to go away. I don't know Father very well at all. What if he's mean? I want to stay here. I just want to stay here. I want to stay here and have music lessons again. But I don't think I can."

My nanny sighed.

"Well, what's that expression that people always say? When one door closes, somewhere God opens a window. You seem to be living in a windowless house."

I sank lower into the mattress, both confused and hurt. Her tone suggested she was insulting me but I didn't know if I had the right to feel that way since I didn't understand her words. Perhaps I misinterpreted? Regardless, maybe I wouldn't share anything with her again just in case.

Looking away from Sarah, I instead focused on my hands. I found myself staring at the big purple bruise on my wrist which caused me to remember what that lady downstairs, Rita, had asked me.

May I ask what happened to your wrist?

I raised my head and watched Sarah begin to walk toward the bedroom door.

"Wait," I called as her hand reached out for the doorknob.

MORGAN AND KATRINA

"What?" Sarah turned back and placed a hand on her hip.

"I... I know who hurt my wrist."

She looked at me blankly. I waited for a response.

"Okay?" she eventually said. My body faltered slightly at her reaction. I thought what I had said was important.

"What about it?" Sarah asked, when it was clear that I wasn't going to say anything further. I was quiet for a moment.

"I don't know," I said, which was true. I could feel that what I had said was noteworthy but I couldn't explain why.

"Okay," Sarah repeated, turning to leave again.

"Sarah?" I quickly spurted.

"What?" She snapped.

"He's not going to get in trouble is he?" I asked.

"Who?"

"Morgan."

"Him again? Why do you keep asking about him?" she asked.

"Because..." I started to answer but I didn't know what to say. I stared at Sarah as though she might know but it was clear that she didn't.

"Because?" she tried. I didn't respond.

"It's time to say goodnight, Katrina," she said with a sigh.

The door clicked shut and I was alone, with just the sounds of my clock and the wind outside. But I didn't scream. I didn't even cry. I just stared at the back of my door, lost in thought.

Moonlight shone through my window, and if I hadn't been too busy thinking, I might have appreciated how pretty it looked.

Because... Because...

Because why? Why did I care about Morgan? Why was I worried about whether he was in trouble? Why did I want to defend him so badly even after he had hurt me? It made no sense to me. I had no answer and that was terribly frustrating.

A random song began to play in my head. Of all the music to hear, I would have expected The Beatles. Instead it was Beethoven's Moonlight Sonata that floated through my mind, which stunned me. I had no clue where it came from and I didn't understand how it related to what I was thinking about, but I was too tired to try and change it. Instead, I listened to it drift by slowly as I stared up at the ceiling. Why had this song come to me? Then, after a few moments of listening to it, I suddenly realized what it meant. Now the song made sense. As I stared up at the ceiling, still hurt, muddled, and a little scared, my lips twitched against those emotions. For the first time in days, I couldn't help but smile through my pain.

Moonlight Sonata wasn't the answer. The song was only playing in my head in order to reference something else entirely. It was referencing The Beatles song "*Because*"! Which did answer my question of why I cared so much about Morgan. No wonder he had insisted that classical still had its place in the world. Without it, I never would have realized...

Love is all, love is you.

Yesterday
Morgan

*S*HIT!!!

Oh, holy hell, I'd really screwed up. I *royally* messed up this time. And I couldn't back track out of the situation.

I killed her, didn't I? It was completely my fault. That woman was dead because of me. Me! Okay, so I didn't actually touch her, but did that really matter? I still was the one to cause her to fall, right? So technically that was still helping. Oh, I killed her. I'd done the one thing I'd promised myself I would never do again.

I paced back and forth in my living room like a frantic dog, one arm across my stomach and the other positioned so I could chew the nails on my fingers. I had been pacing since I arrived home, my thoughts spinning out of control over what had happened a few hours before.

They questioned me, of course. What was I going to do, run? That would have looked too suspicious. No, I had to wait, and it had been more awkward than anything I'd ever been through. The guests at the party had given me accusatory looks which had me sweating like a sinner in church. I'd told the police the truth, of course, at least as much of it as I could. *Yes, hello, Officer. I got so angry that my vampiric side exploded, and it scared her to death.* What a story.

And, oh, poor Katrina! I hadn't meant to scare her so badly! I was so caught up in the moment; and what are you supposed to do when a child sees someone die right in front of them, anyway? Of course my reaction was to shield her. She was already sensitive as it was. Maybe some children could handle that kind of thing but not her. I thought it was the right thing to do.

Oh my god, what if I caused her so much trauma that she would need a therapist? Should I offer to pay for it?

I stopped pacing and looked around the room. What should I do? What should I do? I couldn't just stay here making circles like a chicken, could I?

What if I just... left? I thought. *What if I just I packed all my things right now and ran? Wouldn't that be nice? Just take off with no one knowing and high tail it out of here.* It was an appealing thought. I had done it before, why couldn't I do it now?

Surveying my possessions with crazed eyes, I considered which ones I would take with me. It felt as though I only had a matter of seconds to decide, which was ridiculous, but I was panicked. I felt nauseous and could barely stand still.

I was surprised to see that most everything I owned I could, in fact, take with me. Not the furniture, of course, but I didn't really care about that anyway. Huh. I never really realized until now how little I owned.

Where would I go? I guess it wouldn't make a difference as long as there was a funeral home hiring. If I wanted to move, couldn't I just go anywhere I wanted? I supposed as long as it was well enough away from this town then it didn't matter.

No, what about money? I couldn't just... well, wait. I had been paid a ridiculous amount of money for those music lessons. How long could I survive on that if I just lived out of my car until I found a place to work?

I didn't even have to do the math. That woman had paid me more for five months of lessons than I earned annually as a mortician, and I lived perfectly fine on that salary alone. The amount that woman paid me just to teach her kid for an hour? I still remember my eyes bulging when she told me the salary. Good thing I had already cashed all those checks.

But there was still one problem that could snag everything. I walked over to the fridge and opened the door to peer inside, counting the number of bags I had on the top shelf. *Shit*. I only had enough to last me a little over a month. Of course I did, though. I had been living this whole time going off of what I knew about the shelf life of blood, and I was already bending the rules a bit. That was fine while I was living here but now that I needed to move, I regretted never taking the chance to test how long I could keep them. Damnit, I had never thought about how tied to these I was. If I really did move, I'd only have a month, maybe two months max, before I would need more. If I didn't find a job within that timeframe, what would I do then?

Well, I supposed I'd just have to do what I did in the beginning. Hunting wasn't exactly my specialty, but a single rabbit could last me four days or so.

MORGAN AND KATRINA

Oh, who am I kidding? This is a terrible idea! Sure, it might work out in the end, but it wouldn't be easy along the way. I would be taking a lot of risks.

I closed the fridge and turned to face the living room. Spotting my tape player on the counter nearby, I quickly leapt for it and clipped it to my belt. I didn't feel like listening to anything, but the idea of having it strapped to my hip felt oddly comforting. It didn't help much, though. My mind was still racing over all the possibilities before me, mainly the negative ones. I felt defeated and useless as my eyes darted around the room. That's when my eyes landed on the covered windows in the living room.

You're a trapped animal, I thought.

God, I needed out of there. I turned and walked down the hallway to my bedroom. I sat on my bed with a sigh, fidgeting and unable to sit still. Looking up at the mirror on my closet door I wondered if I looked like hell. What I wouldn't give to see my reflection again.

Sighing again, I clasped my hands together over my knees and stayed quiet for a few minutes, just thinking. The panic from before was finally starting to settle though I could still feel it vibrating somewhere within my chest. I didn't know what to do. I was too restless to sleep but if I stayed awake, I'd just overthink everything. Before long, a song wormed its way into my mind.

One day you'll look to see I've gone... For tomorrow may rain so, I'll follow the sun...

Slowly my thoughts returned to Katrina. *That poor girl,* I thought. What was she doing right now? Was she crying? Was she lying in bed unable to sleep because her mother was killed? What was she thinking right now? Did she blame me? I wouldn't be surprised if she blamed me for everything. I'd blame me. I *did* blame me.

I totally messed up her life. She was just a normal ten-year-old girl before I came along. Yes, she was being abused, but what happened tonight surely couldn't be considered 'saving' her. If I hadn't entered her life, she'd have been much better off. She wouldn't have had to witness a death. She'd probably have grown up to be some kind of... of... well, actually, I didn't know what she'd grow up to be, but she would have been set for life regardless. Now what was she going to be? An anxiety ridden recluse, no doubt, all because of me.

If only I could turn back time... I longed to re-start everything. But, of course, that wasn't going to happen. It hadn't happened all those years ago and it wouldn't happen now. How long before I learned my lesson? I had made the stupid decision to become what I was, and I had to take responsibility for that. This situation was no different. How many times had I told myself that this would happen? *Don't talk to people. Don't let them in or they're going to find you out and then everything is going to fall apart.* Standing up from the bed, I walked with heavy steps to the closet. I continued to berate myself in my head as I pulled down a suitcase from the top shelf and placed it onto the bed behind me.

I had to leave. There was no choice. I had to move soon anyway, so why not now? Then I could restart with a stricter lifestyle. No more socializing for me, not beyond work, anyway, which would be fine. If I was careful and played my cards right, there'd be no sad tomorrow.

MORGAN AND KATRINA

Moving almost mechanically, I packed my suitcase in a calmer manner than I would have expected. My mouth settled into a frown as I thought about what I was doing. Running away felt cowardly and yet it was the only option that made sense.

When all of my clothing had been packed, I shut the suitcase and moved to the rest of the house to gather any other belongings I needed. Since I owned so little, I didn't bother trying to find secondary luggage or even boxes to put it all into. Throwing it all loosely into the car was perfectly fine by me. The only thing I absolutely needed to have a compartment for was the blood in the fridge and food, which, after being stowed away in a cooler I'd forgotten I had in the garage, was all set to go. Once everything I wanted to take with me was piled on the couch and coffee table, I began to make trips out to the car. Luckily, it was nighttime, because using my umbrella would have made things difficult. Almost everything fit into the trunk although I did put all of my tapes in the front seat.

When I finished packing the car, I stood in the living room once more and looked around to see if I had missed anything. Eight years I had spent in this house, eight miserable years. Well, maybe not all miserable. The last few months had been okay.

I shook my head and cleared my throat. This wasn't the time for tears. I stepped toward the front door, understanding that once I left, I wasn't going to return. The thought crossed my mind that I didn't get to say goodbye to Mike and a sharp pain shot through me. I shook my head yet again to clear away my regrets.

Fully ready to go, I gripped the doorknob with one hand. Then my eyes floated over to the little table that always sat next to the front door. I knew right away that I had forgotten to check it. I knew because I remembered what was inside it.

With a steady hand I reached for the drawer knob and pulled it, guilt spiking through me as I looked down at the little flashlight that bounced forward.

Don't you like teaching me? she had asked.

I swallowed as the memory floated into my mind. My hands shook and I couldn't look away from the object in the drawer. Instinctively my fingers floated up to press play on my cassette player. I needed something to drown out the silence.

"*She loves you, yeah, yeah, yeah... She loves you, yeah, yeah, yeah...*"

Immediately I shut the player off, silently cursing it as I did so. I kicked myself for having treated Katrina so badly at our final lesson. And, of course, for what had happened to her mother. That wasn't a kick–that stabbed at me. And on top of it all, I was just going to up and leave without so much as a "goodbye?"

My shoulders drooped and I exhaled sharply from my nose. I couldn't leave town before making a pit stop at her house. An apology was due, a big one, and a proper goodbye as well. If there were still officers around, I'd just have to wait it out for them to leave. If she was already taken to foster care then, well, my hands were tied. But I had to try. I couldn't leave without trying to apologize at the very least. I couldn't live with myself if I didn't.

I just hoped I'd make it in time.

The Two Of Us
Katrina

I listen for your footsteps coming up the drive...

Sleep wasn't coming. My head swam with too much information and I kept going over everything on an endless cycle. Sometimes I would think of things as far back as two months ago. More often than not, though, my thoughts would settle on what had happened in the kitchen a few hours prior.

Listen for your footsteps but they don't arrive...

I had been trying to sing to myself in my head to distract myself. I didn't want to remember what had happened ever again, but I could never get past the first few lines of whatever song I tried. Just when I thought I was lost in song, a flash of Mother would appear in my head.

Her head snapped back so neatly in my memory. So quick. So sharp. I could remember the exact way her hair looked, flowing back as it flung out. I could remember a lot of things about that moment, actually. The way her hands reached out to grab at the air. The way her feet slipped out from under her, so fast. I even remembered the pepper grinder skittering across the floor like a frightened mouse. I remembered so much detail. It made me shiver.

Did it hurt? What did she think as she was falling? Where was she now? When she came back, would she blame me for what had happened? I shifted under the sheets and raised my hands up to cover my mouth with my knuckles. I didn't know the answer to any of my questions, and yet I couldn't stop thinking them.

I sniffed, suddenly aware of an odd scent. Immediately I shoved my hands back under the sheets. They smelled like pennies.

A chill ran up my spine as I pictured how alone I was in my room. There were so many places for things to hide. So many places for people to hide. So many places for *her* to hide. I imagined Mother standing perfectly still behind my closet door, waiting for the moment I'd fall asleep. The door would open by itself and she would emerge. She wouldn't walk, she'd float over to the bed to bend over me, bleeding and unable to close her eyes, just staring at me. Would the blood drip onto me? Would she grab me? What would she do? I could feel the hairs on the back of my neck stand on end. For some reason, picturing her doing nothing but leaning over me scared me the most. Just the idea of her watching me from behind the closet door was enough to put me on edge.

I pulled up my knees to my chest as quickly as I could. I had pictured her hands reaching out from the end of the bed to touch my feet. My imagination was taking hold and I couldn't stop it. One minute she was behind a door, the next she was under my bed. There was even a moment where I refused to turn over in my bed, as I feared that she would be lying next to me. The only thing I could think of was Mother, and I was convinced that she was somewhere in my room.

My eyes widened as suddenly I heard a scraping noise outside the window to my right. It was like a large and heavy *something* was moving across the edge of the roof that stuck out just below my windows. At first, I couldn't move. I was paralyzed by the thought of what it could be. Was it an animal? A second scraping noise came, this time closer to the left side window. That was *not* a stray cat. This sound was caused by something much bigger and, going off of what I had just spent an hour worrying over, I was not about to let myself turn over and possibly see Mother's face staring at me from outside the glass.

I squeezed myself into the smallest ball I possibly could, covering my ears and tightly shutting my eyes.

Go away... go away... I pleaded silently. *Please go away...*

A new sound caused me to gasp. It was a muffled voice coming from the left-hand window, so quiet and muffled I didn't even bother to investigate what it might be before thrusting the bed covers over my head in a panicked rush. Even though the voice I heard sounded deeper than hers, I was even more convinced that it was Mother.

My heart was beating fast. Burying myself as deep as I could go within my bed, I flinched when the next sound came: tapping. I covered my mouth with my hands so as not to let a single peep escape my lips.

The tapping continued. I tried to tell myself that if I just stayed quiet long enough, the sound would go away, but after several long seconds of trying to ignore it, it was apparent that whatever was causing the noise wouldn't leave anytime soon. Finally I decided to be brave.

Turning slowly in my sheets to face the direction of the window, I peeled down the covers to

MORGAN AND KATRINA

allow my eyes to peek out from underneath. I gasped when I saw orange colored hair.

Excitement immediately replaced my fear as I carelessly flung off my bedsheets. In a flash, I scrambled out of bed to race to the window. My eyes hadn't fooled me! Morgan was there, crouching on the narrow roof that stretched out over the floor below, one hand pressed against the window. I grinned at him. I had wanted so badly to see him and now he was here.

Suddenly, I could feel the smile on my face fading. Now that he actually *was* here, I remembered how he treated me at the party. I thought about how cold and distant he had been, and how much I had been shunned the whole time. Was I forgiving him so soon? The more I stared at him now, the more I realized that I wouldn't. I might be happy to see him, but it was becoming clear that I didn't trust him as much as I did before.

Morgan sat unmoving, staring at me with sad eyes. Could he sense how I was feeling or was something else making him sad? Wait, why was he here in the first place? Was he here to say he was sorry?

As if to answer my thoughts, Morgan pointed at the window latch. I frowned, irked that he would want to come in without so much as an apology first. To show how I was feeling, I crossed my arms and took a step backwards. He seemed to sigh and then he motioned with his hands that I wouldn't be able to hear him without opening it. *Oh...*

Embarrassed, I walked forward and unlatched the window. He waited patiently for me to open it, but I refused to let it swing further than an inch or so. Pressing my mouth to the small crack, I whispered to the vampire before me.

"You're not invited," I said.

"Katrina, I've been at your house twice already. I don't need to be invited anymore."

I pursed my lips, irritated at my own mistake.

"But that doesn't mean I'm coming in," he assured. "I wouldn't do that unless you allowed me to."

I didn't respond, still feeling unsure. Shifting my weight between my feet, I lowered my hands to my sides, leaving the window only partially opened.

"I don't need to come in anyway," he said after seeing how uncomfortable I was.

Still watching him carefully, I chewed the inside of my lip. He looked back at me, then sucked in a bit of night air to resettle himself.

"Katrina, I came to apologize."

I raised my head slightly, trying hard to not look pleased.

"I didn't treat you well at the party earlier. I ignored you and purposefully tried to keep distance between us. I was doing it because I thought it would be the right thing to do since you would be moving away anyway. I thought maybe if we each pretended the other didn't exist that it would be easier to handle being separated. But I was clearly wrong, and I see that now. I'm sorry for treating you so badly."

I just looked at him silently, considering his words. He nodded after a few moments, then took another breath.

"And..." he started again. "I wanted to ask how you were feeling about what happened earlier."

Immediately, I averted my gaze. My fingers rushed up to interlace and fidget. I found myself unable to meet Morgan's eyes so I found a nice spot on the wall to look at instead.

MORGAN AND KATRINA

"You don't have to say anything if you don't want to," he said. "We don't even have to talk about it at all if you don't want to, but I at least wanted to say I'm sorry for grabbing you. I should not have done that. I thought it was the right thing to do at the time, but that was my mistake. And I'm sorry for frightening you."

"I don't want to talk about the kitchen," I responded quietly, still refusing to look at him.

"That's alright," he said. "Is my apology okay, at least?"

After a long hesitation, I nodded.

"Okay. Then I won't talk about it unless you bring it up first." He tilted his head as he watched me. I glanced at him from the corner of my eye, still not wanting to look at him straight on. His expression was strange; I couldn't tell if he was wanting to cry or smile. Just as I was beginning to feel uncomfortable, he spoke again.

"Then I guess it's time to tell you the other reason I'm here."

I nearly looked fully at him, but I didn't want to show that I was curious.

"I came to say goodbye."

My head snapped to face him and my jaw hung open. "What do you mean?!" I demanded.

"Just that," he said, smiling weakly. "I've decided to leave town. It's time for me to move on."

"But... where are you going?" I sputtered, hurrying forward so that my face was just in front of the window's opened crack.

"I don't really know yet," he answered.

Alarmed, I swung the window fully open. I slapped my hands down onto the windowsill and threw my head forward to look straight into his eyes.

"Take me with you," I cried.

Morgan's eyes widened, then they slowly returned to a glassy state and he frowned. "I... I can't," he said.

"Why not?"

"It... it's not that simple," he said, raising his hands slightly. "I can't just... bring you with me. I'm pretty sure that would be kidnapping, technically speaking, of course. I don't have legal custody of you."

Anger rose within me. It was the same anger I had felt in the living room at the party. From the bottom of my toes to the deepest cave of my chest it ballooned, and my face began to crease into a snarl. No sooner had I begun to clench my teeth than tears welled up in my eyes. My vision was going blurry and I could barely see the pity as he watched me. I gripped the windowsill, painfully trying not to cry. He appeared to sense this, as he slowly reached out for my hands. The idea of him comforting me, however, only made me even more mad.

I let out a shriek, lifting my hands high into the air before thrusting them downward as hard as I could onto his thighs. Morgan flinched but said nothing, retracting his hands quickly away from mine. I twisted away from him, stomping into my room as far as the foot of my bed with my fists clenched hard at my sides. At any second I was going to snap.

"I think I deserved that," Morgan muttered at me.

Then there was silence. I assumed he was still there at the window, but I had no clue what he was doing, if anything. Eventually I heard a scraping noise and I could tell by the shadow creeping up over me that he entered the room. I tried to picture hitting him again but strangely I couldn't.

MORGAN AND KATRINA

"Katrina..." he whispered, setting a hand upon my shoulder.

And then I broke.

I didn't hit him like I originally wanted to. The feeling of anger I had felt changed into something else entirely. Instead of turning around and smacking him, I spun around in anguish, throwing myself at him with my arms outstretched. He nearly fell over, his elbows rising into the air as his feet stumbled backward, but I didn't care that I startled him. I collapsed completely onto him, my arms wrapped tightly around his middle as my eyes spilled over with all of the feelings that I had kept trapped inside. I couldn't hold it back any longer.

Carefully, Morgan lowered himself to a crouched position. He placed one hand on my back and the other at the back of my head. Soon enough he was cradling me as I sobbed harshly into his shoulder.

I gripped the back of his coat fiercely, burying my face as far as it would go into him. He let me cry as hard as I needed to while staying completely quiet. Like a trapped animal finally bursting forth from its cage, my tears emptied into him, soaking the shoulder of his coat almost entirely. It was exactly what I needed.

I must have cried for ten full minutes. I wept for everything I had ever been upset about, from how terrible I felt in this house with Mother, to the fact that Morgan was going to leave, and I'd never see him again. The tears even fell for the happy memories I had, mainly how I would never relive them again. Not if Morgan was going to leave, anyway. Music lessons would be over forever. Life with him at all would be over forever. I had known all of this before, of course, since I'd been told I'd be going to boarding school. Somehow, though, it was worse that he was the one leaving rather than the other way around. I felt abandoned and I was desperate for him to stay.

Morgan, meanwhile, didn't move an inch. Occasionally he patted my head or rubbed my back but otherwise he remained completely still. I used this opportunity to cling, like a monkey to him, fully aware of how terrible I must have looked but not caring at all. I thought that maybe if I could just keep holding onto him, then he couldn't leave.

All my pain drained out of me. By the time I was finished, I was laying like a limp rag doll in Morgan's arms, weak and tired. I could have stayed there for hours, helplessly draped against his shoulders with eyes half opened in a daze fixating on the wall.

But I knew it wouldn't last forever. I knew he had come to say goodbye. And I knew that once I was calm, he would have to leave. So, in my frail and vulnerable state, staring at the wall and barely able to move, I asked him again, whispering.

"Please, take me with you."

There was no response right away. I almost wondered if he hadn't heard me, but I couldn't bring myself to say it again. I felt too weak. I didn't want to move, let alone speak.

Then, his shoulders drooped. A long, slow breath released from his lips and I could feel movement from what was probably his head turning to look to the side. Either he was thinking hard or I had confused him, but it didn't make sense for him to be confused. I had spoken quietly, sure, but I was positive it had been clear.

I..." he started but trailed off. My head, which before had felt so heavy that it was impossible to move, now lifted so I could see Morgan's face. Just as I had guessed, his head was turned to the side and he was staring at my bed. He looked troubled, his eyes fixed in that direction, not blinking, and his mouth was creased in a terrible frown. After a moment or two, Morgan silently turned to me. I said nothing as we stared at each other. I didn't want to do anything until he answered.

"Okay," he whispered. "Okay."

My entire body sank in relief, my head immediately fell back onto his shoulder. That one simple word caused me to close my eyes in relief. I had never felt more peaceful. Was it possible to feel so light and so heavy at the same time?

Morgan's arms wrapped me into a tight hug, and he rested his cheek on the top of my head. I hugged him back, trying hard to keep back more tears.

"Are you alright now?" he asked after a few moments, releasing me and looking down. I peeled myself from him and wiped my eyes with my hands. I nodded at him, not wanting to look at his shoulder in case it was embarrassingly wet. He nodded back, gripping my elbows.

"Then it's time to go," he said. "Grab your things."

I nodded again, this time a smile spreading across my face. I stepped back and turned toward my bed to grab my bunny doll but paused and twisted back to leap at Morgan for another quick hug. He chuckled lightly, returning the embrace.

"I'm happy, too. But we have to go as soon as we can. We don't have much time."

"Okay," I agreed, turning around to grab the bunny from my pillow. Then I raced over to my desk drawer to retrieve my tape player. Once I had both of my most treasured items in hand, I returned to stand by Morgan. He had already moved to the window and was looking outside of it cautiously.

"I'm ready," I said. He glanced down at me with a confused expression.

"No shoes?" he asked. "Aren't you going to grab some real clothing?" I frowned, looking down at myself.

"I've never run away before," I murmured.

"I'll help you. Let's get you a bag."

Ten minutes later and we were ready to go. I was dressed in the only outfit I owned that I didn't hate, which was still unfortunately a long dress.

"Can I wear pants when we get home?" I asked Morgan. We were both standing by the open window, ready to step onto the roof.

"You can wear whatever you want," he responded automatically, busy searching the yard. A few seconds passed and then he blinked hard, as if only just now realizing what I'd said. He turned his head to look down at me with a very concerned expression and then knelt down to face me eye-to-eye before speaking.

"Katrina, you have to understand that we might not be living in a real home for a while."

"You said home isn't a house," I said, remembering our first music lesson.

"Do you understand what I mean, though? We may have to live out of my car for the first few months, maybe longer. No more soft and comfy bed for a while. Can you handle that?"

"I think so," I said, nodding. I held the handle of my bag with a dumb smile on my face. Running away with Morgan felt so exciting!

"Katrina, this is serious," he said. "You will never see this house again. You will never see your brother or your nanny or anyone from this house again. If you come with me now, you will never have the same life again. We'll probably struggle with money for quite a while. Are you okay with that? Do you want that?"

I opened my mouth to jokingly say 'all you need is love,' but one lift of his eyebrow and I shut it immediately. His question felt like a trick and I wasn't sure why I couldn't say 'yes' right away without feeling stupid. I waited a while, chewing the inside of my lip and staring at him. Then, a question popped into my mind.

"Will I be a vampire too?" I asked.

"No!" he shouted, his hand shooting up quickly to grab my arm. I jumped in shock and dropped my bag's handle, fearful of what he was going to do.

Seeing my frightened reaction, Morgan's shoulders slumped, and he removed his hand, looking guilty. "I'm sorry," he said. "I reacted without thinking."

I calmed myself, lowering my hands after discovering I had instinctively held them up in defense.

"It's just," he said. He paused before starting again. "You know how I feel about being one myself. I know it's interesting and I know you're curious about it. I'm always going to be here to answer your questions about how it works for me. But being a vampire isn't fun. It's hard. And it loses its charm very quickly. I won't ever do that to you. All right?"

"All right," I said. Admittedly, I was a disappointed but maybe I could ask him again when I was a little older. Bending over, I picked up the handle to my bag and waited for him to move first.

"So... can you leave this life behind?" he asked again. "No more rich money. No more fancy things. What you hold now might be the only things you own for a while. We'll get a place eventually, but for now we have to drive as far as we can. We won't go hungry, but if we don't find a place to stay within the year, we'll be struggling. Can you handle all of that?"

I thought hard for a moment. I wanted to take his words seriously, even if I thought what he was asking sounded easy.

"Do I have to continue the piano?" I asked. I felt the need to clarify.

"Not if you don't want to," he replied with a shrug. "You never have to play it again if you don't want to, although that would be a shame. You're good at it."

"Can I learn the guitar?"

"Of course."

After letting a few seconds of silence pass, I finally nodded. "I can handle that."

"All right. Ready, then?" he asked.

"Yes."

We moved quietly. First, he lifted me up off the floor to place me outside the window onto the roof. Then he followed, making sure to close the window behind him. Once we were in the clear to continue, he motioned for me to stay quiet and we crept to the far end of the house. I wasn't really afraid of how high up we were, but I *was* afraid of someone seeing us. As silly as it was to imagine Sarah out in the middle of the night, I couldn't help but picture us being spotted by her. I found myself peering over the roof's edge as though Sarah was standing just below us. I had to swallow my fear of being discovered as I followed behind Morgan.

Once we reached the edge that we would climb down from, I thought for sure our adventure would be short-lived when Morgan confessed that he hadn't actually considered how we were going to get off the roof. I suggested we get down in the same way that he had gotten up in the first place, but all he replied with was a small mutter involving the word vampire so I quickly dropped the idea. After a few moments of quiet rambling, Morgan finally settled with climbing down the garden trellis with me on his back. Once we were on the ground, he took the bag I was carrying and slung it over his shoulder.

"My car is over there past those trees," he whispered, pointing to the woods that lay past the side yard. "It's a shorter walk than it looks," he added after seeing my expression.

We stepped quietly but quickly. Morgan led the way, looking back every few seconds to make sure I was still behind him. I kept my eyes on the back of his head, trying to shake the scared feeling now bubbling in my stomach. I wasn't scared because I was leaving with him, but rather that something was going to happen to make it so we couldn't go. Instinctively, I kept looking back at the house to check the windows for a face peering out at us, or a light turning on. Twice I even paused after having seen a strange reflection on the glass and had to run in order to catch up with him. Eventually, I forced myself to keep my eyes forward on Morgan. I shouldn't look back, no matter what.

The bright moonlight cast long shadows across the grass. I couldn't help but smile when I realized I was out on the yard in one of my nicer pairs of shoes. *What would Mother say if she could see me now?* I frowned, suddenly disturbed by the thought of her. Shaking my head, I tried to focus only on the man in front of me. When we reached the edge of the dark woods, he stopped walking.

"Okay," he said. "This is your last chance to turn back if you want to. Do you really want to do this?"

I paused then turned around, gazing up at the large white house in front of me. I stared in the direction of where we had come from and I thought of everything I would be leaving behind. *No more soft and comfy bed*, he had said. No more private tutors, no more fancy parties. No more Sarah. No more Charles. No more anything that I had been used to before.

I realized that also meant no more Mother.

Turning back around to look up at Morgan, I took in his features. His expression was blank, but his eyes were still that familiar shade of blue and they shined in the moonlight. I thought back to the first time I had ever seen him. The first time he had ever slipped those black headphones over my ears. The first time I had ever heard music that wasn't symphony. The first time I had ever truly felt home.

"I want to go with you," I said.

"All right," he said with a nod.

The woods were not as scary as I thought they were going to be. They were darker than the yard, yes, but the moonlight was bright enough to filter through the treetops so we could see where we were going, which made it much easier to not be scared. In no time at all we were on the other side, looking at a road with a few houses across it. They were a fair distance away, thankfully, so we didn't have to worry about someone seeing us. I spotted his black car right away and hurried to get to it. I was eager to be on the road with Morgan.

"Front or back?" he asked me when he'd caught up.

MORGAN AND KATRINA

"Back seat," I replied. When he tried to open the door for me, I stopped him. "I want to do it," I said, hitting his arm. He raised his hands, grinning.

Once I was properly settled in the middle seat, Morgan tossed my bag to me. I placed it to my left, then watched as he closed my door and walked around the car to get in the driver's seat.

"Ready?" he asked.

"Yes!" I shouted. "To Penny Lane!"

"More like a mystery tour," Morgan chuckled. He started the car and we pulled out onto the road. At first, I couldn't sit still from being too excited over watching him drive. After a few minutes of silence, though, I started to get peacefully tired and I leaned back, resting my head against the back of the car seat. I rolled my head to the side to watch things go by outside the window. Trees, houses, and signs flickered by as we drove. I watched them lazily, smiling to myself. Turning my head back to look at the rearview mirror, I smiled wider when I saw no reflection. How different things were now than the last time I looked into that mirror. My eyes trailed over to the orange hair in the driver's seat. My chest felt unimaginably warm.

"Morgan?" I asked.

"Yes?" he said without looking back.

"Can we listen to something?"

I could see the side of his cheek get rounder and knew he was smiling.

"What do you want to listen to?" he asked, his voice playful.

My eyes suddenly welled with tears. I felt happy and sad as I grinned at Morgan before telling him what I wanted. "The Beatles."

Acknowledgements

*F*irst and foremost, thank YOU, dear reader, for taking the time out of your day to read this book. You didn't have to. You certainly had plenty of other wonderful books you could have chosen to spend your time with but you chose mine. And that means the world to me. Even if you didn't like it, you gave it a chance, and I couldn't be more grateful.

Second, I'd like to thank my main editor, Mel, for pushing my story from, as I call it, "a teenager to a full-fledged adult". She took the time to really make sure my book could be the strongest it could be and without her encouragement and understanding of what I was trying to say with this story, the book wouldn't be anywhere near what it is today. Thank you for putting so much effort into crafting this story with me. I couldn't have done it without you.

Third, I'd like to thank everyone who helped edit the book in its early stages. The grammar checkers, the test-readers, anyone who helped give me a boost when I needed it. There were quite a few of you and it was thanks to you all that I felt comfortable tackling the next stages of my book's development. Without you all, I surely would have looked a fool approaching any professional editors with my shabby thrown-together manuscript. Thank you for all the support you guys gave me.

MORGAN AND KATRINA

Next, I'd like to give a very big shoutout to my friend, Heather. When I had first made the decision to give this book a major overhaul in plot and story, you were right there by my side to encourage me all the way. Between helping me put together the story structure, researching the time period, editing, looking up how to publish the darn thing, and/or just listening to me babble endlessly about whatever was on my mind about it, you put up with it all. This book wouldn't have taken two steps off of the ground without your assistance and I thank you greatly for it. I think it's safe to say you've single handedly helped me the most out of everyone I'm thanking in this list and it's all due to your patience and willingness to help that I got through this journey at all. I would hope any author has a friend as dedicated as you were throughout this whole endeavor because without you, this would have been an extremely bumpy ride.

And finally... to the one who started it all. The original Katrina. Naomi. Where do I even begin? I care so much about you. And I'm so happy for you in how your life has gone. I know I always said you were bound to do great things and knew you were aimed for much happiness in your life, but not even I imagined that you would one day be where you are now. You have grown to unimaginable heights and still, to this day, I have not met another soul with as much carefree wonder and kindness as you. This is where the story finally ends. You were there when the book was first formed. You were there as I began to gather inspiration for it. You were there when I feverishly spent three days straight, writing the entire thing from beginning to end in what I now call

"The first draft". You supported me, encouraged me, believed in me, and never let me lose sight of my goal. We're finally here. I'm finally writing these words after having finally finished the book. And I cannot wait for you to read the final version. Your affect on this book has been immeasurable and I know it means a lot to the both of us that it's finally published. Thank you. Thank you for everything. Thank you for being there for me. And unknowingly giving me the spark I needed to bring this story to life. I am so incredibly blessed to know you. Please know that I will always think of you whenever I read this story. I think it would be impossible not to. You're amazing. And I am so glad that I know you.

ABOUT THE AUTHOR

When Morgan Marquette was a young boy, he dreamed of someday living out his days as the "old man on the hill" who dressed in strange old fashioned clothes, scared local children with his ominous presence, and caused many rumors to float through the town that he was actually a ghost (influenced mostly by the flowing of his grand and miraculous dark coat in the wind). As of the publication of this book, Morgan has achieved this goal. And would probably deny any insinuation that his household is surprisingly filled with shockingly un-scary things such as a large collection of stuffed animals, a lot of Pokémon cards, and a ball pit.